She wasn't goin[g] ... fight.

Kelly watched as her unwanted visitor opened the car door. Without an umbrella, the tall, broad-shouldered figure pulled up the hood of his jacket as protection against the downpour before striding up the path. She noted he didn't even flinch as the brisk wind slapped the cold rain at him like a sodden whip. Something about his bearing said military. Great. Another one of those Protectors. The last thing she wanted or needed.

As the stranger stepped up onto her covered porch and lowered his hood, Kelly got her second shock of the day. Even drenched, the man was beautiful. Breathtakingly, stop-your-heart gorgeous. Worse, she'd seen his face somewhere—in her dreams perhaps? She didn't remember.

To her shock and disbelief, she felt her body stir to life deep inside. While she tried to grapple with this unpleasant surprise, she drew her weapon, pointing it directly at his heart.

"Inside," she ordered. "Hands where I can see them."

Dear Reader,

Because I support numerous animal rescue organisations, this topic is very close to my heart. When I wrote *The Wolf Whisperer* and I learned the heroine Kelly McKenzie was a shape-shifter who ran a dog rescue ranch, I was thrilled.

Every single day, whether on social media or on the news, I hear another horrific story about animal abuse or neglect. This breaks my heart. I do what I can, giving donations when I'm able, and offering my support in other ways. Eventually, I hope to become a foster parent for rescued Boxers with Legacy Boxer Rescue, a fantastic organisation in my area.

As a dog rescuer, Kelly has a big heart. She gives her love and compassion freely, even to Mac Lamonda, a man who is actually her enemy. She never could resist a wounded animal, even one whose wounds are strictly internal. As for Mac, dare he accept the healing she offers, since her people are the ones who have stolen his children?

I enjoyed writing Mac and Kelly's story and watching them grow as they overcame the obstacles fate placed in their path. I hope you enjoy reading about their journey.

Happy reading,

Karen Whiddon

WOLF
WHISPERER

KAREN WHIDDON

MILLS & BOON

First published in Great Britain 2012
by Mills & Boon, an imprint of Harlequin (UK) Limited,
Eton House, 18-24 Paradise Road, Richmond, Surrey TW9 1SR

© Karen Whiddon 2012

ISBN: 978 0 263 89589 6

089-0312

Harlequin (UK) policy is to use papers that are natural, renewable and recyclable products and made from wood grown in sustainable forests. The logging and manufacturing processes conform to the legal environmental regulations of the country of origin.

Printed and bound in Spain
by Blackprint CPI, Barcelona

Karen Whiddon started weaving fanciful tales for her younger brothers at the age of eleven. Amidst the Catskill Mountains of New York, then the Rocky Mountains of Colorado, she fuelled her imagination with the natural beauty of the rugged peaks and spun stories of love that captivated her family's attention.

Karen now lives in north Texas, where she shares her life with her very own hero of a husband and three doting dogs. Also an entrepreneur, she divides her time between the business she started and writing the contemporary romantic suspense and paranormal romances that readers enjoy. You can e-mail Karen at KWhiddon1@aol.com or write to her at PO Box 820807, Fort Worth, TX 76182, USA. Fans of her writing can also check out her website, www.karenwhiddon.com.

To Legacy Boxer Rescue of Hurst, Texas for all you do to help abandoned and abused Boxers, offering love and medical care, and best of all, hope. I salute you.

Chapter 1

The three-legged dog with one torn ear raised his head, sniffing the air. When he looked at Kelly McKenzie, she could have sworn he gave her a canine smile. Kelly had rescued the mixed breed three months ago from the filthy backyard where he'd been kept, chained to a tree and nearly starved to death.

A bottle of Jack Daniels and ten dollars had been all it'd taken to persuade the mean-faced owner to part with the starving pup. No doubt the fury simmering in Kelly's green eyes had helped convince him. The guy was lucky Kelly hadn't shot him. Only the urgency of the dog's condition and the fact that she couldn't help any animals if she was locked in jail had prevented that. The rescue, the dog took precedence.

With skill and care and love, Kelly had nursed the abused canine back to health. After all, that's what she did. Her calling. She rescued hurt dogs, some of them so mistreated that they lashed out in kind, unable to accept or understand love or kindness.

But not this one. This one had wagged his crooked stump of a tail as Kelly'd unchained him from the tree and lifted him into her arms. Normally, a dog of his type would weigh at least fifty pounds. He'd probably tipped the scale at thirty, at most. He'd felt like a bag of bones.

Bringing him first to her vet, then home, she'd tended to him, with the same quiet patience she gave all of her bruised and battered animals. This one she'd named Lucky and he'd responded to food and love—most likely received for the first time in his short life—with a single-minded devotion. Fully healed both inside and out, he'd proven to be smart and sweet and forgiving. He appeared to have completely forgotten his horrible past. Always at her side, Lucky became Kelly's constant companion.

Or one of them. Glancing around at the six or seven dogs roaming the hilltop near her, she smiled. She always had several rescues she couldn't let go of and didn't rehome, because in one way or another, they were part of her. These beloved animals made up her personal dog pack, all the company she wanted or needed.

To say she kept to herself might have been the understatement of the year. But, by virtue of what she was, her solitary lifestyle wasn't even a choice, it was a necessity. Actually, she'd grown used to it. Truthfully, she was happy and didn't need anything—or anyone—else.

She stood on her land, with her dogs, watching as the sun began to brighten the horizon, and knew that life was good and full. Here in Wyoming at sunrise, even in late summer, the early-morning breeze skated down off the mountains, snapping at her skin with a chilly bite. If any time of day made Kelly want to wax poetic, sunrise would be it.

Her cell phone rang, startling her. Fumbling to get it out of her pocket, she answered.

"Kelly McKenzie?" The thick Scottish brogue was instantly recognizable even though she hadn't spoken to her cousin Ian in years. Worse, this call was not only unprecedented, but strictly forbidden. Except in dire emergency.

"Ian? What's happened?" Kelly asked, gripping the phone. "Is my mother all right?" The last time she'd seen Rose, she'd been grieving over the death of Kelly's father, while faced with the necessity of sending the rest of her family away for good.

"Your mother is as well as can be expected, considering what's happened. It's Bonnie." Ian took a deep breath, audible over the crackling phone line. "Your sister's been captured. And no one can figure out who has her or where she's been taken."

Mac Lamonda despised driving in the rain. And of course, while on this assignment that he'd had to pull strings to get, right after his plane landed in the middle of nowhere Wyoming and he picked up the rental car, rain had begun to fall.

Big fat drops, the kind that almost hurt when they hit your skin. Cold, even though it was the end of August.

Naturally. He would have laughed at the irony if he wasn't so damn exhausted. Exhausted and on edge, verging on furiously giddy. Driving in the rain was…bad luck. A frisson of remembrance skittered up the nape of his neck. People died. People *had* died, and he let himself remember that since, after all, he was on his way to finally start the wheels in motion to regain part of what he'd lost.

His wife, Maggie, had been killed in a car crash in the rain. The car had exploded and the fire had killed her. Her loss alone had nearly destroyed him, but when he'd emerged from the depths of grief to realize that her family had stolen their two children, their combined loss certainly had. The one thing—the only thing— that had kept him going was knowing he would get them back. He had to. Or die trying.

His target, the woman he was on his way to see in his official capacity of Pack Protector, this Kelly McKenzie, was a distant cousin to his wife. She also had a history of being resistant to anything Pack. Since he wasn't going to offer his help, like those who'd come before him, he really didn't care. It didn't even bother him that the very organization he'd taken an oath to serve had now become one he'd willingly betray.

He planned to use Kelly McKenzie as leverage to regain his children. Her for them. If need be, he'd eliminate her, just to show the rest of her thieving family that he meant business. He hoped it wouldn't come to that.

Getting her to let him in might be difficult, but subduing her would be easy. These Tearlachs tended to be a peaceful lot, or so his wife had always claimed.

As he pulled out onto the feeder road heading for the interstate, the rain became a steady downpour, then an outright deluge. In the space of thirty seconds, visibility went from fifty feet to ten, if that. Rain lashed at his compact rental car and he slowed to a crawl, wishing he had the luxury of exiting the freeway and holing up in a motel until the storm was over.

But no, with a fatalistic shrug, he knew he couldn't. Time was of the essence now. She'd let him in. She had to. Failure simply wasn't an option.

Heading east on I-25 out of Casper, he switched on the GPS unit. Though it took some time for the thing to hook up to the satellite, it finally did and the metallic voice came on, announcing his location and the instructions that he should remain on I-25 for 76.3 miles.

Of course. With a sigh, he switched on the radio and forced himself to mentally review the case file one more time, even though he already had the contents memorized.

Subject—female, age 28. Name—Kelly McKenzie. Single, no children, owner of a dog sanctuary and rehabilitation center in Wyoming.

And a Tearlach. Rarest of the rare, virtually an anomaly among their kind. So rare, few had even heard the term. Mac had, of course, though he didn't let on.

During the initial briefing, which had been highly classified, he'd pretended to be surprised to learn that Kelly McKenzie came from an entire family of her kind. When the Pack had learned of them twelve years ago, they'd begun negotiations with the Patriarch, one Douglas McKenzie, Kelly's father, now deceased.

Talks had reportedly been going well until tragedy had forced them to disperse and go into individual hiding. No one knew of Mac's connection with the Tearlachs, and for now, he wanted to keep it that way.

Once the family had scattered to the winds, Kelly was the only one they'd been able to locate, and only because of a chance encounter with a Pack newspaper reporter who'd known her father and had recognized her. The rest of her extended family had managed to stay hidden, despite extensive searches.

Mac knew how extensive. He'd searched privately as well, aware he'd never find his missing children unless he found them.

Meanwhile, the Protectors silently kept an eye on the lone representative of the McKenzie clan, attempting to make contact from time to time, always rebuffed, and always retreating to observe from a distance. Mac had pulled strings to be allowed to be sent to talk to her, preparing to go on his own if his request was denied. Luckily, it wasn't.

The Protectors wanted to have the Tearlachs as allies. After Douglas McKenzie's death, no one had emerged as a new leader, no one had stepped forward indicating they were willing to resume negotiations. So they had begun contacting Kelly, with the plan of remaining in the background, and letting her know they were available should she wish to form an alliance.

After all, they were The Protectors, the Pack equivalent of the CIA and FBI, all rolled into one. They were highly respected among all the Pack, especially now that they'd vanquished the corruption inside their own organization. They were certain that sooner or later, surely even Kelly McKenzie would welcome their assistance.

This time, Mac had been successful with his machinations and he had been sent as their representative. He was supposed to wine and dine and charm her, talk her into agreeing to take a tour of the Protector headquarters.

No one knew that he planned to get the truth out of her, one way or another, use her in whatever way possible to enable him to find his children and bring them home again.

* * *

After hanging up the phone, Kelly paced, restless. She had to come up with a plan, since apparently the rest of her family wanted only to continue their passive lives, remaining in hiding, doing nothing. Ian had said that as far as he knew, they were making no attempt to rescue her sister.

This shouldn't have surprised her. After all, these were the same people who'd refused to organize and avenge her father's death. Green and gullible at sixteen, Kelly had let them talk her out of her pain-filled, planned vendetta, aware as they so carefully pointed out that her father would have wanted her to live.

But no longer. This time, she refused to roll over and play dead. As long as there was a chance she could save Bonnie, she'd take it. Now all she had to do was formulate a method of attack and go for it. Since her father had taken pains to engineer their reputation as peace-loving sorts, no one would even expect it.

The Protectors—or whoever was responsible—would pay.

The weather mirrored her mood, almost as though the downpour with its booming thunder and flashes of lightning fueled her inner turmoil. She blazed through one pot of coffee, started another, then mentally yanked herself up by the scruff of her neck and made herself stop. Overindulging in caffeine would only make things worse. She needed to be calm and focused in order to come up with a coherent plan of action.

The first thing she did was go online and purchase plane tickets to Canada. According to Ian, Bonnie had been living on Vancouver Island when she vanished.

Outside her window, nature raged. Still. Odd.

The force of the rainstorm didn't bother her. The duration did. In Wyoming, a sudden, swift downpour was common. One that lasted all day was not. An omen of things to come? She hoped not.

Still, she couldn't shake the feeling that something else was about to happen. One of her premonitions. Her family had called her the witch of the wood for that reason. Her premonitions usually were accurate.

Finding herself at the front window for the sixth time that day, she frowned. What the...? A soft blur of headlights cutting through the murk as they swung onto her long, narrow driveway.

Immediately, every nerve on alert, she located her pistol and loaded it with silver bullets. Were her sister's attackers now coming to attempt to take her? Holstering the gun, she shook her head and bared her teeth. Let them. She'd make sure they died trying.

As the unfamiliar vehicle slowly approached, one by one her dogs came to attention, climbing to their feet, cocking their heads and adapting various poses of alert anticipation. Eerily still, they listened as though they could hear what, in her human form, she could only anticipate.

Closing them off in the den, she went to the front door and opened it. Standing in the doorway, under the overhang, she drew her weapon and watched as the rain-lashed car coasted to a stop in front of her garage. Since she didn't know exactly what to expect, she was ready for just about anything.

She knew one thing. If her visitor thought she'd go without a battle, they had another think coming.

Annoyed and tense, she watched as her unwanted visitor opened the car door. Without an umbrella, the tall, broad-shouldered figure, unmistakably male, pulled up the hood of his jacket as protection against the downpour before striding up the path toward Kelly. She noted he didn't even flinch as the brisk wind slapped the cold rain at him like a sodden whip. Something about his bearing said military. Great. Another

one of those Protectors. The last thing she
wanted or needed.

As the stranger stepped up onto her covered
porch and lowered his hood, Kelly got her second shock of the day. Even drenched, the man
was beautiful. Breathtakingly, stop-your-heart
gorgeous. Worse, she'd seen his face somewhere—in her dreams perhaps? She didn't remember.

To her disbelief, she felt her body stir to life
deep inside. While she tried to grapple with
this unpleasant surprise, she drew her weapon,
pointing it directly at his heart.

"Inside," she ordered. "Hands where I can see
them."

He blinked, clearly shocked. As he raised his
hands, she saw a muscle working in his jaw,
revealing his anger, as he stepped into her foyer.

Tough.

"Who are you and what do you want?" she
snarled, kicking the door shut behind him.

She could see his aura, that fine identifying
shade encircling him like a faint halo. This—his
aura—told Kelly he was a shape-shifter, like
her. Which meant he was Pack, as she'd thought.
The ones she avoided like the plague. They
were the only ones who had even the slightest
inkling of what she truly was, and they didn't

even know the half of it. They never gave up, especially those known as the Pack Protectors.

She wondered if she was like a trophy to them and if her constant refusal to join them had turned her into The One That Got Away. She also suspected that they'd finally gotten tired of her constant rejections and had resorted to grabbing what they wanted instead. Like her sister.

Ian's phone call proved it. They'd started with Bonnie and now had come for her. But she was ready for them. She'd neatly turned the tables.

"Tell me where my sister is," she demanded. "Or I'll kill you where you stand. I have silver bullets."

The too-perfect-to-be-true man stared at her, silently dripping onto her Italian tile floor.

"You're trespassing," she warned. "I'm well within my rights to shoot you."

Ignoring this, he gazed down at her, unafraid and boldly confident. Then, with water running off his tanned skin like diamonds, he flashed a smile so brilliant Kelly felt it like a punch to the gut.

"Afternoon, *Tearlach*," he drawled.

She froze at the casual use of the old, now-forbidden word. She'd not heard it spoken out loud since she'd been a teenager living in the wild, distant mountains of Scotland, and even then it had been uttered in a whisper, under the breath, with reverence.

Tearlach. Her father had died because of this word. This stranger, this man had no right to use it so brazenly. She felt a flash of irrational anger, which she quickly tamped down. He wouldn't understand. The uninformed never did.

While she formulated a response, the stranger continued to stare at her, his amazing eyes boring into her. "I don't know anything about your sister, but I think you might know about something of mine. How about it, Tearlach? You tell me, and I'll leave you in peace."

Ignoring this, she clenched her jaw. "Did the Pack send you?" she asked. Then, without giving him time to formulate an answer, she dismissed him with a flick of her hand, keeping her pistol trained on him. "Of course they did. I don't want to join your little club, so they sent you to grab me, just like they did my sister. Too bad I'm going to make you tell me where they've taken her instead."

"Put the gun down." Narrow-eyed, he glared at her as if she was the one in the wrong. "Or at least be careful where you're pointing it."

"Answer me and I'll let you leave," she told him. "I promise."

Instead, he smiled again, no doubt well aware of his effect on women. "I'm with the Protectors. I came to offer you our assistance. As many as you need, all armed and ready to help. You say your sister's been abducted? We can help you find her."

She sensed he was ad-libbing, making it up as he spoke. "I'll bet you can." She stared him down. "Especially since you're the ones who took her. Where is she?"

"I don't know." Inconceivably, he smiled again, a pleasant and oddly compelling smile that infuriated her. "We didn't have anything to do with her abduction, I swear to you. You're the only one of your kind we've been able to locate, since your father died when you were sixteen. You are aware he was in the middle of negotiating with us?"

"Liar," she snarled.

"I assure you I'm telling the truth." He met her gaze. "I have nothing of yours, but you do have something of mine. I'll help you if you'll help me. How about it?"

She clenched her teeth. Something of his? What that could be, she had no idea. Nor did she care. "I don't know what you're talking about, but I don't want to hear your lies. You aren't the first one they've sent to talk to me. Now, I'll tell you like I told them. I have no interest in joining your Pack. Not now or ever. The answer will always be no."

As he lowered his hands, reaching for his pocket, she snarled in warning, "Keep your hands where I can see them."

Immediately, he did as she demanded. "I promise we had nothing to do with your sister being taken. We only want to help. Protect and serve, that's our motto."

She cocked her head, considering him. Her sixth sense, which she always trusted, told her this man, no matter what he wanted, was trouble. Nicely packaged, but trouble with a capital *T.*

Problem was, should she let him go? Her sister had been taken, and even if they weren't responsible, once the Protectors learned she'd pulled a gun on one of their men, she had no doubt they'd exact retribution. They were like that, with their pseudo good-guy image, working behind the scenes to cause death and destruction. Her father had made the mistake of trusting them. No one in the family would ever make that mistake again.

"You don't know where Bonnie is?" she asked again.

"No." His blue gaze never wavered. "But I'm willing to help you find her."

This time, she sensed he spoke the truth. Partially. Aware she might be making a mistake, she slowly lowered her pistol. "I have no need of your help. You can go. Just leave. We'll pretend this encounter never happened."

Feeling both oddly hollow and self-righteous all at once, she turned, opening her front door to let him out.

"Wait." Instead, the man actually pushed the door closed, shoving her up against the wall.

Once again she raised her gun. "I'll shoot you," she warned.

To her stunned disbelief, he dared to reach out and touch her bare arm with his cold, wet fingers, ignoring the weapon. She felt a shock go through her, an electrical jolt, which she knew must be because his unusual masculine beauty attracted her. Living alone for so long, she was nothing if not honest with herself. Looking at this man made her desire him, which of course infuriated her. Not now. Especially not now, while Bonnie's life was at stake.

Shaking her head, she bared her teeth as she shook off his grip. "Back off or I'll shoot."

"I hope you told the truth when you said you have silver bullets in that thing," he drawled.

"Otherwise, you know as well as I do that you're wasting your time."

"Of course I have silver bullets."

"Why resort to violence? You could at least let me talk, listen to what I have to say." He shrugged. "For me, violence is always a last resort, to be used when all other avenues are exhausted and I'm at the end of my rope."

Again, truth. This man was nothing if not truthful. Mostly.

"If you'll talk to me, I won't report this to the authorities," he said.

Blackmail. Still, it was effective. Since he had a point, she lowered the gun. Of course she had no intention of trusting him or letting him pretend to help her find her sister, but she could listen to his spiel, and then send him on his way. They always said the same thing, with very little variance. She'd listen and pretend she'd never heard any of it before. And she'd keep her pistol ready.

"I'll give you ten minutes," she said. "If I let you say your piece, after that you have to go. Agreed?"

Instead of answering, he moved on past her. Startled, she followed right behind him into the foyer of her small ranch house, trying to ignore the fact that he was dripping puddles of rainwater on her clean tile floor.

From the bedroom, one of her dogs started barking, prompting the others to join in.

"What do you have in there, a kennel?" he asked, one brow raised.

She didn't even crack a smile. "My personal pack. *Canine* pack," she elaborated, crossing her arms. "Start talking. Your timer is running." Glancing at her watch, she met his gaze. "Right about now."

Instead of jumping to do her bidding, he simply stared at her, one corner of his sensual mouth curved in the beginning of a smile.

Short of manhandling him—and really, as if she could—there was little she could do. They were getting smarter and more brazen, these faceless shifters who made up this Pack of Protectors. Prior to this, they'd always sent females, probably in the hopes that she would bond with them. This time, sending a hot man to try to coerce her, aware that she lived alone, without companionship or sex… Nothing short of brilliant.

That is, brilliant if she were anyone else. But Kelly McKenzie didn't need anyone. Ever. She was fine on her own.

As the seconds ticked past, she felt a flash of fury.

"If you're not going to speak, then go. Leave me alone," she growled, holding herself stiffly in a classic lupine warning, knowing he'd recognize it.

"I can't leave you alone," he said, his deep voice ringing with both sincerity and desperation. "As you've said, your sister's been taken. So have my children. I've come to bargain with you, *Tearlach*. Yours for mine."

Staring at him, she narrowed her eyes. He dared to confirm what she'd only suspected? The Protectors truly had been the ones who'd captured Bonnie?

Disbelief mingling with fury in her gut, Kelly brought her weapon up to bear on his heart. "Don't use that word. Your kind only defile it. I should shoot you where you stand."

Either unwilling or unable to see how close to the edge she was, the stranger stood his ground, meeting her gaze dead-on. She could have sworn rage rather than fear simmered beneath his calm expression.

"Look," he said. "I know your family split up. I'm not saying we have your sister, only that we can help you find her. What I am proposing is a trade for a trade. Your people have something of mine, my kids. I want them back."

"I don't know what you're talking about," she said distinctly. "I don't know anything about any kids."

His clear gaze never wavered. "You might have had the luxury of lying once. But not now, not to me. The stakes are too high. Don't tell me you don't know who I am."

She should just shoot him. But something about him—maybe his firm belief that he spoke the truth—interested her. "I'm sorry. I don't."

Briefly, he closed his eyes. When he opened them again, the deep blue startled her. "Then let me educate you. I'm Mac Lamonda."

The name sounded vaguely familiar. But still, she couldn't place him. "Okay, Mac Lamonda. Now tell me what you mean that I have your kids. If you'd bothered to take a look around here, you'd see there are no children, yours or anyone else's."

His jaw set, he stared her down. "I think you know I don't mean you personally," he spat. "You Tearlachs. Your people. When my mate died, your father came and took them. Without my permission, without my knowledge. I want them back."

Then it clicked. This couldn't be him. He

should have been dead. "You're Maggie's husband," she whispered. "The one who… I'm so sorry."

"You ought to be," he snarled. Then, while she was puzzling over this new development, he jumped her, knocking her gun from her hand and twisting her arms behind her back. And then, just before he began to speak, her front window exploded.

Chapter 2

The blast slammed them to the ground. Instinctively, she covered her face with her arm, breath temporarily knocked out of her. She'd hit her head, hard enough to see stars, and thought she might be bleeding.

What the—?

As she struggled to suck in air, she remembered the man. Mac Lamonda. Her cousin Maggie's widower. Lifting her head—the only part of her she could move at the moment—she saw he'd landed half on top of her. He was motionless, his sooty-lashed eyes closed. She was so stunned and shocked that for a moment she thought he was dead.

But then he moaned and she realized he was only unconscious. Dead weight. Shifting her legs, she managed to heave him off them.

From outside, thunder boomed, startling her. She was hot, too hot. And surrounded by smoke, clogging the thick damp air, making it difficult to breathe. Dimly she became aware that fire roared nearby. Hot. Too close.

One of her dogs barked. Another howled from somewhere near, the sound full of terror. Her chest hurt. Her dogs. Her canine family. Hell hounds, she hoped none of them had gotten hurt. She needed to get them out—all of them. Man, dogs and herself. Now.

But how?

As she staggered to her feet, dread coiled in her gut. Her house was on fire. Her sister was missing. It all had to be tied together.

Eyeing the man again, she checked his pulse, finding it steady and strong. He'd be fine, once she got him outside. After all, he was a shifter, like her except a Halfling. One of the only things that could kill their kind was fire.

Fire. Focus. Her home was burning. She realized she must have hit her head harder than she'd realized. Everything seemed surreal. Out of kilter.

Eyes smarting from the smoke, she looked

around, trying to ascertain both the current location of the fire, and, second, if her enemies still remained nearby. Whoever they were. Whatever they were.

Mac's accomplices? What did they want? They already had her sister. Now they'd come for her. Apparently, they hadn't thought Mac capable enough to do the job on his own.

Thick black smoke rolled in. The roaring of the flames grew louder, tempered by the steady drum of rain and the hiss as the two met. She had to get out of here, now, and take the man with her. But how? He was a large man and she had no illusions as to her strength.

One of her dogs yelped, making her aware again of the immediate danger to them, as well.

Still, she couldn't seem to focus.

Damn.

She got up, staggered to the back door and pushed it open. The instant she did, as fresh, rain-drenched air rushed in, the fire exploded in an angry roar.

Ignoring this, she rushed to the bedroom and opened the door.

"Come." Amazingly, when she gave the command, her voice came out strong and certain, with no hint of panic. The terrified dogs darted past—she counted, all seven of them—barreling outside toward safety and rain and freedom. Kelly staggered after them, then remembered the man. Mac.

"Wake up." She shook him, wishing she were cold enough to simply leave him to his fate. After all, he deserved it. But if she got out of this—and she would—she needed him to tell her where he was holding her sister. "Please, Mac. Wake up."

He didn't move. The heat, the smoke, the fire grew stronger, and still he didn't move. She half thought that this event might be fate catching up with him. When his wife had perished, he should have died also.

But he wouldn't die here, because of her. Left with no choice, she hooked her hands under his armpits and began to drag. Adrenaline-fueled, she made it to the door, over the doorjamb, and outside. Despite the ache in her arms, she pulled him across the soggy grass to the edge of the trees that bordered her land. This should be far enough from the house, since she wasn't sure if there'd be another explosion or even if the at-tackers—whoever they were—were still around.

What was she thinking? Of course they were still around. They'd come for her and most likely weren't going to leave without her.

Her best gun. It was still inside, though she

had a spare in the kennel. Even as she contemplated going back to retrieve it, fire blazed through the living room, destroying what was left of her little house. Her home. Even if there was a fire department in the area, they wouldn't have been able to make it on time.

Still, with a crowd of paramedics and firemen and policemen around, the attackers would be hampered from making a move. For the first time ever, she cursed living in the wilds of Wyoming. She needed help—she glanced at the man lying on his back in the wet grass—exactly what he'd been offering. Little good it did them both now. They were lucky to have made it out alive. And, she amended, fortunate all of her dogs had escaped.

Of course, in the law of "what can go wrong, will," the downpour slowed, becoming barely a misty drizzle instead of a downpour. Still, she knew any amount of rain would be too late to slow down the inferno. She needed to face facts—she would lose her home. Still, she was lucky.

Mac moaned, drawing her gaze. He stirred, struggled to sit, before falling back to the damp earth. Kelly walked over to him, crouching down to help him sit up. No one had come to rescue him. Maybe she'd been wrong about the attackers being his people. Though she didn't see how that could be, perhaps another party had jumped into the thick of things.

"You're okay," she said softly. "I got you out."

"What the—?" He blinked, wiping at his face with his hand. "What happened?"

As she opened her mouth to answer, another explosion sounded. Kelly winced. That had been the propane tank, on the western side of the house. The flames roared up again, spitting and hissing, undeterred by the misty rain.

Something moved over by the barn. A shape too large to be a dog. The attackers.

"We were attacked," she said, leaning in close and talking urgently. "And they're still here. For now, we'll have to work together. Can you change?" She waited while he tried to process that information, aware they didn't have a lot of time.

"Change?" He nodded, wincing at the pain as he did. "I think so. Why?"

"Because I think if we want to have a prayer of capturing them, we're going to need to change to wolf."

He'd have to wait to get information from her. Worse, she'd saved him. Despite himself, Mac liked that instead of wanting to flee, she wanted to go on the offensive. Even better, she was right. Every instinct screamed in agreement that they needed to change to wolf. They could run faster, attack harder and fight fiercer.

Crawling up to all fours, he nodded. "You first," he said. "I'm still regaining my strength."

She gave him an intent look, her long-lashed green eyes appearing to glow in the murky light. "We are together, as one," she said, immediately blanching as she spoke. "I can't believe I just said that. But it's necessary. *Mo Anam Cara.* Do you understand what this means?"

Though a chill skittered up his spine, he didn't—at least he didn't think so. Yet he vaguely remembered seeing something like that in the file and, before that, hearing his wife laugh about it, calling it only superstitious nonsense. Words she was to say to protect him, though they would bind them together. Though she'd never done so and he hadn't cared.

And now…this woman wanted him to do what? Repeat them after her? Whatever.

Damn, his head hurt. He couldn't think. Did he have to say something similar back? If so, what? And why? He knew this, though he couldn't remember what or where he'd heard it. "I…er…"

"You've got to reply," she repeated softly, her

low-pitched voice vibrating with urgency. "I'll say it again. We are one, Mac Lamonda. *Mo Anam Cara.* Do you understand?"

Again he felt the same chill snake up his spine. Ridiculous. They were only meaningless words. Shaking it off, he grimaced. Though he wasn't sure if repeating her words was what he should do, he jerked his chin in a nod. "Fine, we are one. Now what?"

As he spoke the words, she froze, her gaze searching his face as though waiting for something else. When he didn't elaborate, she finally nodded. "It is done, then."

"What's done?"

Instead of replying, she pointed toward the barn and another building that looked like a large kennel. "Change and follow me, okay? I think I'll definitely need backup."

When he nodded, she took off. One second she was moving away from him, the next—Mac couldn't believe it. To his shocked amazement, she changed in midair, like that fake wolf in the *Twilight* movie. One moment, she was human, a woman charging in a full-out run. The next, a giant wolf with a glossy coat the exact same sable color as her human hair. Her clothing, torn and shredded, fell to the ground in tatters. Eyes glittering in the smoke, she turned and eyed Mac, waiting.

Damn. He shook his head. Not only was she a beautiful woman, but an absolutely gorgeous wolf.

Quickly stripping off his soggy clothing, he tossed it on the ground, wincing as his head throbbed. Taking a deep breath, he mustered his strength and began his own shift into wolf.

His change, while quick by Pack standards, wasn't as flashy or dramatic as hers, but the instant he was fully wolf, renewed strength and power flowed into him. Changing had been the right thing to do, attackers or no attackers. As human, his capacity to fight was limited to whatever weapon he had at hand, including his fists. As wolf, he could use his entire body; his ferocious essence would be leashed and tamed no longer.

She touched her muzzle to his, taking his scent and giving him hers. Next to her, he felt invincible, a phenomenon he'd never experienced, even when running as wolf with other Protectors. Heady.

Side by side, they moved forward. Immediately, the scents assailed him, amplified a hundred times stronger than anything his pitiful human nose could detect. In addition to the overriding smell of smoke and fire, he could scent dog and man and wet earth and leaves, along with something more, something awful— the scent of decay.

He knew this scent. It meant vampire. The walking dead. He growled, glancing at her before he leapt forward. Baring her teeth in a snarl, she followed, her four feet as swift and sure as his on the muddy ground. His wolf coat made a much better barrier against the wet, damp cold than anything designed by humans.

Mac stopped. As Kelly came up beside him, he stared at the three hooded figures now facing them. All vampires? No, he also smelled flesh and blood and life.

Metal flashed. One of them had a gun.

He glanced at Kelly. Side by side, his wolf form dwarfed hers. Despite that, he sensed she was equally powerful and dangerous. Their gazes met briefly, before they returned their attention to the others. Their enemies.

One of the three made the mistake of moving, using that gliding run peculiar to vampires. Instantly, Mac took him down, slashing at the undead corpse with his powerful teeth and claws. Though the action wouldn't kill the vamp, unless he remained out when the sun rose, it would take him out of commission for now. One less vampire to deal with.

Two remaining. Were they human, vampire or shifter? Something about one… He sniffed, catching a whiff of blood and skin. Half-human, half-shifter. Halfling, like him? Even as he pondered, the vamp made a move toward him, while the other circled around Kelly.

No time to think. Mac acted instinctively, leaping forward, teeth bared, hitting him directly in the chest. He slammed into him, the other's body oddly hollow, not whole or solid like that of a living creature, but a husk, a shell. The undead. Another vamp.

Baring his fangs, he went for the creature's throat, planning to take him down the same way he'd taken down the other. A loud bang went off, too close. Pain and heat sent him reeling back, flinging him off the vamp, as though a giant hand had lifted and thrown him. Shot. He'd been shot.

Dammit. But nothing he hadn't survived before. Except this time, the wound felt different.

The bullet—hard, foreign—seared through him, white-hot agony trailing in its wake. What the…? Not a normal bullet. A silver one. That meant his life was over. Suddenly he realized what she'd meant when she'd said they were one.

If he believed the superstition he'd read in the case file, now he couldn't die unless she died, too.

No way. He had no time to believe in fairy tales, preferring reality. Even his own wife, Maggie, a Tearlach herself, had discounted it as nonsense. She'd even found it amusing, refusing to ever say the ritualistic words to him.

Sure as hell, no words had been able to save Maggie. After her death, he'd wondered if saying them would have made a difference. Other than prolonging his life without her, he didn't think so.

Steeling himself, he thought of his children. Twins, barely eighteen months old when they'd been stolen from him. They'd be two and a half now, nearly three. Would they even remember him?

And now this new wrinkle in things. This Kelly had told him they were one. The ritualistic words. And he'd agreed. If the superstitious nonsense was true and he lived, that would mean she'd saved his life. He would owe her. He'd owe a Tearlach, his sworn mortal enemy, part of the ones who'd stolen away what remained of his life.

He had to get them back. He mustn't fail,

couldn't fail. Isobel and Caleb would be coming home.

That is, if he didn't die. A silver bullet was always deadly. No exceptions, except Tearlachs. If the legend of her protection wasn't true, then he would die here, without even seeing his and Maggie's precious children ever again.

Either way, he wouldn't go down easily. Defiant, he clenched his teeth and struggled to get to his feet, refusing to cry out or even acknowledge the pain.

A silver bullet. Hell hounds.

With every breath, the dangerous metal spread silver poison throughout his body. He knew he must get the slug out if he wanted to buy more time.

The bullet had to come out. But how? As he tried to focus, his vision faded in and out. He held on to what reality he did know for certain. Cold misty rain, hot blood in his veins and— looking up—the sheer viciousness of his assailant's grin as he watched Mac suffer.

The second shock—that Halfling was no vampire. That shifter looked vaguely familiar. A Protector? Surely not. Because if he was, that would mean Mac had been played for a fool all along.

Mac's vision blurred and he sank to his knees.

Having taken Mac out, his attacker turned away, lifting his gun and sighting the weapon on Kelly. Unable to do more than watch, Mac grunted with pain and turned his attention toward his own wound.

The bullet must come out.

Grimacing, he bit at his own leg, teeth connecting with fur and muscle and sinew. Bracing himself, he counted to three and then yanked, biting back a yelp, snarling instead.

Bullet must come out. He repeated this like a mantra.

Ruthless, he tore at his own flesh, searching for the slug. Finally, his teeth connected with metal and he clamped down on it, gagging at the acrid, bitter taste of silver, mortal enemy of his kind.

As it exited his body, bringing with it muscle and sinew and skin, blood welled up in the wound, pouring from the gaping hole in his matted leg and dripping from his teeth, the coppery bullet metallic and poison in his mouth.

Evil. He spat it on the ground, then eyed his wound. Must stop the bleeding. After all, blood was irresistible to a vampire. Even, he thought dazedly, shifter's blood.

A hiss came from above. He looked up, knowing what he'd find. The vampire had gotten back up and faced him, no doubt attracted by the scent of fresh blood. His glowing red gaze appeared transfixed by Mac's wound.

Of course. As he struggled to hang on to fading consciousness, he wondered what would happen if the vampire drank his blood as he lay dying. Would he then be reborn, one of the undead, a new form of being, a lupinc vampire?

Right. He groaned. As if there could ever be such a thing. Though Tearlachs existed, so why not?

As he peered up through a haze of pain, the vampire leaned closer, white fangs gleaming. It was going to bite him. Seriously? He bared his teeth in self-defense.

Kelly appeared, growling low in her throat. She forced the vamp to back away from Mac, keeping the monster from defiling a dying wolf and drinking and draining his blood.

Mac closed his eyes, letting out breath he hadn't even realized he was holding. Hounds help him, he was glad.

The shifter appeared and lifted his gun. Kelly snarled, and leapt forward at the exact same moment that the bloodsucker did.

Bang. Once. Bang. Twice. And then a third time. Kelly kept going, apparently undeterred despite having taken three bullets. Three *silver* bullets. Or had they gone into the vampire?

Damn. Despite his pain, Mac couldn't help but be impressed.

Dropping the gun, the shifter spun on his heel and took off in a speed-blurring run. The vampire, too, had vanished, nowhere in sight.

Blood dripping from her wounds, the wolf—Kelly—did not pursue.

Mac must have blacked out then. The next thing he knew, Kelly—in human form—cradled him in her arms. She gently shook him awake.

"Change back," she urged softly. "I need you to become human. Let me take a look at your wound."

Struggling to focus on her incredibly beautiful face, he took a deep breath and willed himself to shift back to human form.

He was so weak that shifting to man took longer than usual. But finally, it was done and he lay, naked and bleeding, in her arms.

Her blood-soaked arms.

"You were shot, too," he croaked. "Three times. Right?"

"No." She sounded supremely unconcerned. "Only once, and I already took care of that. Right now, we've got to stop your bleeding."

Already took care of... Damn it. The benefit

of being a Tearlach. Invulnerable to anything and everything, except fire. Despite horrific injuries, Maggie would have healed, would have lived if the car hadn't exploded. He let himself drift with the pain.

"Where are your clothes?" she asked.

Dazedly, he looked about for something to use as a makeshift bandage. "Over there." He pointed.

She grabbed his sodden hoodie off the ground. "This will work. Hold still."

Wrapping the hoodie around Mac's leg, Kelly tied off a makeshift tourniquet.

"I hope this will stem the bloodshed. If you were full-blooded, a nonsilver-bullet gunshot wound would heal almost instantly. But because you're a Halfling…" She shrugged. "It'll take a bit longer."

He couldn't take offense, because she was right. Halflings healed only slightly faster than humans. Not that it mattered. None of that mattered now. No shifter, full or half, lived after being shot by a silver bullet.

The Tearlach crap be damned. They were both going to die. Strangely enough, this knowledge brought him peace. Truth be told, he had nothing, really, to live for. If he couldn't have his children, he was ready to go.

Unless, the niggling thought wouldn't go away, the legends were actually right about Tearlachs and their magical powers. If they were, he wouldn't die. And neither would she.

Mind-boggling and probably the product of a dying mind. Wishful thinking. Yet once it had occurred to him, the thought would not go away.

Being around Kelly could save him. Might save him... No. Would save him. The true significance of the words she'd spoken. *We are one—Mo Anam Cara.* Spoken by a Tearlach, that meant he was under her protection. Which meant, in theory, like her he couldn't die unless by fire.

Therein lay the appeal of her kind to the Protectors. And to their mutual enemies.

So there was a distinct possibility he might live. But first, as a fresh wave of agonizing pain swept over him, he realized he'd have to go to hell and back.

Mac moaned, drawing Kelly's weary gaze. Now that their attackers had vanished, her first responsibility was to make him as comfortable as she could. She needed to get him in out of the damp, chilly mist. Despite his being the enemy, her impulsive binding of them together meant she couldn't abandon him now.

Her house was in ruins. The other explosion had taken out several of her dog runs, though it hadn't damaged the main kennel building or—she hoped—hurt any of the dogs.

Luckily, she'd kept a small office inside the kennels where she frequently did paperwork on a battered computer. There, she had a futon that could double as a bed, a shower she used to bathe the dogs, a toilet and a fridge. Nothing fancy, but until her home was rebuilt, this would be where she'd have to live.

And where she'd take the Pack Protector while he recovered. It wouldn't be easy, the first time recovering from a silver-bullet shot. She remembered her first time, back when she'd been a wee girl of twelve. No, this man would suffer greatly on his road to recovery. By the end of it, he'd probably wish he was dead.

Again she eyed him. Luckily for him, he'd passed out from the pain. Now, how to get him inside the kennel. While the adrenaline rush earlier had enabled Kelly to get him outside, she doubted she could replicate that feat again.

Yet she couldn't simply leave him here in the rain.

"Hey, Tearlach."

To her shock, Mac had raised his head and called for her, his voice weak but steady.

"Don't call me that," she chided. "Now more than ever, it's important that you forget you ever heard that word."

He didn't ask why. She thought maybe now he understood. Then, to her amazement, he pushed himself up on his elbows.

"Help me up," he said, his voice gaining strength.

"Do you think you can stand?" His resilience amazed her. Still, she'd be surprised if he managed to stand, never mind walk. "If you can, I'll help you walk to the kennel. It's warm and dry and there's a place you can rest. And it should be safe. The dogs will alert us to any danger long before it reaches us."

Jerking his head in a nod, he pushed up to his feet. Though she rushed over to offer her shoulder for support, he waved her away, staggering a few steps forward before halting. Though he was breathing hard and swaying slightly, he looked a far cry better than he had just five minutes before, which meant he was healing fast. Almost as quickly as her.

Honoring his strength, she kept back, though close enough to offer aid if he needed it. "Let me know if you need my help," she said.

Squinting at her, he didn't respond. Instead, he lurched another three or four steps toward the kennel, then rested. Though he held his shoulders up, he kept one hand pressed against the bandaged wound in his leg. From what she could tell, the makeshift tourniquet had been effective. Only a little blood seeped from under his hand to run down his wet and muscular leg.

He healed like a full-blooded shifter rather than a Halfling. Or, she reflected, maybe that was because she'd taken him under her protection.

As they made their way slowly toward the kennel, her dogs, still stunned from the explosion and gunshots, swirled around them, agitated and nervous. Though she was far from calm herself, she spoke soothingly to them, working at projecting a serene attitude, knowing it would help relax them.

Once inside, she dried him off as best she could, taking care to touch the still-healing wound gently. Though he must have hurt, his stony expression gave nothing away. As he watched her, his blue eyes were hooded.

Waiting for him to ask why she'd saved him—a question she didn't know the answer to herself—she had to fight to keep from being all thumbs, which was not normal for her. She'd tended lots of wounded creatures in her time, though none of them had been so blatantly masculine, nor as beautiful.

When she'd finished her ministrations, he lay back on the futon and went to sleep. Kelly wrapped him in a soft blanket, attempting to make him as comfortable as she could.

Once Mac was taken care of, she rounded up the other dogs that still roamed outside, wanting to bring them in before full darkness fell. As soon as she had them all accounted for, blessedly unharmed, she returned with them to the kennel apartment where Mac still slept.

Peeking at the wound, she was pleased to see it had healed even more. As if it had been sutured, the jagged tear in his skin was beginning to close. His body had already brought itself back from the brink of death and was well on the road to healing, much faster and less painfully than she'd expected.

Suddenly exhausted, Kelly dropped into her office chair. Eyeing the handsome shifter, she knew she had one more task ahead of her. Once Mac recovered, she would have to explain that the gift she'd given him came with strings. By telling him that they were one, and by his acceptance, they were now bound together for life. Kelly was pretty darn sure he wouldn't be happy about that. Hounds, she wasn't entirely thrilled herself.

But what had she been supposed to do? Let him die in front of her? She who had trouble killing an insect? So in an impulsive moment, she'd said the sacred words—only to protect him—and the thing was done.

Would she have regrets? Only time would tell.

And, she couldn't help but wonder if he already knew. He'd been married to a Tearlach. Surely he and Maggie had undergone the ritual. Or had they? After all, Maggie had died and he had lived. Still, she'd never heard of a Tearlach marrying without performing the necessary binding. But could a shifter be bound to two women, even if one died? She didn't know.

Again she eyed Mac. At the rate he was going, it shouldn't take him more than a good night's sleep to heal. For his sake, she hoped he'd spend most of that time unconscious. Less painful that way.

Chapter 3

As the afternoon drifted into evening, Kelly remained in her chair, watching him. She found herself tracing the lines of his rugged face with her gaze, pondering the strength of his profile and the breadth of his shoulders.

He'd been married to her cousin Maggie. Though Maggie was dead, that made him family. She'd sworn the oath with him, bound him to her, and he was hers now.

This feeling—it had to be desire. She'd read about it, heard songs about it, but until now, she hadn't been touched by it. It felt like a small flame building inside her; she felt a longing to touch him, to press her lips to his bronze skin, for an unspeakable, unthinkable *more*.

Shaking herself back to her senses, she pushed to her feet. Perhaps her lonely exile was finally getting to her. She'd never met a man who affected her the way this one did. Of course, living out here in the wilds of Wyoming, she met few men, other than her neighboring ranchers. And they certainly didn't make her want what she couldn't have.

She reminded herself that he'd mentioned trading her sister for his children. Though she doubted he actually had her sister, he might know where she'd been taken. His kids were a different story.

Even if he brought Bonnie back, Kelly couldn't guarantee the return of his twins. While she hadn't heard anything about his kids being taken, it sort of made sense. Any child born of a Tearlach must be protected, and with their mother dead, her mate should have died also. That was the way of things. Once Maggie had died, the children had to be protected. Their gifts were too highly valued, too much of a temptation for someone merely after the prize a Tearlach's gift could bring.

If they'd been allowed to remain with Mac,

their lives would have been in danger from the moment they hit puberty.

That night, she made a pallet on the floor and slept, drawing her dogs around her like a shield. The kennel had a functioning alarm, which, though not monitored, would at least alert her to any intrusion. If the attackers came back, at least she'd have some kind of warning.

But the night passed uneventfully, and she woke in the morning feeling rested and completely healed. The man—Mac—still slept, though his color had improved and she judged that he was very close to being one hundred percent improved.

While waiting, she purified the area, drawing the ritual from instinct and memories. She set up an altar, a small replica of the one she'd had in her home, using some candles she'd dug out of a drawer and a half-burnt stick of incense.

Then, she bowed her head and offered up a prayer, though to what god, she couldn't say. In the end, she supposed it didn't matter to who or what she prayed. She—and her family, as well as this man who was now bound to her—would need all the help they could get.

First, she had to take care of her dogs. In the closest town, she had one person she trusted. Ben was human, without any knowledge of shifters or vampires or, most important, Tearlachs. He'd come forward two years ago, wanting to volunteer for the dog rescue group she'd founded. He often helped her save a doomed dog, both fostering and helping to transport them, often from across the country. He'd even stayed with Kelly's personal dogs once or twice when she'd felt the urge to travel. She often called him her big brother, only half-jokingly. She knew if she ever really needed him, he'd have her back, just like a real brother.

Ben answered on the third ring. "Kelly! It's been a while, way too long. What's up?"

She could picture him, the eternal hippy with his too-long gray hair pulled back in a thick braid and his uncombed beard going in every direction. Ben was retired career military and she supposed his wild appearance was his way of rebelling at years of being told what to wear and do. He was also a former sniper and a crack shot.

"I need your help." Briefly, without giving too many details, she outlined the situation. Years ago, she'd hinted vaguely to Ben that she'd done a stint of undercover work, highly classified, and she called on this cover story now.

"Call the police," Ben advised. "See if they

can send a few state troopers out. Sounds like you need some firepower."

Kelly didn't even bother to respond. She just let Ben think about what he'd just said.

"You can't involve the authorities, can you?" Ben finally asked. "That's why you called me."

"Exactly."

"What do you want me to do?"

"Watch my dogs. I know this is asking a lot—"

"Nah. It's okay. You know I love your pups. How many are you up to these days?"

"Seven house dogs. Plus more in the kennel. If it's okay with you, I'll bring my seven out to your place. The others will need transporting to a temporary foster home."

"In other words, me." Ben's dry tone contained a hint of amusement.

"I couldn't ask you to take them. My seven are enough."

"How about I pop out there daily and feed them? Would that work?"

Kelly thought for a moment, then reluctantly answered. "No. Too dangerous."

"For me? I thought it was you they're after."

He had a point. "True, but I can't say for sure they won't be back. I don't want you anywhere in the vicinity if they do. They're more deadly than I can say."

Ben snorted, but he gave in. "Fine. I'll take your word for it. Let me make a few phone calls about the kennel dogs and I'll let you know. When do you want to bring yours over?"

"The sooner the better. Today? Tomorrow?"

He whistled. "You are in a hurry, aren't you?"

His tone made her want to smile. Immediately, she quashed it. "I've got to get on the road."

"Hunting or fleeing?"

This time Kelly had to fight to keep from laughing. "What do you think?"

"I think I wouldn't want to be whoever you're after when you catch up to them. You sure you don't want me to round up my buddies? We could help you out."

Ben and his friends referred to themselves as the Redneck Posse. Kelly suspected they'd all once been part of the same Special Ops unit, but she didn't know for sure. She'd never asked and Ben had never volunteered the information.

"Thanks, but that's not necessary." She could imagine his reaction if she told him her attackers had been vampires and shape-shifters. "I need you here more."

"All right, then. Just thought I'd offer." Rather

than disappointed, Ben actually sounded a bit relieved.

"And I do appreciate that," she said.

"How long should I expect you to be gone?" Ben asked, probably more out of curiosity than anything else. He lived alone, with one dog and an ancient parrot.

"As long as it takes," Kelly answered. "I have no idea. That's the best I can do."

"See you tomorrow, then."

Hanging up the phone, she turned again to study Mac. One of her rescue dogs, a pit bull mix named Brandi, who'd only recently been given house privileges, had gone to sit by the man's side. The large animal's posture was alert and watchful, as if she was guarding one of her pack mates or her best friend.

This stunned Kelly. Brandi generally avoided people. Kelly had been working with the former dog-fighting casualty for three months now and the animal barely allowed her to touch her coat. Now the burly dog sat by the side of the ill man as though compassion was her middle name.

Interesting. If she had time, she'd study this in more detail. Brandi's behavior could mean a breakthrough for other dogs that had suffered at the hands of dog-fighters.

But with time running short, Kelly could

focus only on Mac, doing what she could to ease his suffering while he rid his system of the poison. For the next several hours, she sat vigilant by his side along with the dog, keeping him clean and trying to get the occasional bit of liquid into his parched mouth, wiping it up as it ran down his chin.

It shouldn't be much longer now. The wound continued to heal at an amazing rate. As the fever shook his muscular body and he thrashed about in the covers, Brandi would whimper. When she laid her square-shaped head on Mac, the man quieted instantly. Though the smell of poison tainted the air, the animal didn't seem to notice or care.

Beside Mac on the table, his cell phone vibrated. Snatching it up before it could disturb him, Kelly debated answering. Someone as beautiful as this one must have a significant other, not to mention family and friends. Most likely they were worried that he wasn't returning their calls.

"Hello?" she answered.

"Who is this?" A masculine voice, full of suspicion.

"My name is Kelly McKenzie. I—"

"The Tearlach?" He sounded skeptical, which was good.

"You people keep calling me this," Kelly snarled, only half acting as she forced rage into her voice, building up so she could sound convincing as she spoke the first lie. "I don't even know what the word means."

"Right. Whatever. Look, this is Donald, of the Society of Protectors. Put Mac Lamonda on. I need to talk to him."

Glancing at the man still unconscious on her futon, Kelly sucked in her breath and prepared to tell the second lie. "He's gone," she said. "He left."

Then, before Donald had a chance to question her, she closed the phone, hanging up on him. Immediately, she turned the cell off, in case he called again.

There. That was done. The subterfuge necessary to protect her sister had begun. Regardless of which scenario was true, them believing he was gone couldn't be anything but good. If Mac Lamonda was working with the Protectors to capture her, with him gone, they'd waste precious time trying to contact him before they'd send others. By then, she'd have vanished. If he was working alone and, as a renegade, had captured Bonnie in order to trade her for his children, he'd have no backup.

Win-win. Though she wouldn't consider it as such until Bonnie was free and safe.

With a sigh, she dropped the cell to the ground and stomped on it hard, crushing it beneath the heel of her shoe until it no longer resembled anything phonelike. Then she picked up the pieces and carried them to the trash bin.

Turning, she began heating up a frozen dinner in the small microwave. Luckily, she kept a well-stocked freezer in the basement of her home and the fire hadn't damaged much down there, except for leaving an abundance of sooty smoke and ash. She had no electricity, but living on a remote ranch, all she'd had to do was fire up the generator.

Soon, the soothing scent of macaroni and cheese filled the room.

Turning, she found Mac sitting up in bed, watching her. A moment of surprise stunned her—his eyes were so unbelievably blue, after all—and then she felt a pang of recognition so immediate, so deep, she couldn't catch her breath.

Recognition? That made no sense. She'd never met this man before, anywhere. If she had, she knew she'd never have forgotten.

Mac's ever-present watchdog Brandi raised her head, eyeing Kelly with a watchful gaze that looked eerily similar to the man's. To her surprise, despite the tantalizing aroma of food, the animal didn't move from her position at the edge of his bed.

"Hey." Mac gave her a weak smile. His raspy voice made him sound as if he'd just woken from a long, luxurious nap instead of a near-death fever. She found it sexy as hell. Unfortunately.

"Hey, yourself," she said briskly. "I was just making some supper. Are you hungry?"

Searching her face, he frowned. "I don't think so. Not yet, anyway." Glancing at the nightstand where his phone had been, his frown deepened. "Were you talking on my cell phone a minute ago?"

Ah, the moment of truth, time to tell him she'd lied to his employers as to his whereabouts, even insinuating that he may have died. Though reluctant to begin, Kelly knew it was necessary. She didn't have a choice. That didn't mean she'd enjoy it. "Yes," she answered. "I was."

He nodded, as if her intrusion into his personal business was perfectly normal. "I see. Who were you talking to?"

Changing the subject, Kelly asked a question instead of answering. "Do you realize what happened? You were shot with a silver bullet. You almost died. But you didn't."

Inane chatter, but sometimes a simple pointing out of the facts was necessary before hitting him with the big one.

Mac's frown deepened. She saw the exact moment he remembered. Everything.

"Silver bullets. Hell hounds." For a moment he glanced down at his leg, wincing. "I remember. You're right—I shouldn't even be alive. How'd I get in here?"

"I helped you. Mostly, you walked."

"Seriously?"

She nodded. "You lived because you're under my protection. You won't die. We are one."

Gaze locked on hers, he swallowed hard. "So it is true. You really can do this? When you said we were one, that's what you meant?"

"Yes." She took a deep breath. "You were married to my cousin. Didn't Maggie ever discuss this with you?"

"No. She thought all of this was a big joke."

Now he'd succeeded in shocking her. "Being a Tearlach was amusing to her?"

"You'd have to understand her sense of humor. But yes, she thought the rest of her family took it all too seriously."

Careful now, she tried to figure out how to

phrase her next question. "Besides what you learned in the Protector's file, how much do you actually know about us?"

"How much did Maggie tell me, you mean?" She nodded.

"Very little." He sounded bitter. "I didn't even know about the protection thing until I read the file. We were together three years and she never said those words to me."

Careful not to show her shock, Kelly nodded. Luckily, Mac didn't understand enough to realize the ramifications of this. She did. Maggie had not considered Mac, her husband and the man whose children she'd borne, her true mate.

Which meant there might have been another. Enough to make her wonder if Mac indeed was the children's real father.

She said none of this, aware he certainly wouldn't appreciate it. Yet the only other option was that Maggie had wanted to ensure that if anything happened to her, their children would still have a father.

"Tell me what you know," she urged.

"Are you immortal?" he asked, his expression serious.

"No. And neither are you, now that you're under my protection." She avoided using the more honest phrase *bound to me.* "Tearlachs eventually do die, of course, usually of old age, but nothing else can kill us. Except fire. That never changes."

Eyes narrowed, he swore. "So the only advantage over being a regular shifter is that you can withstand silver bullets."

At a loss for words, because there was more, so much more than that, she swallowed. "I—"

"Damn. I don't see what the big deal is. No wonder Maggie joked about it. Tearlachs aren't really all that different than regular shifters. So you can withstand a silver-bullet wound. So what?"

"You'd be dead if it weren't for that," she pointed out. "And you forgot to mention our ability to confer this gift on another person."

"True, and thanks for that. But I still don't understand why everyone is so eager to form an alliance with the Tearlachs."

"The ability to withstand a silver bullet could come in handy in the event of a multispecies war."

To his credit, he caught on immediately. "In other words, if the humans came against us like they did back in the Middle Ages."

"Exactly."

He didn't appear convinced. "How likely is that? It's—"

"Far-fetched." She dropped into the chair at the side of the futon, aware she had to tread carefully. Though she'd never had to have this conversation with someone, she'd heard stories of others who had. What she bestowed was a gift, a treasure beyond price. Yet the recipients didn't always view it that way.

"Why me?" he asked, as she'd known he would.

Keeping her expression neutral, she lifted one shoulder in a shrug. "Because you happened to be there when I was attacked. I didn't want to have your death on my hands."

"I see." His bemused look told her he didn't. "If this is such a good thing, then why didn't my wife…"

She felt a knife twist in her heart. "I don't know," she answered. She wanted to ask him if Maggie had loved him, but wasn't sure she wanted to know. It was too personal and, ultimately, none of her business.

Odd. Completely and utterly strange. She'd never been one to shirk things and had always believed in straight-on honesty right from the start, but she didn't think she could handle any more of this.

Trying to think, she looked away. Was she required to inform him how deep the bond she made between them went? Or would it be better to let him find out for himself?

Choosing the latter, she rubbed her hands together.

"Now," she said briskly. "You've asked your questions. I want to ask a few of my own."

"Go ahead."

Her turn. Kelly stared at the man, wondering what questions she should ask to get the most knowledge in such a short span of time. She'd chosen him, like it or not, by an impulsive act of mercy. Now, she needed to find out what sort of man she'd picked.

She'd always trusted her dogs' judgment of people. They all loved Ben, which was part of the reason she trusted him.

Brandi, the golden-eyed pit bull with the battered ear, never strayed from Mac's side. She adored him. Kelly suspected that it might be a case of one damaged individual drawn to another, as if the dog recognized a kindred spirit.

Maybe that rationale would explain why she'd given something so sacred to a complete stranger. Sometimes, she felt like one with the damaged dogs. Something she'd never admitted, not even to herself, until now.

Putting such thoughts from her head, she

forced herself to focus on what she needed to know.

"Have you remarried?" Though he didn't wear a ring, she needed to get this out in the open.

One brow went up. "Maggie's only been gone eighteen months."

"That's not an answer."

"No. What about you?"

"This isn't about me," she said, her tone impersonal. "I don't have the benefit of a folder with all your personal info inside like you did."

"Fine." He shrugged. "Ask away."

She wished she was better at this or, at the very least, had some sort of checklist to operate off of. Something along the lines of "ten things to ask before you bind yourself to someone." Only, in her case, it would be too late.

The deed was done. Once given, her protection could not be taken back.

Therefore, she persisted. "Do you have any brothers or sisters?"

"No. I was an only child. And, before you ask, my mother is still alive. She's a shifter. I never knew my human father."

Gently, she asked the rest of it. "You and Maggie had two children, if I remember right. A boy and a girl?"

He glared at her. "Twins. Caleb and Isobel. They're three. I haven't seen them since their mother died."

She noticed he held himself stiffly, as though by moving less he could make himself invisible, invulnerable or both. Though she'd never had children, she could definitely relate. She missed her family. She understood very well how the pain of loss never went away, just diminished slightly over time.

She didn't show her pity, aware she wouldn't want his whenever she spoke of the loss of her own family and the death of her father. She already knew he felt as if he'd laid his soul bare in front of her, a distinctly uncomfortable feeling. Compounded by the fact that they were virtual strangers... She bit her lip and forced herself to look at him.

Now he looked away. A moment passed, a bit of silence broken only by the jagged sound of his breathing. When his gaze finally returned to meet hers, she saw anger lurking in the depths of his blue eyes. A second later, it was gone, quickly banished.

She sighed, well aware of how sorrow could eat you up from the inside out. "It's not easy, is it?"

"No. Even after all this time..." As he trailed

off, the rawness of his repressed emotion lurked in his voice. Of course, the anger that blazed in his eyes told her what was coming next.

"I want my children back." Leaning forward, his gaze captured and held hers. "Honest to hounds, if you have an ounce of compassion, you'll help me."

She said nothing, unwilling to make promises she couldn't keep.

Finally, he nodded, his jaw set. "Why are you doing this? What's your reasoning?"

"I want my sister back. So we do have something in common."

"Then why won't you work with me?" His rough voice spoke of his emotion. "If I can get your sister for you, will you make sure I find my children?"

Though she knew she should lie, she couldn't force the words from her suddenly closed-up throat. When she finally did, she only repeated the question that he'd never answered. "Do you have my sister?"

Slowly, he shook his head, his bereft expression letting her know it pained him to do so. "No. Nor do I know where she is. I can tell you that the Protectors aren't the ones who took her. I was only bluffing earlier, because I'd hoped you could lead me to my kids."

Since he'd given her a truth, she could only respond in kind. "I don't know where your children are, either. I wasn't even aware that they'd been removed from your custody."

"Stolen," he snarled. "Don't make it sound so civilized. I was at the funeral home, planning for her funeral, for Christ's sake. Someone from Maggie's family—*your* family—swooped in and grabbed them. They couldn't even attend their own mother's funeral. Maggie's family had disowned her, so I had to bury her alone."

The words hung in the air between them. Despite herself, Kelly's eyes filled with tears.

"You're crying?" he said, his tone filled with an odd combination of wonder and anger. "Why?"

Lifting one shoulder in a shrug, she sighed. Then, she gave in to temptation and reached out and touched his jaw, feeling the stubble like sandpaper against her fingertips. After the first reflex, a nearly imperceptible jerk, he froze.

Feeling completely stupid, she took her hand away. "Sorry."

"Yeah." He stood, placing one leg in front of the other as if testing his own strength. After a moment, he began to walk, slowly at first, increasing his stride as he gathered confidence.

"Can we stop with the fifty questions?" he asked.

"For now. But I'm sure there's more I'll need to know later. I'm trying to get to know you," she said.

"Again, why?"

Once more, she offered the truth. "I'm hoping to learn something that will explain to me why I offered you my protection."

He stared. "You speak as if giving your protection is an unusual thing. Is it that rare?"

"Yes. Extremely. We can only do that once in our lives."

Again his face closed in, letting her know he was thinking of Maggie, the wife who had chosen not to give him the precious gift, who had never truly been his mate.

"Why does it matter?" he finally asked, the devil-may-care smile at odds with the bleakness in his gaze.

"Believe me, it does." And that was all she'd say on this. For now.

Chapter 4

"Don't think you can shut this down so easily," he said, and he laughed. Something about the masculine sound made heat flare inside her.

Not good. Not good at all.

"You've got to at least answer my earlier question. Who called my phone?"

Crap. She'd hoped he'd forget.

She held up a hand. "In a minute. I need to ask one more question first. Do you know who is behind this? My sister's abduction, the attack yesterday, all of it."

"No."

Oddly enough, she believed him. Continuing to hold his gaze, she nodded. "You're privy to inside information. Do the Protectors have any idea who took Bonnie? Any clues where she might be?"

Instead of answering immediately, he dragged a hand through his choppy, dark hair. "It wasn't in the file. But our intel has led us to believe that whoever took her is coming after each of you. They want to grab your entire family, one at a time."

"No surprise there," she said ruefully. "That's why we all scattered to the four corners of the earth. My father knew this would happen. Then last night? Was that what this was all about?"

For a moment he looked dazed. "Was it only last night?" And then, before she could respond, "Why do you think? Of course that's why they attacked us. Why else?"

Restless, she began to pace back and forth in front of him. "I'm not sure. They shot me. And you. They didn't capture me. It didn't make sense."

"That's because you fought them off."

"Maybe. But still, it doesn't make sense."

"You know, you might be right." He grimaced. "But I'm thinking they didn't expect you to fight. Most of your people do not."

"I have never understood that. Even your people think we're all pushovers. That's why your boss was so shocked when he called." The instant she heard herself say the words, she wanted to recall them. But then, she knew she could only put him off so long.

"My boss? That's who you were talking to? What did he want?"

"I'm guessing to see if you were dead or alive. I think he knew about the attack. I really think the Protectors are behind this."

"No way." He rubbed his mouth. "We don't operate that way." Then, eyes narrowed, he studied her. "What did you tell him?"

She took a deep breath, then gave him the truth. "I said you were gone. That you'd left."

Swearing, he looked as if he'd like to hit something. Instead, he held out his hand. "Give me my phone."

She didn't move. "No. Listen to me. It's vitally important that they believe you've gone."

"That's bull. I would have called in." He held out his hand. "My phone. Now."

"I can't do that," she told him. "I destroyed it."

As he stared at her, fury blazing from his eyes, a muscle worked in his jaw.

"Listen to me," she continued. "Hear me out. I don't think you can trust your employers."

He snorted. "Of course you don't. Look, I

realize you're upset. You just were attacked, you lost your house, had to save a stranger's life and, on top of that, your sister's gone missing."

"And someone tried to kill you," she pointed out. "Let's not forget that."

"I haven't." Crossing his arms, he looked away. "But I can promise you those weren't Protectors. They were vampires, for hound's sake."

"And one shifter."

"True, but he had to be a renegade. Maybe even a Feral. What shifters work with vamps? Not Protectors."

"I don't know. That's your territory. Are you saying Protectors never work with vampires?"

He thought for a moment. "Not usually."

Hearing the hesitation, she pounced. "But it has happened?"

Reluctantly, he nodded. "Very rarely."

She pressed her point. "I think they set you up. But you being here worked against them. They wanted to grab me and failed."

His closed-off expression told her he wasn't buying it. "And what about me? Why would they do such a thing to one of their own?"

"Means to an end. They were willing to sacrifice you."

He didn't want to believe her, she could tell. Yet something in what she said must have resonated with him since he didn't discount it right away.

"Can you prove this?" he asked finally.

"No. But I can't disprove it, either. Until we can do one or the other, I'd say we go with the assumption that they did."

Immediately, he shook his head. "I'm sorry, but I'm not buying it."

"Then give me another alternative," she cried. "Something besides a senseless, random attack. They were armed with silver bullets. They had a purpose."

"Yes. To capture you. But it wasn't us. For the last time, the Protectors don't work that way." He stared at her for so long she fought the urge to fidget.

"I don't agree."

"Fine," he finally said. "Let's just agree to disagree until we have more information. Where do we go from here? What's the plan?"

She couldn't help but notice the way he said "we" rather than "you."

"I want my sister back. I'm going to find out a way to rescue her." Taking a deep breath, she looked at him. "And, if you help me find her, I'll do my best to help you get reunited with your children."

Still watching her closely, he didn't appear convinced. "How do you propose to do that?"

"I'm going after them."

"Just the two of us? I don't think that's a good idea."

"Why not?" she asked, using the same calm, measured tone she used to sooth a spooked dog. "You're a trained Protector and I'm a Tearlach. It'll be enough. We'll be fine."

"You know, that's why I was sent to you. To offer you the help of the Protectors."

"Their help comes with too many strings." Again she leaned in close, aware he still didn't know all that being a Tearlach entailed. "I want *you* to come with me. Singular. Not them. I don't trust them."

He lifted a brow. "Why the hell not? At the risk of beating a dead horse, you have no proof that they took your sister—in fact, since I was sent here to talk to you, that really argues against that idea. If we were in the habit of simply grabbing what we wanted, I would have captured you myself."

To that, she snorted. "As if you could."

His slight smile told her he was letting that one go. "You've got to do better than that. If we're going to be partners, we've got to be honest with each other. Why don't you trust the Protectors?"

Taking a deep breath, she told him the truth. "Because they killed my father." Though she tried to rein it in, bitterness colored her voice. "The Protectors are responsible for tearing my family apart."

Silence fell while he processed her words, his expression grim. "Though I'm sure you have your reasons for believing this, your father was working with us, not against us. We were allies when he was killed."

"I don't believe you. I need proof."

"Why?" he asked. "From what I've seen of you, you seem to operate on hunches and supposition. Kidnapping someone really isn't the sort of thing we do."

"Maybe not now. But I know differently. Think about what your organization was less than a year ago. Protectors were nothing more than paid assassins. They exterminated anyone who didn't conform to a predetermined set of narrow rules. They were corrupt through and through. So don't tell me it's not possible."

He bowed his head. "True. But those individuals and their followers are all gone. They've been punished. Things are different now." Taking a deep breath, he watched her, no doubt waiting for her to speak. When she did not, he continued as if she had.

"You speak of us with such rancor." Watching her the way a wolf keeps an eye on a sunning snake, he grimaced. "Since you feel that way, why did you save me? I'm a Protector. My loyalty is with them."

"Still? Surely after this, you must have doubts."

"Why would I?" He spread his hands. "You've given me no proof, no evidence. You were attacked and we both were shot. That's all we know."

He had a point. All she had were her hunches and, while they were rarely wrong, she had no proof.

"Furthermore, why do you want me to go with you? You don't know me. If you don't trust them, you shouldn't trust me, either."

As if she had a choice. One impetuous act, and here they were. Stuck together for the rest of their natural lives. Only he didn't know that yet.

With a sigh, she realized she'd have to tell him the rest of it. "Let me try to explain. As I told you, you're under my protection now. Now that we've said the words and completed the ritual, we're bound together. This is not something I take lightly."

"Bound together? For how long?"

"For a while," she said vaguely, aware he'd probably press for more details. How could she tell him that they were, theoretically, bound together for the rest of their lives? Did he really need to know that in her world, a Tcarlach spoke those words only once? To the one who would be their true mate? Not just to some random stranger, no matter how beautiful he might be.

Oh, what a horrible mistake she'd made. Still, when she imagined him lying dead in a pool of blood, she knew she'd do the same thing again.

Apparently, her words were enough to make him suspicious. "Why do I get the feeling that there's a lot you're not telling me? You're feeding me bits and pieces of the story. I need you to spit it all out. I'm listening."

"I'm not ready to do that yet." She met his gaze, being as honest as she could. "Sorry."

"Then give me back my phone."

Stubborn man. If she had an ounce of sense, she'd hand him back the pieces of his cell and send him on his way before either one of them got hurt.

But she couldn't. That was the crux of it. She flat-out had no choice. He didn't have a choice, either. If he wanted to pretend he did, that was up to him. He'd find out the truth sooner or later.

"I'm not giving you back your phone. I've already destroyed it. Look, we're bound together, you and I. Like it or not. I said the words, saved your life, and there's a debt to be paid."

As they locked eyes, something clicked in his gaze and she knew he had begun to understand.

Dipping his chin, he finally acknowledged the truth of her statement. "You're right," he said. "I'll go with you. I do owe you for my life, and I always repay my debts."

Honor, she thought sardonically. Rare among shifters these days. As if he truly had a choice. Careful not to show any emotion, she nodded. "Thanks."

"Hold on." His smile contained a hint of mockery. "I'm not finished. I'll go with you, but in return, you have to promise me one thing."

She crossed her arms. "Go ahead."

"If on the chance you're wrong and the Protectors are not behind this, will you agree to at least talk to them?"

She considered. "Maybe."

Immediately, he shook his head. "That's not good enough."

Hiding a smile, she finally nodded. "Fine. If

you're wrong and can prove it, I'll talk to them. No promises beyond that."

With that, he seemed satisfied. "All right, then. It's settled. Where are we going and when do we leave?"

"As soon as you're well enough." She glanced at her watch. "I want to make sure you're all healed. Maybe a few more hours, maybe tomorrow. We'll have to take the house dogs to a friend in town."

He nodded, then shoved aside the sheet and swung his muscular legs to the side. Pushing to his feet, he waved away her clumsy attempt to offer support.

"I've got it." Swaying slightly, he looked like a sailor trying to find balance during rough seas. Jaw clenched, he grabbed the side of the futon and, using it to steady himself, took a tentative step forward.

Then another. When he looked at Kelly, grinning, she felt an odd knot in her chest.

"I did it," he said, sounding triumphant. "I'm good to go." His smile widened as he examined the shrinking patch of skin where the bullet wound had been. "This is freakin' amazing. You can't even tell I've been shot."

Such was the blessing—or the curse—of being protected by a Tearlach.

While she was pondering this, Mac disappeared into the bathroom and closed the door behind him.

As the day moved on, his strength improved. At lunchtime, he was starving, eating three sandwiches and an entire bowl of chips, plus an apple and two pickles.

"You look good." She gave him the honest compliment. "But you're not fully healed yet. Rest, if you can. We've got a long trip tomorrow."

He smiled wryly. "Yes, Nurse Kelly. Whatever you say."

At that, she couldn't help but laugh.

"You're right, I need to lie down," he said. When she nodded, he went straight for the futon, her pit bull Brandi settling on the floor at his side. Closing his eyes, just like that, he fell asleep.

She watched him doze, unable to help herself. Whatever force that drew her to him tormented her, making her want to climb up on the futon and curl into his side. She restrained herself, just barely, and kept one eye on the time.

An hour later, the sun had begun to travel toward the horizon and he woke up. It was time to go.

Crossing to his side, she rubbed Brandi's head

lightly before scowling at him. It occurred to her that her best armor might be an unpleasant attitude and she tested that now.

"Are you well enough to travel now? If so, we need to go right away."

"At dusk? Why not in the morning?"

How to explain the instinct that guided her life?

"Because we have to leave now," she said. Nothing more.

To her surprise, rather than arguing, he got up and stretched, drawing her gaze. "I'd like to brush my teeth and freshen up, and I'll be good to go."

"Let me pack a bag," she told him, making her voice cold to show she had no reaction to the warmth of his male beauty. "Not that I have much—almost everything I own burned in the fire. I assume you have one in your car?"

"Yes." He watched while she threw together a few things. "What about the dogs? I'm guessing it will be safe enough to take them to your friend's place in town, if we do it quickly. Are we taking all of them? Even the ones in the kennel?"

Despite herself, she laughed. "No. Not the kennel dogs. Ben said he'd stop by here once or twice a day to check on them."

"Ben?" He stared at her for so long she became uncomfortable. "Who's Ben?"

"A good friend, nothing more," she said firmly.

After he'd freshened up, he rejoined her in the main room. "Let's hit the road." Leading the way, he held the door open for her. "After you."

"Stay where I can see you," she cautioned, refusing to give in to his charm.

He dipped his chin in acknowledgment, his slight smile knowing. "Still don't trust me, eh?"

"Not entirely," she admitted, checking to make sure her spare gun was loaded before holstering it. She grabbed a box of extra shells, just in case.

Watching all this, he held out his hand. "Since mine was an apparent casualty of the fire, if you have another spare, I'd like a weapon, too."

She ignored him, continuing to pack her ammo.

"I gave my word," he said quietly. "I never go back on that."

Instead of answering, she motioned for him to follow her outside. "We're going to leave now." Checking her weapon, she motioned toward the door. "If and when I feel the need, I'll make sure you're armed. Right now, keep your eyes open for trouble."

She could tell he didn't like that. The frown line between his eyes deepened and his mouth tightened, but he didn't respond, other than to comment on what he plainly viewed as her paranoia. "I don't think they'll be back so soon."

Outside, the early-evening sky looked gray and cloudy. They'd taken a few steps from the house when the sound of an airplane made them look up.

"There." She pointed at the single-engine plane in the sky. "Still think I'm wrong?"

Grabbing her arm, he cursed as he pulled her back toward the house. "Get inside."

Slamming the door closed behind them, Mac faced her, breathing hard. "We don't know for sure that was them."

"No, but do you really want to take a chance?"

He crossed to the window, standing to one side and peering through the drapes. "Is there a place around here for a small plane to land?"

"Other than fields, no. The nearest airstrip is ten miles or more away."

Eyeing her, he appeared to be considering. "I don't think they'll risk trying to land in the pasture. What direction is the airstrip?"

"Due north."

"That's the direction they're heading." He

pointed to a speck in the sky. "If we're going to leave now, we need to hurry."

Nodding her agreement, she opened the door. "Let's go." They headed straight to his car and she waited impatiently while he retrieved his bag from the trunk.

"Is it yours?" she asked, indicating the Malibu.

"No. It's a rental."

She flashed him what she hoped was an apologetic smile before bending over and slashing the passenger-side front tire with her pocketknife. "Come on." She moved on, heading toward her garage at a trot.

"Why'd you do that?" Keeping pace with her, he sounded only mildly curious.

"Because now you can call the rental car company and see if they'll send somebody to retrieve the car. After all, you have a flat tire."

He said nothing, but the look he gave her brimmed with disapproval, which made her feel as if she had to elaborate. "You can tell them you had to get to a meeting, so you left it on this ranch in the middle of nowhere."

"Sounds like you have everything planned."

Again, she got the distinct sense that he didn't approve.

Though she told herself she didn't care, it still rankled. "I like tying up loose ends."

At the entrance, she led the way to her workshop slash garage and punched in a code. The overhead door swung open. Inside the cool darkness where she kept her cars, both vehicles sat untouched and undamaged by the fire. "Come on," she urged again.

Inside, he stared. "You have both a Corvette and a Hummer H2?"

"That wasn't in your file?" She couldn't help her sharp-voiced reply.

Stone-faced, he shook his head. "No."

Half wishing he would react and half wondering why she seemed to be spoiling for a fight, she opened the back of the Hummer to reveal an assortment of plastic kennels. Then she whistled for the dogs. They came running, tails streaming out behind them. One by one, Kelly directed them up into the back of the SUV, lifting the smaller ones and letting the larger dogs jump. They seemed to sense her urgency and moved quickly, obeying without fuss.

The last to arrive was Brandi, who stood with her side pressed against Mac's leg, plainly not wanting to leave him.

"Brandi, up," Kelly ordered. To her disbelief, the dog didn't move.

Not looking at her, Mac stepped forward and patted the floor inside the Hummer. "Brandi, up," he said, repeating her command. The dog responded immediately, leaping gracefully into the Hummer and going inside her crate.

"She's mine," he said, smiling. "Whatever happens, when this is over, she's coming with me."

He thought they could simply part after this. Telling herself that he didn't know, this still both stunned and infuriated Kelly. Careful not to show her reaction, she flashed Mac an utterly fake smile. "We'll see."

Now that all seven were inside their kennels, she closed the tailgate.

"Are you ready?" she asked Mac, keeping her voice pleasant. "We've got to go now."

Meeting her gaze, he nodded and held out his hand for the keys.

For a moment she only stared at him in disbelief before shaking her head. "You're not driving. For one thing, you're not completely healed yet, and for another, this is my vehicle. Furthermore, I know my way around here and you don't."

"Are you always so bossy?"

Looks like she wasn't the only one spoiling for a fight.

"Come on," she told him. "Let's go."

He didn't move. "I think all this Tearlach stuff has gone to your head."

She let her breath out in a huff. "Stop trying to provoke a fight. We don't have time for this."

"They have to land the plane and drive ten miles. I think we have a few seconds to spare." Moving closer, he stopped when he was inches from her face. "A fight might be just the thing," he drawled. "You want one, too. Maybe it'll clear the air."

"We really don't have time for this," she repeated, using her most bored voice. She gave him a dismissive look and turned to move away.

Instead, he grabbed her. Yanked her up close, chest to chest, muscular arms imprisoning her. Then, while she was still sputtering, he covered her mouth with his.

Instantly, she froze, words and arguing all forgotten. He was big and solid and smelled like sun and grass.

As he slanted his lips over hers, she thought he meant to punish her with the hard demand of his kiss. She wanted to resist, would resist; after all, she didn't even know how to respond. Though he could not know it, she had never been kissed before.

So she stood, hanging on to her anger like a

shield, while he pressed his mouth against hers and she tried not to react.

Then something changed. The tone, the tenor, the slight hitch in his breathing, the rapid tempo of his heart against her breast. Though he didn't push, it was *more* and she responded to it like a flower opening her petals to the sun.

She found herself parting her lips and when he slipped his tongue into her mouth, she swayed, dizzy, against him. He tasted her and suddenly she couldn't get enough. Now she pressed against him, feeling the unfamiliar swell of his arousal with something akin to wonder.

This…this was what it was like, the thing she'd been forbidden to have?

As the thought came to her, she realized how close she stood to the edge, to being out of control. She pushed him away, hard, and stumbled backward, wiping her hand across her mouth.

He stood, unmoving and staring at her, expression hooded, then without commenting, he turned and went around to the passenger side, climbing up and buckling himself in.

"Let's go," he said, apparently unfazed and giving her an impersonal smile that she felt like a punch to the gut.

Then, because any reaction she showed— even revulsion—would be a victory for him, she climbed up in the driver's seat, fit the key in the ignition and started the car.

What the hell? Maybe this Tearlach binding thing went both ways. If she ever saw her mother again, she'd have to ask her.

As she backed up out of the garage, a maroon Ford Explorer screeched from around the side of the building and swung sideways, effectively blocking them in.

Chapter 5

"Looks like I was wrong about the time. Do you know them?" Mac asked, eyeing the maroon SUV and wishing he had his gun.

"No. Brace yourself," she said, her voice only the slightest bit husky. "If I have to, I'll run into them. This Hummer can push them out of the way."

She sounded so certain, but he had his doubts. The thing was big, but it wasn't a tank, after all.

"You're probably right, but let me have your pistol." He held out his hand. "Just in case."

She shot him a glance, but didn't hand over her weapon.

With a sigh, he lowered his arm, glancing in

the backseat where the dogs had grown agitated in their kennels. "They know something's up."

"They usually do." Voice impersonal, she returned her attention to the other vehicle. "Good thing they're secured."

He had to admire the way she sounded so cool, confident and collected.

Kelly revved the engine. "Hang on," she told him.

Both front doors of the other vehicle simultaneously opened, meaning there were at least two of them. Probably more, in the back.

Fingers itching for a gun, Mac waited for the back doors to fly open, disgorging a whole slew of bad guys with weapons pointed at them. This time at least, he thought wryly, they wouldn't be vamps. Too early in the day for them.

But no one else exited the vehicle. Instead, the two men in dark suits turned to face the Hummer, peering into the dark garage with hands raised high to show they were unarmed. They looked like government workers—FBI, CIA or...Protectors.

As he tried to see their auras to determine if they were human or shifter, Kelly turned to him, green eyes panicked for the first time.

"Protectors!" she said. "Get down! You're supposed to be dead. They mustn't see you."

Oh, for the love of… Though he shot her a glare, he complied, unclipping his seat belt and sliding down until he rested, back to seat, just beneath the dash.

"Satisfied?"

"Yep. I hope they didn't see you," she said without looking at him, voice tense, gaze still fixed on the strangers. Again she revved the engine, but kept the vehicle in Park with her foot still hovering over the accelerator.

"I doubt it."

As he was about to urge her to get going—no telling when the suits would pull guns and start shooting at them—she shifted into Drive.

"Hold on." Jerking the steering wheel to the right, she jammed the accelerator to the floor.

The massive SUV shot forward and they rammed the Explorer's front quarter panel hard, metal screeching.

As Mac pushed himself up enough to see, the men in suits scattered.

"Get back down," Kelly ordered, shifting into Reverse and backing in preparation for another hit.

Muttering curses under his breath, he complied. Even though they weren't currently in their wolf bodies, they were shifters, and letting her take the dominant position went against everything he believed in. As soon as he was a hundred percent, he promised himself that would change.

She slammed the Explorer one more time. The other vehicle shuddered and slid a few feet.

"Once more ought to do it." Reversing quickly, she repeated the process. This time when she rammed the Ford, she succeeded in pushing the other vehicle out of the way enough to let them past.

"Success!" she said, the excitement in her voice making him wonder if she'd high-five him next.

He really wished he was driving instead of her.

As she floored the Hummer, the powerful engine roared as they tore off, leaving a cloud of dust behind them.

Pushing himself back in his seat, Mac clicked his seat belt on and turned, glancing back to see the other men scrambling to get in their damaged vehicle and give chase.

"You'd better hurry," he commented. "They're about to come after us."

"Okay." The look she shot him wasn't friendly. "I'm doing the best I can."

"Anytime you want to switch, I'm ready. I'm great at evasive driving," he said, quite cheerfully, he thought, despite the fact that he had his teeth clenched.

"You really are a control freak, aren't you?"

Her comment added insult to injury. "I'm a skilled driver," he told her. "And since the motive is to get away from the bad guys, I'd think you'd take all the advantages you could get."

"I drive just fine."

"And there's the difference," he pointed out. "You drive fine. I drive…excessively well. Also, I need a gun. I refuse to be an unarmed target anymore. If you still think I'm going to try and use it against you, then you need to get over it."

"Are you finished?" she asked. For the first time he noticed her white-knuckled grip on the steering wheel.

He tamped back both his frustration and his irritation. "For now." Glancing back, he saw the Ford was still hanging in there. "Can that thing catch us?"

She snorted. "Doubt it. This Hummer might be heavy as all get-out, but it can move better than that. Just to be sure, I'm going to drive like a bat out of hell, so you'd better hang on. I'll show you some excellent driving." She said the last with a straight face.

True to her word, she blazed down the side roads, taking the entrance to the freeway at what had to be at least sixty-five. Behind them, their pursuers accelerated also, minutely closing the gap between them.

"I'm not sure the freeway is the best—"

"Hush." Cutting him off, her mouth twisted. "Right now I can't deal with both you and driving."

"They're gaining," he pointed out, probably needlessly. "Better step on it."

Gripping the steering wheel, she muttered something under her breath that sounded like *damn Protectors.*

"You know," he said, without looking at her, "in my line of work, we're taught to look for facts instead of jumping to conclusions. How can you be certain they were Protectors? I didn't recognize either of them."

"Do you know every single one?"

"Of course not."

"Who else would they be?" She shook her head. "You are so in denial."

That rankled. He had to bite back a hasty cutting remark. "How about we agree they weren't on our side, whoever they were?"

"Fine." She kept her attention on the road and her hands gripping the steering wheel. Still without looking at him, she asked, "Why'd you do that, back there?"

She meant the kiss.

"I don't know," he answered honestly. "Gave in to impulse, I guess."

"Well, don't do it again."

"I won't. Believe me." He sighed. "Mind telling me where we're going?" he asked.

"To drop off the dogs."

Keeping his tone pleasant, he continued, "I mean after that."

Switching lanes without signaling, she stomped on the accelerator and, despite its bulk, the Hummer leapt forward.

When she finally glanced at him, she appeared confident, not worried. He couldn't decide if this was a good thing or bad. "Well, before you showed up, I had planned to head to the airport and hop a flight to Vancouver, Canada. Now there's you to consider, and I have a feeling those goons will be watching the airports. So we're driving there instead." Her sideways glance revealed little. "I'm assuming you have your passport?"

He nodded. "Of course. But why Canada? And more specifically, why Vancouver?"

This time, her look plainly indicated she thought he asked the question simply to irritate her. "My sister was last living on Vancouver

Island when she was taken. From Vancouver we can catch a jumper plane to the island."

This made no sense to him. Wyoming to British Columbia was a long way to go merely to look for clues.

A quick glance back showed their pursuers had fallen back, though they were still doggedly chasing them.

"Surely you don't think your sister's still there?"

"No," she answered, cutting to the middle lane in between a pickup and a Cadillac, passing a minivan, before swerving back into the left passing lane. "But I'm hoping I can find out something to give me a clue where they've taken her. It's all I have to go on, unless..."

He pretended not to get it. "Unless what?"

"Unless you know something you're not telling me."

Christ. It took everything he had not to groan out loud. "We've already been over this. Look, I know exactly how you feel, knowing someone you love is in danger and feeling powerless to help."

"Because of your children."

"Exactly. Not a moment goes by that I don't worry about them."

He took a deep breath, more to calm himself than anything. "What about the rest of your family?" he asked.

She shot him yet another dark look from an apparently endless repertoire of them. "What about them?"

"Look, I'm only asking if they can help you. Your sister's been taken and you've been attacked. It seems as if whoever is behind this is going to try to take them one by one. Rather than going to Vancouver Island to look for clues, wouldn't it make more sense to head out to where one of them still lives and wait for the abductors to show up to grab them?"

For a second she didn't respond, making him wonder if she was actually considering the idea.

Then she glanced at him with a mocking, sardonic smile, and he realized he was wrong.

"Is that the plan? Talk me into revealing their location so your cohorts can follow me?"

His cohorts. Whatever. Turning in his seat, he looked for their pursuers. The Ford Explorer still hung in there, about five cars back.

"At least they're not shooting," he said.

"Probably because they don't want to endanger you."

"For the love of…" Shaking his head, he swore. "You're actually serious? They've already injured me. What is wrong with you?"

Lifting her chin, she shot him a knowing glance. "Nothing's wrong with me. And don't give me that false I'm-so-injured crap. As possibilities go, it makes perfect sense. You've told me how dedicated you are to your job."

"Look, I'm not doing undercover work, or whatever you seem to think." Quietly, he reiterated what he'd said earlier. "I gave you my word, remember? Plus, as you so nicely pointed out to me, I have a debt to repay."

After a moment of silence, she nodded.

"Sorry," she said, her tone dry. "Maybe that was a bit far-fetched. While you have the distinct advantage of knowing all about me, I still know absolutely nothing about you."

As peace offerings went, it was a small one. Still, with a woman this prickly, he'd take what he could get.

Grimacing, he conceded her point. "True. It hasn't been that long since I showed up on your doorstep, managed to get shot and you had to save me. I won't soon forget that I owe you my life." He swallowed, then continued, "But you should know, I don't like being beholden to anyone. It sticks in my craw."

She flicked him a gaze and he saw he'd startled her. For a moment, he thought he might have reached past her invisible barrier. Then, she snorted and he realized he was wrong.

"Pretty good job of trying to make me feel I can trust you," she replied. "Save it."

He didn't understand her way of thinking. "If you mistrust me so badly, why not just dump me off somewhere and go on your way? Why keep me with you, especially since you seem to think I'm about to betray you at the earliest opportunity?"

"Because I really think they'll try to kill you if you're not with me," she said slowly.

Frustrated, he clenched his teeth. "Either I'm one of them or I'm not. Make up your mind."

"You can still be one of them and be in danger."

"That makes no sense."

"I'm aware of that." She shot him another look, her lovely mouth twisted. "But I frequently have these sort of premonition things. Insights, if you will. I can't explain them, but they come true more often than not." She motioned behind them. "Looks like we've lost our tail."

Turning to look behind them, he saw no sign of the Ford Explorer. "That's odd, since we're still on the freeway. Unless they got off, took a shortcut and are planning on cutting us off farther on."

"Now who's paranoid?" she asked, but she was smiling.

At least they were talking.

"Don't slow down. You never know, they might have had another set of guys take over, knowing we wouldn't recognize the vehicle."

Though she shook her head, she did as he asked, continuing to accelerate. Glancing at the speedometer, he saw they were going well over ninety miles per hour.

But she appeared to have relaxed somewhat. Something she'd said earlier...

"You say you have premonitions, right?" At her nod, he continued, "What about now? What do you see happening now?"

"I can't turn it off and on like that. I wish I could, but I have absolutely no control over when it happens."

He considered this, not entirely sure he believed in second sight, especially since Maggie had always discounted its existence. Still, Kelly was different. He supposed he was willing to consider the possibility. If nothing else, talking about it made good conversation.

"But you had a premonition about me, right? When?"

"When you showed up on my doorstep. Actually, I had two premonitions that day. I knew something bad was going to happen, just not what. And then, when I saw you..." She fell silent.

"And? When you saw me, what did you... see?"

"Oh, it's not like that," she replied immediately. "I don't actually 'see' things, like a vision. It's more of a knowing, a gut feeling."

He nodded to show he understood, though really he didn't. Her tone had softened somewhat, and he'd prefer to keep it that way. "Like intuition?"

"Maybe. But a bit more precise."

"Gotcha," he said. This woman intrigued him, for more reasons than her jaw-dropping good looks. She was a puzzle, layered in ways that his uncomplicated wife, Maggie, hadn't been. Oddly enough, he felt drawn to her, though he'd be the first to admit it had been a while since he'd been with a woman, any woman, which could be the reason. That, combined with her unselfconscious sensuality...

He looked up to find her eyeing him oddly. "Are you all right?" she asked.

"Yeah. I'm fine." Giving himself a mental shake, he knew he'd have to be careful. Things like lust could cloud his judgment, which led to mistakes.

Barreling down the freeway, they had to be hitting speeds approaching one hundred. In the back, one of the dogs whined, causing several of them to join in.

"I thought we were going to drop the dogs off at your friend's in town," he pointed out.

"We are."

"But we're on the freeway. Haven't we passed whatever town you meant by now?"

"The closest town is thirty miles away." She sounded amused. "We're headed there now. Once we get the dogs taken care of, we'll be traveling northwest. I've got to sit down with a map and figure out a route."

"Do you have a contingency plan?" he asked. "Just in case that doesn't pan out?"

"No. It will work out. That is the only plan." She didn't appear to find anything wrong with this. "We'll see what happens from there."

As a Protector, hell, as a rational *man,* he was deeply uncomfortable with such vagueness and said so.

"That's the best I can do." She shrugged. "Sorry."

"Don't you think they'll either be waiting to intercept you on the way or waiting for you once you arrive?"

She frowned, giving him a suspicious look.

"Is that a warning?" As if he were calling the shots, working with her pursuers.

In an instant, they were right back where they'd started, as though they'd never made any headway at all.

Like a roller coaster. Up, then down. He'd had enough. "Look, I don't know what your deal is, but you either stop the deprecating and derogatory remarks, or I'm out of here. I don't care about your premonitions, I'll take my chances."

"You gave your word," she reminded him, her voice level as she threw his own words back in his face. "What about the sacredness of that?"

For a moment, he saw red.

"That's it." He pointed, aware both his voice and his hand were shaking from the effort of keeping his temper under check. "Pull over and let me out. If you think I'm riding all the way to the Western Canadian coast with you treating me like dirt, you've got another thought coming. Since you so clearly despise me, I'll just have to figure out another way to repay the debt."

She didn't pull over, but then he really hadn't expected her to. The woman was a mess of contradictions. He doubted she even understood her own actions.

Right now, though, the ball was in her court.

Instead of looking at him, she contemplated the road, her expression frozen in stone.

"You're right," she finally said, shooting him a quick glance that wasn't just a tiny bit apologetic. "I'm sorry. It won't happen again. Unless, of course, you give me reason."

Mac let that one slide. This was a start. "Fine. No more of this you're-the-enemy stuff, okay?"

Slowly, she nodded. "Okay."

"Good. Now maybe you can explain to me the real reason you wanted me to go with you."

"Because you know more than you're telling me," she admitted. "And I'm not calling you the enemy, but I know you aren't telling me everything. You mentioned trading my sister for your kids. Why would you say that if you didn't have a good idea how to get to her? So, don't bother to deny it."

"I was desperate," he admitted. "I didn't know what else to say to get your attention. I've been searching for a Tearlach—any Tearlach—for the past eighteen months, ever since they grabbed my children. You're the first one I've found, and that only because of a job assignment."

"Still, you showing up right before the attack seemed awfully convenient," she said with a half smile.

He rolled his eyes. "Let me get this straight. You think I arranged getting myself shot with a silver bullet to prove you are what the file says you are, let you save my life and am still holding out on you?"

"I—" Glancing in the rearview mirror, she swore. "They're back. We have a tail again. How they hell did they find us?"

He shook his head. "It's not like we went any-where. We're still on the same freeway."

"True." She swore again. "Why didn't you tell me to get off?" Without waiting for an answer, she continued, "The next exit takes us to Ben's place, but I'm going to drive past. I can't bring trouble to his doorstep. He didn't ask for any of this."

"Take the exit anyway," he urged. "Just don't go directly to Ben's. We'll have a better chance of losing them once we get off the freeway."

"All right." She gave him a grim look. "Where do we go? Any ideas?"

Incredulously, he nearly opened his mouth to retort. She'd been so bossy, so determined to be in charge, and now she was asking *him* for advice?

Careful to hide his reaction, he swallowed hard and mentally counted to three before speaking.

"Since we can't travel with seven dogs," he said, "we've got to drop them off. We lose these bozos, and circle around. I want you to call Ben and arrange to meet him somewhere else. We'll move them from our vehicle to his, and then take off."

"Any idea where we should meet?"

"I don't care. A shopping mall, a convenience store, a gas station. Anywhere there are lots of people and cars. It's easier to disappear in a crowd."

"All right, then. I have to admit, this is the first time I'm honestly glad you have the experience you have."

He said the first thing that came to mind. "You're saying you're glad I'm a Protector?"

After only an instant's hesitation, she nodded. "Yes."

"Thank you. Now, call Ben, arrange a meeting place and then lose these goons. After we drop the dogs off, we might want to consider trading this out for another vehicle."

"Trade in my Hummer?" Wow. This *was* progress. Again, he managed to keep his face expressionless.

"No. Park it. Then we grab another car. Something different that they won't recognize."

"Steal a car?" She sounded so shocked that

he had to smile. "I'm not breaking the law if I can help it. That's the first thing I learned about staying hidden—don't do anything that'll put you on the radar."

She did have a valid point. Still, they were driving a huge Hummer. Like no one noticed that?

"Fine. We'll keep the Hummer. Even if it is highly recognizable. Maybe after the second or third time we find ourselves with a tail, you'll understand what I mean."

"Maybe I'll just lose them again." Giving him a grin he could only describe as shit-eating, she yanked the wheel to the left, cutting off a dump truck in the process and barely avoiding taking a direct hit to the rear passenger side.

"Damn." He swore out loud.

Careening down the exit, she took the first side street, then another left, then a right, finally pulling into a small grocery store parking lot and driving around to the side, where she pulled into a space between the trash Dumpster and the building. The huge Hummer barely fit.

"We have a clear view of the parking lot from here, and won't be easy to spot," she told him, her voice rich with satisfaction. "Let's see if they find us this time. If they do, we'll know they have a tracking device."

Ten minutes passed. Then fifteen. At twenty, Kelly started getting antsy, shifting in her seat.

Finally, he took pity on her. "I think we can safely say we lost them."

"Good." She dug out her cell phone. "Let me call Ben and arrange to have him meet us. We're less than ten minutes from his house."

Call made, she finally relaxed. Turning and speaking to her dogs—who'd been remarkably quiet—in a soothing voice, she seemed confident again, almost friendly.

A few minutes later, a faded blue Chevrolet van pulled into the lot and slowed. Pulling a U-turn, it slowly backed up toward them.

"That's Ben," she said, smiling the first genuine smile Mac had seen since he'd met her. She pushed open her door and jumped from the Hummer, moving with an energy to her that made Mac wonder.

He thought about following but, not wanting to interrupt her private time with her friend, decided to stay put. He'd help them transfer the dogs, assuming they needed it.

The big man who emerged from the van wasn't at all what Mac had expected. Built like a linebacker, the human had long gray hair pulled back in a Willie Nelson–style ponytail. This contrasted with his military bearing, but

Mac had seen a fair share of men who, once released from the restrictive military life, went the opposite direction.

Mac watched as Ben hugged Kelly, a look of naked longing flashing over the other man's lined face. Stunned, Mac looked away, realizing Ben wasn't aware of an onlooker's presence.

When he looked back, they were no longer hugging. Kelly was talking animatedly, gesturing at the Hummer. A moment later they walked around the driver's side and opened the back.

Mac got out and walked back there, meeting the other man's hostile gaze with an easy smile. Kelly introduced them and he held out his hand. Slowly, Ben took it, looking from Mac to Kelly and back again.

"How do you two know each other?" he asked.

"Long story," Mac said. "We really don't have a lot of time."

Acknowledging the truth of his words, Kelly reached for one of the smaller dog crates, lifting and transferring it inside Ben's van. "He's right," she said. "Sorry, Ben. I'll have to catch you up later."

Either Ben was used to rejection or he'd realized he'd never have a chance with her. Expression calm, he nodded and grabbed the largest crate, the one containing Brandi, the pit bull mix. Lifting it as if it weighed next to nothing, he carried it over to his vehicle and set it down gently.

With his gunshot wound still aching, Mac stuck with the smaller crates. In about two minutes, they'd transferred all the dogs to the van.

"I really appreciate you doing this," Kelly said, giving Ben a quick hug. "Make sure and stop by my place at least twice a day, okay?" She didn't see the wounded expression that flashed in the other man's eyes as he met Mac's gaze.

Mac dipped his chin in silent acknowledgment before glancing at his watch. "We need to get going," he said.

Immediately, Kelly turned and went to the driver's side. Opening the door, she gave Ben a jaunty wave, watching as he got in his van and drove away.

"Now we're off," she said, either forgetting to don her crabby attitude or mellowed by her brief encounter with Ben.

Mac thought her eyes looked suspiciously bright, so he suspected it was the latter. "Exactly how close are you and Ben?" he asked, dismayed at the sharp pang he felt at the thought that they might be more than friends.

"He's like a brother to me," she said quietly, starting the Hummer. As the engine roared to life, she shook her head. "I know he'll take care of my dogs, but I can't help but worry about them. They're my family, especially since I don't get to see my real one."

As they pulled back onto the service road, her cell phone rang. Keeping one hand on the steering wheel, she answered.

"Hello?" Whoever was on the other end must have shocked her, because she froze. Listening, she nodded once or twice, but didn't speak. A single tear trickled down her cheek.

Chapter 6

Mac waited in silence until she concluded the call, gripping the phone and never uttering anything else except a whispered and choked goodbye at the end. Finally, she closed the cell. When she raised her head and looked at him, bleak sorrow darkened her gaze.

"Are you all right?" he asked, pointlessly, since it was perfectly obvious she was not.

Mouth working, she tried to speak, and finally settled on shaking her head.

Somehow, he knew what she was trying to say. "They've taken someone else, haven't they?"

"Yes." She nodded. "One of my cousins. Ian's sister Katie."

Though he didn't know if she would welcome his comfort, he was unable to keep from reaching for her. Instead of embracing her, he touched her arm.

"I'm sorry. I can't imagine what this must be like for you, having to stand by helplessly while your family is snatched, one by one." But he did know. His children had been stolen in exactly the same way. Pain stabbed him at the thought.

Narrowing her eyes, she studied him. He braced himself for a suspicious question, but instead she lifted her chin.

"We're no longer standing by doing nothing," she said, her mouth set in a hard line. "Just like you have never stopped looking for your children."

He dipped his head, acknowledging the truth of her words.

"And we've never been helpless," she said.

"What do you mean?"

"You Pack people think you have us pegged, but you don't know the half of it." Her voice wavered. Looking away, she cleared her throat.

"Are you all right?" he asked again, not knowing what else to say.

"Yes. No." She spoke the contradictory words as if trying to make up her mind. "Sorry. I'm a bit of a mess right now."

She took a deep breath before continuing, "That phone call was from my mother. This is the first time we've spoken since my father died twelve years ago."

Surprised, he raised a brow. "You haven't spoken to your own mother in twelve years? That seems a bit extreme, doesn't it?"

With a shrug, she discounted his words. "It wasn't safe."

"Hmm." He let that one go. "Neither one of you appeared to have much to say to each other after all that time."

She gave him a small bleak smile, making him wonder if she was aware of how desolate she looked.

"Mom didn't have a lot of time to talk," she said. "But that's okay, since I'll be seeing her soon."

Aware he had to tread very carefully, Mac nodded. "What do you mean?"

"My family is getting together. While I'm not sure that's a good idea, nobody asked for my opinion. Since my dad died, my uncle Danny has been calling the shots."

"Getting together? Which means there'll be more than one Tearlach in the same place?" A prickle of excitement filled him. If all the Tearlachs gathered, then maybe… He couldn't help but wonder if his children would be there.

Kelly appeared oblivious to his train of thought.

"Exactly. Since two of us have been taken, they've realized this isn't going to stop. My uncle has called a meeting." Twisting her hands together, she sighed. "I'm worried the abductors will find out about it and it won't be safe for anyone."

"I agree with you there," he said, relieved that she had finally seen reason. "We can make it safe."

"How?"

"Let me make a phone call. The Protectors need to know about this. Your family needs assistance. They can help. It's a win-win. The Protectors will be glad to provide security."

"No." Her sharp tone matched the look she gave him. "That's exactly what I'm talking about. Letting anyone find out will be dangerous. No one needs to know about this. No one, most especially not them. Do you understand?"

"Then you shouldn't have told me."

"That's why I didn't give you any specifics," she retorted. "Now, are you with me or against me?"

Since arguing would be pointless, he slowly

nodded. "I'm with you." She was wrong, but until he could prove that to her, she wouldn't understand. Plus, he didn't want to jeopardize the possibility that he might be able to see—and take back—his children.

"I probably shouldn't have even told you," she continued in a brisk voice. "Now I have to decide whether to bring you or drop you off somewhere."

Crud. She had to bring him. And he couldn't let her even begin to suspect why.

Feigning disinterest, he looked out the window. "I'd be happy to wait in the car while you attend your meeting."

"That won't work," she said immediately. "I'm afraid to let you out of my sight."

"I don't even have a cell phone," he pointed out.

"True, but there are still payphones here and there. The last thing I need is for you to find one and call your buddies. I can't put my family at risk like that."

He hid a smile. She was smart, he'd give her that. However, if he called in anyone at this point, it would be one or two of his friends to act as reinforcements in helping him rescue the twins. Nothing more, nothing less. If she and her people didn't want the Protectors' help, he wasn't going to foist their services on them.

Though, until now, he'd been completely up front with her, she didn't need to know that he'd be on her side only for as long as it suited him. If push came to shove, if it came down to her and the Tearlachs versus getting his children back, she had to know what he'd choose.

He had to believe she'd do the same.

"It seems to me you've already decided what to do with me," he said, keeping his voice neutral.

She gave him another cutting look while she drove. "True. I don't trust you not to tell the Protectors. Especially if your children are involved. That's why I haven't told you the location."

He kept quiet, waiting, wondering if she'd realized his plan.

Finally, she sighed. "But you're right. I have to keep you with me, though I honestly don't know if they'll let you in. Especially when they learn you were married to Maggie."

Married to Maggie. Not Caleb and Isobel's father.

At her words, he bit back the urge to correct her and bowed his head, rubbing the back of his neck while he tried to think. Maybe Kelly, never having been a mother, didn't truly realize the depth of a parent's love and dedication to their children.

He *had* to get into the meeting, even if the twins weren't there. Finding out who'd been the one to take them and where they were being kept hidden would be the first step toward recovering them.

"You know," he said slowly. "Though you might not think I realize exactly how rare this meeting is, I do. And I think you don't understand how dangerous it will be if your adversary learns of it. Does your family comprehend the risks?"

"Yes, of course." She bit her lip, indicating she still wasn't happy. "Why do you think we scattered after my father's death? The location of the meeting is not only secret, but will be heavily guarded."

This was a new one. "Guarded by whom?"

"My people. We have our own trained fighters, I'm certain."

Which meant she really didn't know for sure.

"And you haven't told them about me?" he asked.

"Not yet." This time, she didn't bother to try to hide the suspicion in her eyes. "Mac, what are you planning?"

"Me?" He feigned innocence, aware she'd probably see right through him. "Nothing."

She sighed. "Look, I told you I'd look into what happened with your children, but I'm going to have to tell my family who you are, especially since I'm bringing you near them. So clear your mind of any plans involving heroic child snatching."

"Look," he said slowly. "You have to realize I can't promise you anything, especially where my children are involved."

"But—"

"On this, there will be absolutely no compromise," he interrupted. "Knowing what you know about me, I still don't understand why you didn't get rid of me before now."

"I couldn't," she said in a small voice.

Ruthless, he continued, wanting no further lies between them. "Kelly, I'm truly grateful to you. I'm glad to be with you, glad to help in any way I can, but you have to know my kids come first with me. Forever and always."

"Of course." Her mild tone surprised him. "I completely understand and I respect you for it. My family used to be important to me, as well."

Used to be. He wondered if she realized how harsh that sounded. "If you get what I'm telling you, then I still don't understand your reasoning for keeping me around. Mind explaining?"

"Not now. As for understanding, in good time, you will," she answered, her voice dark. "All too soon, believe me."

"You make it sound…dark. As if it's something horribly awful."

"Maybe it is."

"If so, then I'd rather be prepared. Why not simply tell me now and be done with it?"

She shook her head. "Maybe later." The finality in her voice told him she'd finished discussing this particular topic.

Another bit of mystery and, from the stubborn set of her chin, one she wasn't budging on. Since he had more important things to focus on, such as using her to locate his children, he let that one go, for now. She'd said later. He'd hold her to that.

They passed a semitruck painted to look like a giant American flag. As they pulled up alongside him, the truck driver honked his horn. It played a few bars from the song "America the Beautiful."

Mac grinned, exchanging a glance with Kelly, glad to see the trucker had been able to coax a reluctant smile from her.

"That was weird," she said, still smiling.

He thought of telling her she needed to smile more often, but decided that wouldn't be welcome. Maybe it would be better to keep things on a strictly businesslike level from now on. That way no one got hurt when the inevitable letdown took place. Which it would, eventually. Even he could see that far ahead.

"All right, then. Tell me this. What does your family hope to accomplish?"

"What do you think?" She sent him a wry look. "I mean, they've already taken two of us now, both females in their early twenties."

"Does anyone have any idea why?"

"No." She drummed her fingers on the steering wheel. "There have been no ransom demands, nothing."

"And you're sure this wasn't just a random thing like what happens in the human world? Jealous boyfriends, stalkers, something like that?"

"We're not allowed to have boyfriends," she told him.

His mouth fell open. "Not allowed? By who?"

"By our law, Tearlachs can only mate with Tearlachs."

"Why?"

She shrugged. "I don't know. I was never told—I guess they thought I was too young. I was only sixteen when the family split apart. Now that I'm twenty-eight, you'd think someone would have bothered to fill me in, but no one has."

"Tearlachs aren't allowed to mate with regular shifters?" he repeated, still more than a little stunned.

"Yes. And you must realize this. That's why Maggie was ostracized by her family, by our family. Don't tell me you didn't know."

He hadn't. "Maggie spoke little about her family. From the way she talked, I assumed her parents were dead."

"Nope. Her father is my uncle Danny. He and her mother, Audrey, are very much still alive. But because of Maggie's disobedience and marriage to you, they told her she was dead to them."

"I met some of her family," he protested weakly. "Not her parents, true. But I met her brother."

Kelly stared at him, obviously surprised. "You met Reggie? That's odd, since he never struck me as much of a lawbreaker."

"He obviously loved his sister more than some stupid rule," he retorted.

"Maybe so." To his surprise, she agreed. "It's

hard to follow laws when you don't know the reason for them."

"Is this rule possibly tied to the two missing girls? Think about it. If they wanted to break the no-mating-with-others rule, wouldn't it be more simple to just disappear, rather than risk their family's censure?"

"Maybe. But that's not what happened." Her tone indicated that was all she wanted to say on the matter.

He had no choice but to take her word for it. "Fine. Then assuming the two girls' disappearances *were* acts of malice, how is your family going to get them back?"

"I don't know. That's what the meeting is for. By coming together, we plan to find them and stop this once and for all."

"How?"

She grinned, surprising him. "At the risk of repeating myself, there are a lot of things you don't know about us."

Of that he had no doubt. Though the report the Protectors had given him had seemed comprehensive, he now believed it wasn't. Whether intentionally or not—now he was getting paranoid—it was short on information. The Tearlachs had long been a secretive bunch, and he was beginning to realize that what was known about them was only what they'd chosen to reveal.

They fell into a companionable silence. Though she'd given him no inkling of their destination, this time they were driving in a southeast direction. Definitely not toward the west coast.

Once she relaxed, she began whistling while she drove. Past cornfields, the tall stalks waving in the ever-present breeze. Through flat prairie and farmland, where the nearest tree seemed miles off and the cloud-dotted blue sky stretched to eternity and beyond.

Though the scenery didn't vary much, it felt familiar and comforting. The Heartland of America. Soothing, despite its monotony.

Her whistling fit right in. Glancing at her, he saw that she was smiling.

"You're happy."

Shooting him a glance, she shrugged. "Maybe. It's more bittersweet. I haven't even talked to my mother or my sister in twelve years. Since my father was killed, I've lived like an outcast. It's been easier not to care. I'm assuming everyone's life has been the same as mine."

"Assuming? You don't know?"

She shook her head. "We've been forbidden from making contact."

"At all? Why?"

"Less risk of being found," she said simply. "There are ways of anonymously keeping everyone informed. That's easy in this digital age. We all have webpages, and we all use an avatar for a profile picture."

"So just no personal contact."

"No." She sighed. "Though I have to confess that Bonnie and I cheated slightly. We kept in touch on Facebook, under fake profiles. That's how I know my sister didn't have a boyfriend. She would have told me if she'd met someone. Bonnie was alone, just like me."

"Then how did your family find out she was abducted? Through you?"

"No." Her expression turned troubled. "We're supposed to post our status weekly, on every Wednesday, without fail. When Bonnie didn't post, a query was sent anonymously to her webpage address. When that didn't receive a response, someone called her personal cell phone. My cousin Ian is in charge of maintaining everyone's contact records. That's who called me. And who also learned that Bonnie was missing."

"So Ian called her cell and no one answered?" He dragged his hand across his chin. "That seems pretty inconclusive to me."

Signaling a lane change, she waited until

that was complete before glancing at him. "Oh, someone answered. A man. He told us in no uncertain terms that he had Bonnie and if we tried to find her, he'd kill her."

As the day dragged on and the miles added up, Kelly began to feel the effects of the sleepless nights and stress-filled days. Her eyelids began to droop and despite her best efforts, she had difficulty keeping them open.

Mac, ever observant, noticed. "You look like you're about to doze off. If you want to nap, I'm perfectly happy to drive," he said. "If you're planning on driving straight through, you can't stay awake forever."

Another yawn while she mulled this over. Then, surprised to realize she was actually considering it, she glanced at him. "I don't know..."

"You've got to trust me sometime." He spread his hands, smiling to take the sting off the words. She couldn't help but notice the elegance of his hands, the fingers long and slender, made for playing a musical instrument or caressing a woman's skin.

Whoa. Her face heated. Where had that thought come from? Must have been her exhaustion messing with her mind.

Her stomach growled. Maybe it would help if she got something to eat.

With this in mind, she took an exit that advertised a fast-food restaurant. Pulling into the parking lot, she killed the engine and stretched. "I don't know about you, but I'm starving."

Just thinking about a big juicy hamburger like the one advertised on the glossy poster in the restaurant window made her stomach growl again.

"I could eat," he said. Though he sounded lighthearted, his clenched jaw spoke of his annoyance. Probably because she hadn't agreed to let him drive.

As they walked to the entrance, his stomach growled loudly and she smiled. "I can tell."

After a moment, he smiled back. Warmth spread through her as their gazes locked. Then she shook it off and reached for the door.

He beat her to it, holding the door open for her. Hesitating for one second, finally she dipped her chin and brushed past him.

Inside, they stood next to each other at the counter like a real couple, which felt odd. She ordered a large burger and fries, unsurprised when he ordered twice that amount for himself. After all, he was male, he was a shifter and his body was still recovering from the silver-bullet wound. He'd need to eat lots of protein to keep up his strength.

Carrying their loaded trays, they found a small table and pulled out chairs across from each other. Not speaking, each unwrapped their meals, chowing down in companionable—and she thought, contented—silence. His earlier annoyance appeared to have vanished.

Despite the size of his meal, he finished before she did. Leaning back in his chair, he watched her munch on her fries, his expression unreadable.

"One thing I don't understand," he said. "Why'd your family split up to begin with? I understand with your father getting killed, the world must have seemed like a dangerous place, but the logic about separating the entire family escapes me. It just doesn't make sense."

She stiffened, her previously relaxed feeling dissipating, just like that. Slowly and deliberately, she finished the last two fries, swallowing and wiping her fingers on the napkin before she lifted her chin to answer.

"My father knew that someone, our enemies, and by that I assume he meant the Protectors, would come after us." Taking a deep breath, she was proud of how dispassionately she was able to speak.

Mac's hard expression told her he wasn't buying it. "Again, vague. Paranoid, even. But let's go with this theory. Your father believed your family was in danger. Instead of organizing a group to fight the threat, making an army of Tearlachs, so to speak, he ordered you to split up and hide? Does that make sense to you?"

"No." She looked away. "The splitting up wasn't his idea, it was my uncle Danny's, his brother. My father was in the middle of making plans for the entire family to go into hiding. Together."

She went silent, wondering how to continue. This evidently prompted him to urge her to continue.

"Then what happened? I know you said a Protector killed your father, but you didn't say why."

Taking a deep breath, she glanced at him, steeling herself to tell the rest of it. "He'd gone to town for supplies, and someone—a Protector—attacked him."

"You're positive it was a Protector?" he asked.

"I only know what I was told," she answered.

"By whom? Your father?"

"No. He never came home. Uncle Danny told me and Bonnie what had happened."

Mac waited, for which she was grateful. No

doubt he was aware from the tortured look in her eyes that she needed a minute to gather her composure. She took a deep breath, willing herself calm.

When she continued, her voice was once again steady. "My father called my mom from a payphone and told her what had happened. She begged him to be careful, to come back to her. She even told him to kill the Protector. I heard because I was in the kitchen with her when he called. I've never seen my mother suffer so much anguish."

She glanced down, wondering why telling him this brought the old pain back full force. She'd honestly thought she'd come to grips with the loss of her father and then almost immediately losing her entire family. Her entire support system, her sense of security, all destroyed in an instant. She'd been only sixteen and sometimes felt she'd lost her youth at that tender age.

Over time, a decade plus two years, the sorrow had become somewhat blunted, softened with the passage of the years, as she moved from her teens into her twenties. She always felt far older than she should have.

Her father's death had changed everything. All of the children—she and her sister and cousins—had been split off and shunted off to places unknown. Countries and continents divided them. Because of one act of violence, all their young lives had been disrupted, destroyed.

They could never get this back. And yet they went on living, all of them. She had to assume it was the same with them. The world continued turning, the sun rose and set and life went on.

It wasn't like she'd ever forgotten it, and often she relived in her dreams the night her entire world had been unspeakably altered, but this retelling felt so raw, as if she was experiencing it all again. Maybe that was because this was the first time she'd retold the story out loud to another person.

Or maybe it was Mac, trying not to show sympathy, though his deep blue eyes shone with it. For some reason, this made it all worse.

"Maybe that will change," he said. "Now that your family is getting back together."

Nodding, though privately she hated to get her hopes up, she took a long drink of her diet cola. "I'd like that, but I kind of think this Texas meeting is a one-time-only thing."

Crud. She froze. The instant she'd finished speaking, she realized she'd told him more information than she'd wanted. Though he'd have to find out sometime. And that didn't narrow it down too much. Texas was a huge state.

"Texas?" He raised a brow. "We're heading to Texas?"

Miserable, she nodded.

"Have you ever been to Texas in August?"

"No. How bad can it be?" she asked.

Shaking his head, he frowned. "Compared to Wyoming, you'll think you've traveled down into the bowels of hell."

"So it's hot." She shrugged. "I can handle it. The only time we'll be outside is at night when it's cooler."

"It's not much cooler after dark." He smiled to take some of the sting off his words. "Though I guess it depends where in Texas we're going. I've heard the Davis Mountains out in far west Texas got snow on May 1, so maybe it's better there. I know the higher elevations are drier, at least."

She glanced at him again, wondering how much to reveal. "We're not going west," was all she said, before a huge yawn overtook her. Damn sneaky things.

He saw. "We're either going to have to stop for the night or you're going to have to let me drive," he pointed out again. "I don't want to have an accident because you fell asleep at the wheel."

Stifling another yawn, to her own surprise

she nodded. "You're right. I was planning on driving straight through, but you haven't had any more rest than I have." She pointed out the front window toward the building across the street.

"We'll stay at that motel."

He turned to look where she pointed, at one of the many generically bland motels that dotted the scenery of all U.S. interstates. At least it didn't look like some cozy love nest.

He startled at the thought, since even the idea that he'd think she'd even want to shack up in some motel was crazy. Not only did she not have the time, but she'd made it clear that she believed in following her Tearlach rules.

There'd be no hanky-panky that night, and they'd both do well to remember that.

Chapter 7

"Are you ready?" Jumping to her feet, she drained the last of her drink and carried her tray to the trash bin.

"Sure." Following, he did the same, wondering at her fortitude.

They returned to the Hummer and drove across the street. After she pulled into the driveway, she located a spot close to the main entrance and parked.

"What about a credit card?" he asked. "We can't use mine because it's company issued and they'll know. And if anyone is tracking you, they can easily find you if you use one of yours."

She gave him a tired smile to let him know

she'd already thought of that. "I've got it covered," she said. "We all were issued special credit cards and IDs to use if the need ever arose. I brought those with me."

"Wow. I'm impressed by the thoroughness by which you Tearlachs used to remain hidden."

"Shhh." Hushing him, she glanced around. "Please don't use that word. Everything was planned by my uncle Danny."

Though his expression plainly said he thought she was being paranoid, he apologized. "Sorry. I'll try to remember."

The bored desk clerk checked them in, giving them, at her request, a room on the first floor at the end of the long I-shaped structure. She asked for only one card key.

"We're sharing a room?" he asked, the humorous tone telling her he asked just to needle her.

"Of course." Trudging down the hall, she didn't even look at him. "There should be two double beds."

"And if there's not?"

"Then one of us will be sleeping on the floor."

He went silent since he didn't have to ask which one.

Finally, they located their room and, with one

pass of the card key, opened the door. The room, decorated in garish shades of yellow, orange and brown, did indeed have two double beds.

Right now Kelly thought they looked like the most comfortable beds she'd ever seen. She felt like she could sleep for days.

While a hot shower sounded appealing, it seemed like too much work.

"Though I'd really like a shower, I'll wait until morning." Pulling back the bedspread on the bed closest to the door, she avoided his gaze.

Suddenly hyperaware of him, she didn't know what to do first. "I'm just going to go wash up and then the bathroom is all yours."

He nodded, gazing at the television. She wondered for a half second if he were suddenly tongue-tied and feeling overly warm, like she was. She wondered what he wore to sleep in. Boxers or briefs, the age-old question. Or… nothing at all. The thought made her flush. If normally he slept in the nude, she hoped he'd leave his boxers on tonight.

Grateful for an escape, she grabbed her bag and fled to the bathroom. Though she glanced longingly at the shower, she settled for washing her face and brushing her teeth. She debated sleeping in her clothes, but knew she'd be much more comfortable in a T-shirt and terry-cloth shorts.

In the other room, she heard the television click on. Thank goodness. That meant he wouldn't be staring at her when she exited the bathroom. She hoped.

Hurriedly changing, she glanced at herself in the mirror, trying to screw up her courage. She could do this. She had no choice.

Taking a deep breath, she opened the door. Wearing a faded T-shirt and her old, comfy shorts, she walked nonchalantly to her bed. Only when she was underneath the covers with the sheet pulled up to her chin, did she let out the breath she hadn't even known she was holding.

Finally, she was safe.

Mac tried not to stare as Kelly emerged from the bathroom, but he couldn't help glancing at her. He wondered if she knew how sexy she looked in the too-large, soft T-shirt. From the sway of her large breasts underneath, he could tell she wore no bra. And her short-shorts revealed that her legs were long and shapely.

Damn. He wanted her. Still. Again. Now.

His body stirred as he imagined cupping her in his hands, lifting her T-shirt and tasting her skin with his mouth. He could see her reaction if he skimmed his hands lower, inside the waistband of her shorts, could practically feel her rising desire as she writhed against his hand.

"Stop that," she ordered in a strangled voice, her face bright red.

"Stop what?" Though he tried to sound innocent, the husky rasp of his tone made him unconvincing.

Color still high, she wouldn't look at him. "I can tell what you're thinking. I don't know how, but I can. So stop thinking that. I just want to get some sleep."

He had to bite his tongue to keep from teasing her with a sexy innuendo. Things would be better for both of them if he let that pass without comment. Even though, personally, he found making love first a great way to get a good night's rest.

"Sorry." Clearing his throat, he cast about for some way to rapidly change the topic. He supposed he could talk about the weather, or the hotel, or the drive— something, anything. But instead, he pointed toward the door, knowing this would be the fastest way to change the subject. "How do you know I won't sneak out once you're asleep?"

His comment had the desired result. She looked up, embarrassment forgotten, her frank gaze direct. "I don't. But as you've said repeatedly, I've got to start trusting you sometime. It might as well be now, right?"

And with that, she effectively gained his cooperation. Not that he'd planned on making a break for freedom, but she'd ensured he'd stay, with her words of trust. He did want her to have faith in him, so much so that the desire went far beyond his duty of a Protector on assignment. He didn't want to think too deeply about what that might mean.

Using the remote, he turned the television off. The silence at first felt deafening. Crossing the room to the bathroom, he made sure to give her bed as wide a berth as the confines of the room would allow. The entire way, he felt her gaze on him, burning into his back.

"Do you need anything?" he asked, steeling himself to turn and face her, glad his arousal had somewhat subsided.

Shaking her head, she reached for the light and gave him a small, halfhearted smile. "Sleep well."

He shook his head, trying to clear it, and managed a smile of his own, right before she turned out the light and slid under the sheet.

"You, too," he said, entering the bathroom and closing the door behind him. He wondered if he ought to take an icy shower. Instead, he splashed his face with cold water and brushed his teeth, before changing into an old T-shirt of his own.

When he emerged into the dim room, she'd rolled onto her side and had her back facing him. She didn't move, no doubt pretending to be asleep, though he could tell by her breathing that she was not.

His bed was surprisingly comfortable, and it took him only a moment to get situated before he, too, turned off his light. He thought sleep would not come easily and that he was definitely in for a night of restless tossing and turning, but he fell asleep almost as soon as his head hit the pillow.

When he woke, still in darkness, well before dawn—at 3:30 a.m. according to the digital clock on the nightstand—he could tell by her measured breathing that she was deeply asleep.

His body ached—he'd awakened fully aroused. No surprise there. He still wanted her. Badly.

For a brief moment he allowed himself the unspeakable luxury of imagining climbing from his bed and crossing the short space to her. Lifting her covers and sliding in next to her, smoothing his hands down the soft material of her T-shirt, then caressing the warm skin underneath.

Imagining this made him grow even more aroused. Then, as if she participated in his fantasy in her dreams, she moaned.

The sound, low and sensual, nearly undid him. Oddly enough, her words from earlier came back to haunt him.

It was almost as if she'd read his mind.

Was that one of the things Tearlachs could do? He'd seen no mention of this in the file, but Kelly had told him there was much that the Protectors didn't know.

Uncomfortable with his arousal now, he forced himself to think of something else. Ice fishing in the winter on the frozen lakes in his native Minnesota.

With his ardor cooled considerably, he was finally able to drift back to sleep.

Waking at her usual time of 6:00 a.m. as precisely as if she'd set the alarm, Kelly stretched. What dreams she'd had. Sensual and seductive, they'd made her body ache with longing and need.

She glanced at the bed next to her, where Mac still slept. As she watched him, his eyes opened, startling her with their blueness.

"Good morning," she said, feeling unaccountably shy.

Pushing himself up on his elbows and staring at her, he didn't crack a smile. "You hinted earlier that there were more things Tearlachs could do. Is reading minds one of them?"

Immediately she shook her head. "No, of course not."

He narrowed his eyes. "Then yesterday, when you said you could tell what I was thinking, what was that?"

"I have no idea." But she did, sort of. And she knew if he really thought about it, he'd reach the same conclusion himself.

But, since she wasn't quite ready to tell him how deep their binding went, she said nothing.

And, as she guessed he would, he sensed that. Crossing his arms, he glared at her. "What are you keeping from me?"

Of course he'd recognize the truth. She sighed, aware she probably wouldn't be too convincing, but what the hell. She had to try. "Nothing." She smiled, a patently false smile. And, though doing so felt childish, she unobtrusively crossed her fingers behind her back.

"I don't believe you." Sitting all the way up, he swung his long legs over the side, immediately drawing her gaze. Hounds help her, her mouth went dry at the sight of him wearing only boxer shorts and a T-shirt that did little to hide the muscular planes of his body.

When had she ever met a man so beautiful?

Never, she answered herself, knowing she had to train herself to become immune to the powerful lure of his masculinity.

"Why are you lying to me? If we're going to be in this together, as a team, we've got to tell each other the truth. So what gives?"

"What gives?" she repeated, stalling for time. How to tell someone as fiercely independent as Mac Lamonda appeared to be that he was now tied to her for the rest of their natural lives?

You don't just blurt something like that out. No, they had to know each other a lot better and the timing had to be a hell of a lot better than this for her to tell him.

Maybe then he'd even welcome such news.

Chiding herself for such foolishness, she managed a much more genuine smile. "Are you always so crabby in the morning?"

"No," he shot back, giving her a layered look that she couldn't interpret. "Are you always so cheerful?"

"Pretty much," she said agreeably, unable to keep from admiring his backside as he strode to the bathroom.

As the door closed behind him, she let her smile fade. She couldn't help but realize that she was playing with fire. And if she wasn't careful, as cliché as it sounded, she'd definitely get burned.

After they'd both showered and dressed, they checked out and walked over to the little café next door to wolf down some eggs and bacon and toast. When they'd finished their meal, Kelly paid with cash and handed Mac the Hummer keys.

"What's this?" he asked, expression guarded.

"I was thinking it's your turn to drive," she said nonchalantly, careful to hide her smile. "If you want to, that is."

Instead of answering with words, he unlocked the vehicle and climbed up on the driver's side. As she climbed up beside him and fastened her seat belt, he flashed her a grin so stunning in its masculine beauty that it took her breath away.

"I've always wanted to drive one of these things," he said. "I assume since you said we are going to Texas, that we're still heading south?"

"Yes." She sat back in her seat, willing herself to be calm as he exited the hotel parking lot, then took the ramp up onto the interstate.

"Are you nervous?" He glanced at her hand

and she realized she'd been drumming it on the dashboard.

"A little," she confessed. "I never realized I was so much of a control freak."

He laughed and, after a second, she found herself joining in.

"Let's see what kind of music they have out here." She began fiddling with the radio, more to keep her thoughts occupied. She needed to keep her mind off driving more than any real desire to hear a few tunes.

An old Patsy Cline song came on.

"I love that song," they both said, almost simultaneously. Feeling self-conscious, she reached for the dial and turned the volume up.

Still, the truth she'd left unsaid hung in the air like day-old smoke in a bar.

She knew she'd have to tell him sooner or later, but quite frankly, she found the entire situation humiliating. True, she'd been alone for the past twelve years and had never had a serious boyfriend, but to go binding herself to the first attractive male she met? And worse, he was not a Tearlach.

Seriously stupid. Despite the strong pull she felt toward him, she'd been raised to know better than that. And, now that they were traveling to the family meeting, everyone that mattered to her would know about what she'd done. She'd be outlawed, exactly like Maggie had been.

She could imagine what her mother would say. Thinking that, she felt a flash of anger. Her mother had sent her away at the tender age of sixteen to fend for herself. She ought to count herself lucky that Kelly hadn't ended up pregnant.

Put into this perspective, her rash impulsiveness with Mac didn't look half-bad. Shaking her head at her odd method of rationalization, she wondered what the rest of her family would say. Oddly enough, their reaction didn't worry her as much as she'd thought it would.

A sideways glance at him while he drove distracted her, the tug of him pulling at her. He had that power over her, though she thought she did a pretty good job of keeping that little fact hidden. For a moment she got lost admiring him. His bare arm, tanned and covered with fine brown hair. The compelling blue of his eyes, his rugged, masculine features, his arrogant confidence and seriously dangerous smile. One look and she felt like she could melt.

But it was more than his physical appearance, though she truly loved that. His essence, so rugged, so vital, attracted her. And, despite his pain and his determination to regain his missing children, she saw kindness in his smile. Even toward her, a Tearlach, a member of the family who'd taken his kids. He was a good man, this Mac Lamonda. And an honorable one, judging by his behavior since he'd given her his word. A walking set of contradictions. Bad for her since she'd never been able to resist solving a puzzle, any puzzle.

She truly liked him. She who had few friends, and with the ones she had she carried her loyalty to a fault, would call him friend. If he offered. And the fact that she wanted so much more than friendship would be tucked away, out of sight, buried deep.

Squaring her shoulders, she looked away before he remarked on her scrutiny. So she liked him. Big deal. It wasn't like she loved him or anything. Hounds, she barely knew the man.

Shifters, like their wild counterparts, mated for life. Mac Lamonda was now, for better or worse, her mate. Only, he didn't know it yet.

Though she'd bet he'd figure it out soon. On her end the binding grew stronger and Mac grew more and more appealing the longer she spent with him. If she'd found him attractive before, now he appeared downright irresistible to her. She yearned to experience more of his kisses, his touch, all the rituals of being in love that she'd been, by virtue of her solitude, denied.

If she'd been more experienced in the ways of men and women, she supposed she could have seduced him, made him desire her as much as she did him. But she had no idea how, just as she didn't know how she was going to tell him the truth.

The route they took, down I-25 through Colorado, was both unfamiliar and beautiful. Snow-capped mountains gave way to city, and the traffic snarls in Denver had Mac fuming with frustration.

Studying the map, she saw they'd go through Colorado, down to New Mexico, breaking off on Highway 87 at Raton, to make their way to Dalhart, Texas. Then they'd pick up 287 to Amarillo, through Childress, Vernon, and Wichita Falls.

She'd never been to Texas. They had a long day of driving ahead of them. Traveling south in Colorado, she leaned back in the seat and closed her eyes. Might as well take a nap. Feeling remarkably secure with Mac driving her Hummer and with the sun warming her, she fell asleep.

In New Mexico, they stopped in Raton and had lunch at a tiny Mexican café. With her sitting across the small tiled table that tilted so badly he had to take several sugar packets and stick them under one of the legs, he felt oddly comfortable, like they were a couple. Gazing around the tiny, half-full restaurant, he saw other couples, both young and old, and two entire families, three generations all eating together. Surrounded by chatter, some of it in Spanish, and laughter, he felt a longing for this kind of life, the kind he'd had once, before his wife had been killed and his children stolen from him.

The life he would have again, he vowed. And Kelly was going to help him get it back, whether she liked it or not.

When the waiter came, Mac ordered a cold Corona with lime. He drank it slowly, eschewing a glass so he could tilt the cool, sweating bottle to his mouth. Kelly had iced tea, unsweetened and freshly brewed.

"It's flavored with mint," she said with surprise, clearly pleased.

By the time the food came, they were both starving. As the waiter unloaded his tray on their table, from the looks of the huge platters of piping-hot food, the wait had been worth it. The burritos were huge and full of ground beef, seasoned with onion, green chilis and fresh cilantro, with a drizzle of cheese, salsa and guacamole on top.

The first bite brought an explosion of flavor and he tried to chew slowly, in order to savor it, but his hunger overrode that desire, and he ate with gusto, happily devouring the food.

Kelly could eat only half of hers, and Mac barely was able to stuff the last few bites of his into his mouth.

Satisfied, he leaned back in his chair. "Now it's time for a nap," he joked.

Closing her eyes, she nodded and groaned. "I'm stuffed, but in a good way."

The oddest thought—that he could get used to this—came and went. His former life had nothing to do with her and neither did the life he wanted in the future. Glancing around the room, he watched a young mother feeding her toddler in a high chair. Thinking of his children, he felt that familiar ache in his chest. How he missed them.

Not for long. Not for long. He shook his head and signaled for the check. While he waited, he glanced at Kelly. "Now what? On to Texas, I assume?"

Slowly, she nodded. "Do you still want to drive?"

"Of course." Surprised that she even had to

ask, he glanced outside at the Hummer parked across the street. The distance and the grimy window made the vehicle appear even more menacing and tanklike.

He liked that.

Together they walked outside. As they were about to cross the street, a beat-up old pickup came careening around the corner. Mac reacted instinctively, one arm shoving Kelly back into the brick building. He fell backward, and the truck went past, spraying them with dust and Latin music at the same time.

Wide-eyed, Kelly helped Mac up. "Are you all right?" she asked.

"Fine." He had the oddest urge to crush her to him and hold her. Squashing that, he studied her instead. "What about you?"

She shrugged. "I'm okay." Looking beyond him, she glared into the distance. "What the heck was wrong with that guy?"

"Who knows?" He allowed himself to take her arm, and they crossed to the Hummer. "I'm just glad it wasn't another attack."

Once they'd left Raton behind, they took Highway 87 east, heading toward Clayton. This meant they lost the highway and had long stretches of only two lanes, many with no-passing stripes.

Of course they got stuck behind a motor home, seven cars ahead. By the time Mac was able to pass it, he was thoroughly irritated.

The monotony of their surroundings didn't help. The unbroken horizon and the scenery—if you could call it that—stretched on for mile after mile. Wave after wave of pastures and fields, broken up here and there by clumps of gnarled, scraggly trees, all framed by the cloud-less, bright blue skies. Occasionally, they saw a group of white-tailed deer grazing alongside cat-tle. As pieces and piles of volcanic rock began to appear next to the pavement, in the distance he could see the domelike mound of Capulin Volcano.

As she'd been doing periodically since leav-ing Raton, Kelly turned in her seat. "Still noth-ing," she said. "There's a couple of cars way back there, but none are close enough for me to think they're following us."

"Good." He didn't tell her that he'd been watching the rearview mirror ever since they'd left Raton. But her words reassured him some-how. Maybe it was the confirmation that nothing stood out and there were no repeat vehicles, but he finally began to relax.

He pointed out the volcano. "The last time

it erupted was between 58,000 to 62,000 years ago."

"So that's why the roadside is littered with volcanic rock," she said.

"This entire area is part of the Raton-Clayton volcanic field. I've actually hiked up the volcano to the rim. Up there, you can see four states— New Mexico, Texas, Oklahoma and Colorado."

"I remember when Maggie did a travel blog under her assumed name about that trip." She gave him an uncomfortable look. "Sorry. I didn't mean to bring that up."

"That's all right," he said, and to his surprise, it was. It used to be he couldn't even hear his dead wife's name without feeling pain. "I didn't even know she had a blog."

"That was before the twins were even born." She gave him a sideways glance. "There were pictures of you with a beard and long hair. I wouldn't even recognize you now.

"Speaking of Texas, how much farther to the Texas border?" she asked.

"About an hour and a half, give or take a few minutes. It depends on how fast we go."

"Okay, then." She gave him a sweet smile. "Then if you don't mind, I think I'll go back to sleep."

He laughed, oddly charmed. "Go right ahead.

You need to be rested up so you can take your turn at the wheel."

On 287 out of Amarillo, they were able to pick up the pace. Mac thankfully accelerated, glad once again to have a four-lane highway. Beside him, Kelly still slept.

He took the opportunity to study her. Without her guard up, her classical beauty softened. Her perfect skin, so silky smooth, made him long to caress her. When he'd first met her, her startling beauty had surprised him, but she seemed to grow even more lovely each day he spent with her. If he let himself dwell on it, he knew he could easily become obsessed with her.

Family relationship aside, Kelly bore absolutely no resemblance to his deceased wife, Maggie. He should know—after all, he'd spent an inordinate amount of time looking for some tiny similarity. Whether chin or eyes, or skin or hair, the two women were nothing alike.

The disparity didn't end at appearance. Maggie had been boisterous and loud, impetuous and impatient. A whirlwind of energy, she never seemed to sit still. Laughter had come easily to her and when she'd flown into a passionate rage, her rants had been legendary.

In contrast, Kelly exuded a sense of quiet serenity, which seemed to be at odds with the raw sensuality he sensed in her. Whereas Maggie had blown into his life and taken him by storm, the more time he spent with Kelly, he realized she appealed to him for the opposite reason. She seemed to be growing on him, endearing herself to him by a steady sort of stealth.

He supposed that was a blessing. He'd sure hate to be stuck in a car for days with a woman he couldn't stand.

Now if he could just get this tug of sexual attraction under control, things would be pretty darn perfect.

At one point, he caught himself humming along to the radio. He'd been keeping an eye on the road, changing lanes frequently and varying his speed, all the while watching to make sure they didn't have a tail.

The sunlight shone brightly, reflecting off the vehicles in front of him and hurting his eyes. The monotony of the scenery made him feel restless, but all in all he had a good feeling. Unless a helicopter appeared in the sky, he figured they were safe for a good many miles. Maybe even all the way to wherever they were going.

Beside him, Kelly stared out the window, dozing off and on. She seemed relaxed, more relaxed than he'd seen her since she'd slept the night before. An entire day stuck in a car will do that to you.

The red car seemed to come from nowhere. He hadn't noticed it before, and a car like that begged to be noticed.

As the bright red Camaro hugged his bumper, Mac braced himself for something worse. True to his prediction, the sports car swerved as if to pass them, despite the no-passing stripes, and pulled up alongside him on the left, on the wrong side of the road.

As he registered this, the Camaro's passenger window came down. Mac saw the glint of the pistol and slammed on his brakes, a split second before the attacker fired.

Chapter 8

The huge Hummer shuddered and tried to skid right, but he was able to correct it easily.

Kelly came awake with a small gasp. "What's happening?"

"We've been followed somehow. They're shooting. Hang on." Pulling off the road, he stomped on it, kicking up clouds of dust. "We're going off-road."

Ahead of them on the blacktop, the Camaro braked also, fifty feet or so ahead, and went into a spin. The driver overcorrected and the shiny new sports car hit the cement barrier, traveling at least seventy miles per hour.

With a horrible crunch of mangled metal, the

red car went up and over and rolled, traveling across the northbound lanes of traffic, narrowly missing a large semi and a minivan, before coming to rest on its roof.

"Look out," Mac muttered, jamming his foot down hard on the accelerator and sending them shooting past, still on the dirt and hitting every rut and hole with teeth-jarring intensity.

Expression anguished, Kelly turned in her seat to watch behind them. "I think it's on fire. Should we go back to help?"

"Hell, no. Someone on the northbound side will stop and call 911. We need to get out of here. Now."

She said nothing, which he took for agreement.

Once they were far enough past the now-fiery wreck, Mac drove up the embankment back on the pavement. Now that the original surge of adrenaline had left him, he felt the beginnings of anger setting in. "Truth time, Kelly. I need to know what's going on."

Staring back at him, her expression impassive, she gave a slow shake of her head. "I don't know any more than you do."

"Why don't I believe you? Everything you've said has been incredibly vague. I think you know more than you're telling me."

Unaccountably, her beautiful green eyes glistened with unshed tears. He steeled himself, aware that a woman crying to deflect a man's anger was the oldest trick in the book. Maggie had been particularly good at that.

He waited. Twenty seconds, thirty, then forty-five. When she still didn't speak, he heaved a sigh. "Fine, you win. At least tell me where we're going."

"Fort Worth," she said clearly. "The Stockyards."

"The Stockyards?" He swore. "Are you sure?"

"Yes." She gave him a curious glance. "You don't sound happy. Why? You don't like cattle or something?"

He made a rude sound. "You know as well as I do that cattle are skittish around us. But the Fort Worth Stockyards really don't have cattle, unless you count the exhibition cattle drive they do every day for tourists."

"I've never been there. If it's not a real stockyard, then what is it?"

"Kind of a touristy place. The Cowboy Hall of Fame is there, as well as Billy Bob's and several other bars. There's shopping and restaurants and it's generally packed with people. Human people."

"Then that makes sense. From what you're

saying, our kind generally avoid the place, right? Therefore, it sounds like a perfect area to have the big meeting."

"Convoluted logic."

"But good. You know they'll never check there."

He had to admit she was right. "Fine. Let's see how many horses and cows we can spook."

"I thought you said there were no—"

Touching her arm, he grinned. "Kidding, Kelly. Just kidding."

The sun had dropped below the horizon by the time they pulled into Fort Worth. Traffic was steady, congested but not too bad.

"We're staying at the Omni Hotel." She sounded nervous. "Close to someplace called Sundance Square."

Though he groaned mentally, because Sundance Square was yet another area jam-packed with people, he said nothing.

When they reached the hotel, he pulled into the circular drive.

"Let the valet park it," she said. "We won't be needing to drive anywhere tonight."

Which meant what? That the meeting was tomorrow?

As the valet drove off in the Hummer, he followed Kelly to the check-in desk. When she asked for one room, his heart skipped a beat. He didn't know if he could torture himself like that again.

As she took her room key from the desk clerk, she turned to Mac with a smile. "Hopefully, we'll both get a good night's sleep without any more of those random dreams."

Just her mentioning the dream immediately sent his libido into overdrive. Of course.

Watching her cute little backside as she walked to the elevator, he reflected he'd have to use all his willpower to ensure that he didn't climb into bed with her in the middle of the night.

When they located their room and she got the door open, the first thing he noticed was the bed. Singular. One huge king-size bed dominated the room, which was a thousand times more plush than the last one they'd shared.

"One bed," he pointed out unnecessarily.

"And a couch." She sounded positively cheerful. "Dibs on the bed." Crossing to it, she made her point by pulling down the comforter and folding back the sheet.

A sharp rapping sound at their door. They both froze.

"Expecting someone?" he drawled.

Checking her pistol, she shook her head. "I

haven't even notified anyone that we've arrived."

"Just a minute." He checked the peephole. A tall, slender man with red hair stood out in the hall. "Come here and see if you recognize this guy."

Stepping aside so she could peek out, he watched as her expression changed from worry to surprise.

"It's my cousin Ian." She frowned. "I don't know how he knew we were here."

"He probably was watching the lobby. What now? Do we let him in or pretend we're not here?"

Reaching for the chain and undoing it, she shot him a worried smile. "They're going to have to find out about you sooner or later. Might as well be now."

"All right." He stood back as she opened the door.

"Ian," she cried out, as the tall red-haired man wrapped her in a hug. "It's good to see you after all these years."

Instead of responding, Ian stared at Mac. His brown eyes contained no hint of friendliness.

"Who's this?" he asked in a voice full of suspicion.

Looking from Ian to Mac, she licked her lips. "He's a friend."

"A friend?" Ian exploded. "Surely you know better than to bring a friend along to something like this."

Mac crossed his arms, still saying nothing, waiting to see how Kelly would handle this.

She looked down. Then, to Mac's surprise, crossed to him and took his hand. "We've... we're... I've spoken the words of binding with him," she said, rushing the words. "So he's a little more than just a friend."

"He's not one of us."

She glared at her cousin. "I'm aware of that. Yet we are bound. I brought him here because I have no choice. You know how it is."

Ian reared back, jaw clenched. "Does he...?"

"No." She pleaded with her eyes. "I'll tell him in my own time."

Mac glanced at her, no doubt curious, though he apparently knew better than to say anything.

Immediately, Ian's freckled face cleared. "True. And it's not my problem, actually. Or my place to comment. So congratulations." Smiling at Mac, he held out his hand.

"Mac Lamonda." Mac shook.

"Ian McKenzie," the other man said, his tone easy with the slightest hint of a Scottish burr.

"I confess, lad, I was wondering if I'd have to fight you."

"Yeah." Mac chuckled. "I thought the same thing."

Meanwhile, Kelly caught an undercurrent of insincerity, though whether on Ian's part or Mac's, she couldn't tell.

"What's going on, Ian?" Keeping close to Mac's side, Kelly studied her cousin. "Is everyone here yet?"

"Your mother is. She's the one who sent me to get you. She wants to see you before the big meeting tomorrow."

Kelly's entire face lit up, making her breathtakingly beautiful. While he pondered this, his chest tight, she shook her head at him. "Do you mind waiting here?"

"Of course not," he answered immediately. "You haven't seen your mom in twelve years. I wouldn't want to intrude."

"Intrude?" Ian boomed. "You're her mate, lad. How can you possibly intrude? Come along."

Mate? Stunned, Mac was about to correct him when he caught a look at Kelly's face. She appeared to be begging him with her eyes not to argue.

So he didn't. If she wanted her cousin and the

rest of her family to believe they were mated, that was fine with him. In fact, it might even help them trust him enough to let him have his children back.

But now Ian was studying him closely. "You look familiar," he began.

Kelly laughed, the sound completely fake. "That's because he used to be married to Maggie Douglas, our cousin. While she didn't come around the family much, you may have seen him around once or twice at family get-togethers."

"No," Mac put in smoothly. "He wouldn't have. Maggie was shunned by her family after marrying me."

The suspicion back in his gaze, Ian looked at Mac. "Why are you still alive?" he asked bluntly.

"Ian!" Breathless with nerves, Kelly stepped between them. "He was married to Maggie, but they never spoke the words of binding."

The red-headed man never took his eyes off Mac. "Let me get this straight. You were married to one Tearlach and now you've mated with another?"

"I agree it sounds weird." Mac strove for the same lighthearted tone as Kelly had used earlier. "I know it is kind of strange, but what can you do?" Putting his arm around Kelly's slender shoulders, he pulled her close, giving her a loving look and a kiss on top of her head for good measure.

Eyeing the two of them, Ian relaxed. All except his jaw, which remained tight. "I guess you're right. We have little control over what the fates have planned for us." It sounded like a warning.

Though Mac didn't believe in the notion of fate, he smiled and nodded. Not wanting to bring up his children, he thought maybe Ian would mention them. After all, if all the Tearlachs were getting together, his kids had to be around here somewhere.

"Come on." Ian opened the door, giving Kelly a conspiratorial wink. "Let's introduce your mate to your mum. I can't wait to see how she reacts to this."

Next to Mac, Kelly heaved a quiet sigh. "Let's," she replied.

As they strode down the hallway to the elevator, Mac resolved to stay as much in the background as possible. Ian might believe Mac and Kelly were mates, but he should have let the first reunion between Kelly and her mother take place in private.

Once they were inside the elevator, Ian slipped in his card key, but didn't punch in a floor. At Kelly's curious look, he smiled.

"Our mothers are sharing the penthouse suite

on the VIP floor. We've rented several of them, including a large banquet room for our meeting tomorrow."

Eyes wide, Kelly nodded. On impulse, Mac took her hand and squeezed, offering reassurance. Her grateful smile was so brilliant he had to fight the urge to kiss her right there, in front of Ian.

Noticing, Ian chuckled. "True love. How sweet."

Kelly tilted her head. "Have you not yet found your mate, Ian?"

"Nope. And no hurry there," he said easily. "I'm perfectly happy the way things are."

Mac smiled, aware he couldn't say he felt the same, though he did. After losing Maggie, he knew he couldn't bear the same kind of loss ever again. Therefore, Maggie would have been, in reality, his one true mate, his only mate. He tried for a half smile, wondering why this thought felt so foreign, then shrugged it off.

If it helped him get his children back, he'd pretend to be just about anything. Including the mate of a woman he barely knew.

The elevator doors opened and they stepped out.

"This floor doesn't even look like the same hotel," Kelly said. "Even the carpet's nicer."

Ian grinned. "Wait until you see the suite."

As they walked the length of the long hall, Kelly began twisting her hands together. Noticing Mac watching, she gave him a tremulous smile.

"I'm nervous. It's been a long time since I've seen my mom. I'm wondering what she'll think of me."

To his mild surprise, he found himself pulling her close to comfort her. "What do you mean? She's your mother. Even if you'd gotten multiple piercings and tattoos and dyed your hair blue, she'd still love you. I'm sure she's been missing you as much as you've missed her."

"Wise man you have there, lass," Ian put in. "Your mum raised you to be strong, just like all our mums did. When you're a Tearlach, you have to be prepared for anything."

Mac wondered why that was so and even why they still believed it. Maggie had told him the same thing, though always with an ironic shrug and a little laugh. She'd seemed to find the entire Tearlach thing kind of amusingly annoying, and he had to confess, because of her outlook on it, he'd never put much credence in such nonsense.

Until they'd grabbed his children, that is.

Near the end of the hallway, they stopped in

front of the last door on the left. Ian paused. "Are you ready?" he asked Kelly.

Pulling away from Mac, she straightened her shoulders and nodded. "Yes."

Ian tapped on the door, using what sounded like some sort of code. Three sharp raps, then two. Then he repeated the entire thing.

The door opened. A teenage girl with a shock of red hair held it open for them. "Welcome," she said, her accent Australian. Ian stepped aside, indicating with a sweep of his hand that they should precede him.

Kelly took a deep breath, glanced at Ian and did exactly that.

Her first impression was of a crowded room. Some of the people looked familiar, others only vaguely so. She didn't see her mother at first, and while she searched every face in the room, her heart pounded so hard she thought it would burst.

"Kelly?" The soft voice came from behind her, the wonder in it breaking her heart.

Kelly spun, staring at the lean older woman with joy. Her mother Rose's blond hair had begun to silver, though she still wore it long and straight, cascading over her shoulders and down to the middle of her back. Her eyes were still as green in a pale, perfect face, and if there were a few more lines and wrinkles, that was natural considering the passage of time.

She held out her arms and Kelly walked right into them, her heart splintering in half.

"Mama," she murmured, over and over, suddenly a child again and hardly able to bear it.

Smoothing her hair, her mother whispered her name. "Oh, my Kelly. How I've missed you."

At those words, Kelly felt a surprising flash of anger. She'd never understood how any mother could send a child away—only sixteen years old—to fend for herself, alone. Even though her uncle had ordered this, a small, lonely part of her believed her mother should have resisted. Kelly knew she would have, had she been in her mother's shoes.

No matter what the danger, she believed she'd have kept her child at her side.

Though she didn't understand, had never understood, now was not the time for such questions.

"A reunion," her mother said brightly, her eyes bright with tears.

Since Kelly's throat had closed up from her own emotion, she simply nodded and hugged her again, holding her a tad bit too tightly.

. When they broke apart, her mother looked at Mac. "Who is this?"

Instead of answering, Mac looked at Kelly.

Kelly's stomach clenched, but she lifted her chin and made the introductions.

Rose nodded. "Pleased to meet you," she said, before turning again to her daughter. "I take it this relationship is a serious one? Otherwise, you wouldn't have brought him here."

"Yes. We spoke the words of binding a few days ago."

Rose's perfectly shaped eyebrows rose. "Really? He's not—"

"Tearlach," Kelly said. "I know. But I was attacked and he saved my life, so I saved his. I had no choice in the matter."

"I see." Her mother nodded, looking dazed. "Your attack was not reported to me. I'm glad he was there to help you. I honestly had no idea you were serious about anyone."

This proved too much for Kelly to let pass. "I had no idea you knew anything about me at all," she said, her voice tight.

"I know everything about you, from what dog you've rescued last to the name of your friend in town."

"You couldn't be bothered to contact me in

person, yet you had me spied on?" Kelly's voice rose.

"Of course I didn't." Her mother's mouth went tight. "If you'll excuse us," she said to Mac, taking Kelly by the arm. "We need to speak privately." And, without asking if Kelly wanted this, she led her to another room.

Her room, a private bedroom, was empty. Rose closed the door and then patted the edge of the bed. "Have a seat, honey. Make yourself comfortable."

Kelly crossed her arms, ill at ease and unable to articulate exactly why. "I'd rather stand, thanks."

Shrugging, Rose sat, perched on the edge of the bed like a bird about to take flight. "You're angry with me."

"Wouldn't you be?" Kelly retorted. To her mortification, tears stung the back of her eyes. "If our situations were reversed?"

"You were never alone and the family you were sent to live with was well vetted. The Smiths always kept me apprised. They did a good job raising you."

"I left as soon as I turned eighteen. Does that tell you anything?"

Rose studied her with sadness in her face. "You weren't happy?"

"How could I be? Everyone I loved was gone, taken away from me. I didn't even have family with me while I grieved over Daddy."

"Neither did I," Rose pointed out gently.

"But you were an adult. I was just a child. I was heartbroken and confused." She moved closer, studying her mother intently. "You never once called or even wrote me a letter." Her voice broke and, resolutely, she steadied it. "As far as I was concerned, you might have been dead, too."

"Oh, Kelly." Rising, Rose crossed the room and tried to pull a resisting Kelly into her arms. "You know I, out of everyone in the family, couldn't contact you or any of my children. It wasn't safe. I'm so sorry. It broke my heart, too. But I only did what was necessary to keep you alive."

Kelly let herself be held, and even brought her arms up around her mother's slender shoulders to hug her back. "Tell me what really happened, Mother. Why was it so imperative that we all go into hiding and never reveal our true nature?"

Rose shook her head, half smiling, though tears flowed from her eyes. "You'll learn all this tomorrow, at the big meeting. This time we have together, I want to be all about me and you. Tell me about that young man of yours. It seems awfully troublesome that you've just become mates mere days before the big meeting."

Kelly sighed. "Neither of us knew anything about that." Taking a deep breath, she told her mother the truth, relaying the entire story. When she'd finished, she looked up to find her mother studying her.

"You don't think this was a setup? The Protectors had to know he was married to Maggie."

"Even if they did, what difference would it make to me?"

"True." Looking thoughtful, her mother gazed into the distance, as though listening to another voice, one that was inaudible to anyone but her. "Well, either way, Ian and the others will keep a close eye on him. Is he armed?"

Shocked, Kelly shook her head. "No, of course not. He wanted a gun, especially after we were shot at on the way here, but I wouldn't give him one, of course."

"Shot at on the way here?"

"Yes." Kelly told her what had happened. "I don't know what they wanted."

"You, honey. They wanted you. Since they've grabbed the two girls, you're the only other female of childbearing age left."

"I don't understand."

"I'm sorry." Rose winced. When she spoke again, her voice was soft but full of steel. "They are taking all the young females in order to start their own breeding program. That's one theory. The other was even worse—much more sinister."

Her mother took a deep breath before hugging her again. "Sorry to go on like this. I'm just trying to explain."

"Explain what?" Kelly asked.

"Why we did what we did. These people, whoever they are, will stop at nothing to achieve their goal. That's why it was essential that we split up, and imperative that we all hide our true natures."

"I thought it had something to do with something Daddy did," Kelly began.

"Your father tried to stop this—it's why he was killed. Of course, the breeding-program thing is only one of several possibilities. The meeting tomorrow will give you greater details."

A breeding program? That didn't make sense. Her mother had said that was only a theory, and that the others were worse. She wondered if the others made more sense.

"But I don't get why," Kelly said. "I just don't understand."

"Tomorrow," Rose repeated. Taking a deep breath, she cupped Kelly's face in her hands. "Are you certain you're safe with your young man?"

There were very few things that Kelly actually *was* certain of, but oddly enough, this was one of them. "Yes, I am." She lifted her chin proudly. "We're truly bound together. And honestly, if he was going to try and hurt me, he's had numerous opportunities before now."

"He had children with Maggie. You know they've been taken. Don't you think there's a secret agenda with him?"

"Oh, there is. I'm well aware of what he wants." Kelly gave her mother a grim smile. "Though he doesn't know I realize it, he means to get his children back. And really, I can't say that I blame him."

Rose's mouth tightened. "You do understand that's not possible, don't you? They're Tearlachs. As such, his children have been put into the same system you went into. They are in hiding, where they'll remain until they are adults. They are Tearlachs, after all. He has no right to them."

"He's their *father,*" Kelly said. "If he doesn't have the best reason of all to be with them—"

"They must be protected," her mother cut in.

Kelly couldn't see the point in that. "But—"

"No buts." Rose squeezed her shoulder affectionately. Softening her tone, she said, "Come on, let's rejoin the others. We'll talk again tomorrow, after the big meeting. You'll understand better once you have more information. The big picture, as it is."

"You've already painted a pretty bizarre picture." Kelly allowed herself to be led toward the door. "I can't imagine that anything they'll have to say tomorrow will make much more of a difference."

Once back in the crowded other room, Kelly spotted Mac easily. Arms crossed, he stood apart from the others, listening, his expression watchful. As soon as he saw her, he appeared to relax slightly.

She hurried over. "I'd like to go," she said.

He studied her for a moment, unsmiling. "You don't want to visit with the rest of your family?"

A quick glance around the room was almost too much to bear. "No." She took his arm. "I'll see them all tomorrow."

Finally, he inclined his head. "If that's what you want."

Outside in the hallway, she felt like her legs couldn't carry her away fast enough. She didn't want to actually run—good Lord, how much would *that* reveal?—but she got to the elevator as quickly as she could, pressing the down button.

Mac came up behind her. "I take it that didn't go well?"

She shrugged, and then her effort at nonchalance crumbled. Facing the still-closed elevator doors, she struggled to regain her composure.

With a discreet ping, the elevator arrived and the doors opened. Hurrying inside, she blindly punched the button for their floor, keeping her profile averted.

"Are you all right?" he asked. The concern in his voice nearly undid her.

"Yes." She swallowed. "Actually, no. I'm not. I don't know why I'm so upset." Sniffing, she finally swung her gaze up to meet his. "I don't know what I expected, but this wasn't…"

"Enough to make up for all the time spent missing her?"

"Exactly!" Amazed that he'd gotten it so easily, she managed a smile, even if it felt a bit wobbly around the edges.

"So what's on the agenda now?"

Quelling the instant flash of suspicion, she shrugged. "Nothing until the meeting tomorrow."

"And everyone will be in attendance?" he asked, his tone a bit too casual.

"Every adult," she said, then as the elevator

reached their floor, she touched his arm. "No children. I'm sorry."

As they stepped out into the hallway, he swore softly. She debated telling him what she knew about his kids, but decided to wait. Right now the stakes were too high. When this was all finished, then she'd let him know exactly how difficult it would be to track them down and offer to help him find them. For now, she couldn't take any chances.

"Kelly?" Grabbing her arm, he turned her to face him. "Do you know where they are?"

Slowly, she shook her head.

"If you find out anything, anything at all relating to their location, will you give me your word to let me know?"

The elevator doors opened. An older couple, arms around each other's waists, stood waiting to enter. Kelly pushed past them, shaking Mac's hold off her arm and striding down the hall ahead of him.

He caught her easily. "Don't think you're getting off without answering me," he told her.

"I don't know what to say."

Shock and fury blazing in his eyes, he grabbed her and yanked her up close. "How can you not?" he ground out. "These are my children, Kelly. My family, all I have left." His voice broke. "I love them. I need them. Your people had no right to take them from me."

As she stared up at him, her chest tight with the certain knowledge that he was right, she knew two things. First off, she'd do everything, even risk her life, to help him get his kids back.

And second, she was about to kiss him.

Chapter 9

Feeling bold, driven by some kind of sense-less passion that momentarily prevented her from feeling fear or worry or self-conscious-ness, Kelly pushed herself up on her tiptoes and touched her mouth softly, tentatively, to his.

For a moment he only stood frozen. Then, as she moved her lips gently over his, savoring him, she tasted him with her tongue. Still motionless, he made a guttural sound, low in his throat, and encouraged, emboldened, she continued.

Though she felt sure her lack of practice was obvious, she used her tongue to push and tease, acting completely on instinct. She must have done something right. He blazed to life, kissing her back as though his life depended on it.

So this was how it was supposed to be, she thought happily. All the romance novels she'd read over the years had been telling the truth. She could lose herself in a kiss like this. It went on and on and on. She thought she'd died and gone to heaven.

Suddenly, he appeared to come to his senses. Breaking their lip-lock, he inhaled sharply and backed up against the door to their room.

"Kelly," he ground out, his breathing harsh and fast, his pupils dilated. "No fair. At all."

She gave him a slow smile, feeling a rush of confidence in the knowledge that she had the power to arouse him as strongly as he did her. Trying to act nonchalant, she unlocked the door and led the way inside.

"I want to kiss you again," she said, her voice husky. "Right now."

"No." Gripping both her arms, he resolutely held her away. "No more kissing."

Disappointed, she nodded, unable to keep from feeling hurt.

"While I have to admit you're distracting as hell," he continued, "we were talking about me getting my children back. That's more important to me."

"Of course." She nodded again. Despite her disappointment, she couldn't help but admire his resolve. Though her entire body burned and tingled, she took a deep breath, trying to regain her sense of balance. All she could think about was how absolutely wonderful his kiss had been and how badly she wanted to kiss him again. She pushed the thought away.

"The twins are mine and they need me." Meeting her gaze, he held it. "Kelly, I have to know if you're on my side or not."

Stunned, at first she was taken aback. But she realized he was absolutely right. Of course he would focus on his children. "Until now, I never questioned the rules. They just were. While I never understood why Tearlach children had to be hidden and protected, I believed that was how things had to be."

"And now?"

Was that hope shining from his eyes? "Now I think you are right. You're their father. You miss them. You know, in all this struggling for control, I'll bet no one has thought about what the twins are feeling. They must be frightened and sad and missing you horribly."

A shadow of pain flickered in his eyes. "I imagine they believe I've abandoned them. First their mother died, and now I've disappeared from their lives."

Sounded familiar. Just like her own life had been.

"And they're being shuttled around by unfamiliar people to unfamiliar places, when all they want is their daddy to put his arms around them and tell them everything is going to be all right."

He stared at her, a muscle working in his jaw. "You speak as though you know them."

"Not them." She smiled sadly. "But I have been in their situation. After my father died, my entire world was taken from me and I was passed along from foster family to foster family. Oh, sure, my mother claims she vetted them all quite carefully, but that doesn't matter to a young teen who only wants her mom and her dad."

Mac had gone completely, utterly still. "So what are you saying?"

"I will help you," she told him, wiping at her eyes and bringing her chin up proudly. "To the best of my abilities. If there's any way for us to find your son and daughter, I will help you do so."

Now he took a step forward, his dark gaze

locked on hers. "Give me your word," he whispered harshly.

And she wanted him again. Just like that, her sadness was replaced by desire. She licked her lips and felt gratified at the hungry way his gaze followed the movement.

Feeling bolder and more brazen by the second, she moved closer, until they once again stood inches apart.

"I will help you. You have my word," she promised, desire making her voice husky. "I will do whatever I can to help you bring your children back to you."

At her words he made a low sound, a cross between a groan and a cry. He crushed her to him, slanting his mouth over hers, asking for another sort of promise with the hard possessiveness of his kiss.

She melted against him, body tingling, pulse leaping. Her last coherent thought as he deepened the kiss was to wonder if now would be the time, if he'd possess her and in doing so seal the bargain they'd made by speaking the words of binding.

Skimming his hands down her side, he caressed the curve of her waist, the side of her breast. Just enough to tease and make her eager for more.

When he took her hands and guided them to touch him, she let herself explore his flat abs, toying with the waist of his jeans, almost afraid to touch the ridge of swollen flesh that strained against her. Finally, he pressed against her and she had no choice.

"Touch me," he urged. And so she did.

"Oh," she said, shocked and intrigued and exhilarated all at once. Then, unable to keep from feeling it again, she grinned up at him. "I like."

After a moment of what must have been shock, he laughed. A warm, masculine guffaw that, she thought, contained both amusement and affection. If she hadn't seen the heat blazing from his darkened eyes, she would have been confused.

"I'm glad," he told her, pulling her in for a full-body hug.

She gasped as the full strength of his arousal pressed against her. He was huge! Was this normal? Her body tingled and she felt dizzy. Suddenly afraid, she swallowed.

"Are you all right?" he murmured.

With a nod, she pushed away her fear and concentrated on her desire instead. She wanted this man, even though he wasn't a Tearlach and her mating with him was strictly forbidden.

They were already bound by words and the time had come to make the binding permanent.

Tomorrow, she knew, her family might try to take him from her. If she wanted to make sure this wouldn't happen, she knew what she had to do.

Plus, a little niggling voice inside her told her she was looking for any excuse to do what she really wanted to do.

Make love with Mac. No sacrifice, that. A bit terrifying, but only if she thought too much.

Then he kissed her again, deep and passionate, and she forgot about ulterior motives and worrying and fear. She forgot about anything but desire and need and the gloriously hard, muscular body of the man in front of her.

Her knees trembled as he skimmed his hands under her shirt, cupping her breast. She couldn't breathe as he lifted her shirt over her head, helping her out of it, and her heart pounded as he removed her bra.

Should she speak, should she move? Surely there must be something she should do with her hands.

Was she supposed to feel this self-conscious?

Briefly, she wished there was someone she could have asked, someone with whom to share stories, swap anecdotes.

But there wasn't and, as usual, she'd have to wing it.

Shivering, she could only hope she didn't make too many mistakes.

"Are you cold?" he murmured, lips against her skin. Then, before she could answer, his mouth closed over her nipples, sending heat waves ricocheting into her core. He moved his mouth from her breast, searing a path up her neck. "All right?" Lifting his head, gazing into her eyes, he waited for her to answer.

Struck dumb, she nodded. Suddenly it seemed wrong that she was half-naked while he was fully clothed. She wanted to feel his skin, explore his muscles, his hardness, especially *there*. Desire made her dizzy.

Fumbling, she plucked at the buttons on his shirt, making him chuckle.

"Let me help you." With a few quick motions, he had the thing open. Breathing quickly, she slid her hands under the cotton, touching warm, bronzed skin. He sucked in his breath as she stroked his nipples.

Then he shrugged out of the shirt, watching her, eyes dark with desire, waiting to see what she'd do next.

"Your belt," she managed. "It's got to go." Somehow, though her hands were shaking, she managed to unbuckle it, tugging the leather through the belt loops. She kept getting distracted by the telltale bulge of his growing arousal.

Acting on instinct—which really, was all she had to go on—she got his jeans unbuttoned, but hesitated at the zipper. To pull this down would necessitate possibly hurting him.

To her chagrin, he realized this and helped her out. Stepping out of his flip-flops first, the jeans followed. He kicked them aside, standing completely and utterly naked in front of her, fully aroused.

She couldn't tear her gaze away from him.

"You next," he said softly, reminding her she still wore her jeans and, underneath, her panties.

Her face flamed as she began clumsily to remove her jeans.

"Let me." He kissed her again and she gratefully lost herself in the heat his mouth generated.

The back of her legs bumped up on the edge of the large bed. She froze again, wondering what to do next, when he bumped her and saved her from making the choice.

She fell back, glad she'd pulled back the down quilt earlier, sinking into the soft cotton sheets. As he loomed over her, looking huge and aroused and, oh, so male, she shivered again, though whether from fear or desire, she couldn't tell.

As she gazed up at him her mixed emotions must have shone in her eyes because he went still.

"Kelly?" Husky with desire, his voice made her insides do somersaults. "Are you all right?"

Realizing she would have to push him past her inexperience, she reached for him, pulling him down to her. "I will be," she told him, hoping he couldn't see her inner trepidation.

Evidently, he could. "What's wrong? I can practically scent the fear coming from you. Tell me."

Of course he could. He was a shifter, after all. For the space of a moment, she wondered if she should tell him. From what she'd heard, each man reacted differently to learning they would be the first. Some found it a powerful aphrodisiac. Others turned and ran away as fast as they could.

Heart pounding in her chest, she opened her mouth, trying to find the right words. After all, he was going to find out sooner or later.

"I…" Making a motion with her hands, she tried to convey her confusion without words.

He kissed her again, gently this time, holding his aroused body apart from her, touching her only with his mouth. She could feel the heat emanating from him and longed to curl into him like a purring cat in a patch of sunlight.

As he kissed her, sensually seductive without demanding, she changed her mind. She would not tell him with words; she didn't want to take the chance that he would call upon some misplaced sense of honor and refuse to mate with her.

When he tried to raise his head to end the kiss, she wouldn't let him. Instead, she pulled him to her, moving her body against his suggestively. To her shock, the movements meant to seduce him enflamed her own desire, making her burn.

"Please," she managed, caressing him all over except the one place she most longed to touch. "I need you."

Still he hesitated, as though unsure himself. Taking a deep breath, she reached out and curled her hand around the hard length of him, stroking.

He let out a moan, surging against her. "Kelly..."

Suddenly, none of it mattered. Not her lack of experience, his past or the future with the big meeting tomorrow. Right now, she wanted him. Inside her, filling her, making love to her.

Savagely, she swung herself up, aware there might be some pain, but beyond caring. Settling over him, her femininity drawn to his masculinity like a flower draws a bee, she went up, then down, impaling herself on the turgid length of him.

Inside her, something tore and she froze.

"Oh," she said, uncertain how to cope with such a sharp pain.

Reacting to her assault with a savagery of his own, he pushed against her, past the barrier and filling her completely. And back. Then again. In the rush of warmth that followed, the pain began to fade, replaced by something else, something delicious and wonderful.

She gasped, then his mouth found hers and she forgot to even think. Reveling in her own sensuality, she let go, becoming nothing but sensation, unable to tell where she left off and he began.

Her climax took her completely by surprise. It crept up on her, building and building, making her want more, as she writhed against him, matching him stroke for stroke, until everything shattered in a powerful explosion.

A moment later, Mac followed suit, collapsing against her and groaning. Wrapping her in his arms, he held her close, until his breathing slowed enough to speak.

Then, raising himself up on one elbow, he lifted her chin and made her look at him. "Why didn't you tell me?"

Deliciously sated, she gave him a small smile. "I was going to, but I just didn't know how. And then…"

"Things went too fast." He looked positively grim.

"Don't do that," she said, kissing him. "I have no regrets. I wanted to do this."

Still, he moved restlessly, though he kept his arms around her. "I would have done it differently if I'd known it was your first time."

Intrigued, she tilted her head and looked up at him. "How so?"

"I'd have taken more time and gone much more slowly. Most of all, I'd have made sure you weren't hurt."

She pondered this. "I'm a little sore, but not unpleasantly so."

"There's blood on the sheets." He pointed.

So there were a few tiny spots. They'd wash out. All she could do was shrug. "I've been told that often happens on the first time. No worries." She kissed him again, this time a long, lingering kiss that left them both breathless.

"If you keep that up, we'll be doing it again," he warned.

Grinning, she nodded. "I'm up for that."

"Not the first time, you aren't. You'd be way too sore tomorrow." He gave her a quick kiss. "Let's go to sleep. You have a big day ahead tomorrow."

She sighed. Already a delicious lassitude seemed to be creeping up on her. "I don't know that I'll be able to sleep," she said, turning on her side and punching her pillow.

Within two minutes, she drifted off to sleep.

The next morning, she woke still wrapped in Mac's arms. His even breathing told her that he still slumbered.

Easing from the bed, she tried not to wake him, creeping across the room to the bathroom, where after she'd completed her morning toilet, she turned the shower on hot and jumped in.

Did she feel any differently? A little stiff and sore, perhaps. But in a way, she was now a woman in every sense of the word instead of an untouched girl.

Perhaps foolishly, she'd always thought she'd feel completely different. More…womanly, somehow.

Her body tingled as she thought of the way he'd loved her.

Her mate. She savored the words, if only to herself. Though Mac thought they were only pretending, eventually she hoped he'd realize the truth himself rather than her having to tell him.

Once she'd showered and dried off, she emerged from the bathroom to find Mac awake. She went to him and kissed his cheek. "The bathroom's all yours," she said.

He didn't move. "We should talk about last night," he began.

"I'd rather not." Giving him a nervous smile, she crossed to her suitcase and opened it. "At least not this morning. I have too much on my mind as it is."

He didn't push the issue, for which she was grateful. Wrapping the sheet around his lower half, he crossed to the bathroom without commenting, though she could tell from the grim set of his mouth that he wasn't happy.

After the door closed, she sighed and forced herself to concentrate on the task at hand—getting ready for the big meeting. Not only would she get to see the rest of the family she'd been estranged from for the past twelve years, but she'd learn what exactly they planned to do about the abductions and how they were going to get her sister and Ian's sister back.

Unaccountably nervous, she changed clothes three times before finally settling on an outfit. She'd rejected jeans as too casual, a skirt and blouse as too dressy. Finally, she settled on a cream pair of slacks, a button-down cotton shirt and a pair of kitten heels. She took extra time with her long hair, using a flat iron to coax it into perfect straight, choppy lines.

And, though she normally wore only mascara and lip balm, she put on makeup—foundation, eye shadow, blush and lipstick. When she'd finished and she glanced at herself in the mirror, the glamorous woman staring back at her was almost unrecognizable.

Clichéd as it sounded, no longer a girl, but a woman.

She wondered if others could tell she was no longer an innocent. She really didn't look any different, but inside she felt worldly, womanly and experienced. Also, she wanted more. She wanted to do it again, as soon as possible, and more than once. How Mac would laugh if he knew.

As if thinking about him had summoned him, the bathroom door opened. As she turned to face him, on the verge of asking his opinion of her outfit, he let out a low whistle. She smiled, belatedly remembering the sort of mind-connection thing they had going.

But Mac didn't appear to have picked up on that particular sexual direction of her thoughts. Instead, he stared at her with an odd mixture of awe and, strangely enough, fear.

"You clean up well," he drawled.

Despite her nervousness, she couldn't help but laugh. "Thanks." She eyed his khakis and navy polo shirt. "You look nice, too."

He laughed. "Try to sound like you mean it, why don't you? I'm aware I look like a bodyguard or personal trainer in these clothes. I did that on purpose so I'd blend into the background."

Smart man. Her smile widened.

"Are you ready?" he asked.

Rechecking her makeup and her jewelry—large dangling earrings and an assortment of pretty bracelets—she rubbed a bit of lotion on her hands. "Almost. I don't know why I'm so weirded out about this. It's just my family, after all."

He squeezed her shoulder. "Don't worry. I'll be with you."

Biting her lip, she nodded.

"I *will* be with you, won't I?" he asked, eyes

narrowed. "You did clear that with your mother, didn't you?"

"Uh, not exactly. The subject never came up."

He rolled his eyes. "So what are we going to do now?"

"Wing it." She sounded more confident than she felt, which for some strange reason helped. "Play it by ear," she continued. "I'm sure it will all work out."

"I'm not," he grumbled. "But since I don't have a choice in the matter, we'd probably better get going."

Leaving the room, they walked side by side to the elevator. Once inside, he slid in the card key that Ian had given her the night before. The doors closed and they began their ascent to the top floor.

To calm herself, Kelly took in a deep breath, then exhaled. She did this again, trying to clear the clutter from her mind. When they reached their floor and the elevator stopped, she blinked, realizing Mac had been watching her, amusement glittering in his eyes.

All of that vanished the moment they stepped out into the packed hallway. Elbow to elbow, the throngs of people reminded her of a queue waiting to get into a sold-out rock concert.

Unreal.

Immediately, Mac took her arm. "Recognize anyone?" he asked, low-voiced.

"None of these people look even remotely familiar," she said, stunned and shocked and more than a little uneasy.

It was impossible to push through the crowd. While they waited, she continued to scan the faces of the people closest to them.

Still nothing. She shook her head, meeting Mac's gaze. "I don't understand."

"Is it possible they're distant family members?"

"I guess they'd have to be, but honestly, our family isn't this large. There has to be over a hundred people in the hallway alone. It's full from one end to another."

As he was about to reply, she spotted Ian, his shock of red hair a foot above most of the other heads.

"Ian!" She waved, jumping up and down in an effort to make him notice her. "Over here."

She needn't have worried. He made a beeline for her, pulling her in for a quick hug.

"Lass, I've been trying to find you," he said, not even looking at Mac. "We're trying to gather our family all in one area."

"I don't understand." She clutched at his arm.

"What do you mean, seat our family together? Who are all these people?"

Frowning, he glanced from her to Mac and back again. "I'm sorry, I thought I made myself clear. This meeting isn't just our family or even any one family."

"Then who…?"

"All the Tearlachs in the world are here today." Ian waved his hand at the assembled crowd.

"All of them?" Kelly's eyes widened.

"Pretty much," he said cheerfully. "Oh, there were a few holdouts, I'm sure, but we've got nearly a thousand people here today."

"Where did you find a meeting room to hold that many?" Mac asked.

Staring at him, Ian hesitated. After a moment, he answered, "Good question. Actually, the hotel doesn't have any place this big, so we're going to the Bass Performance Hall. We know someone who works there and can get us all in for a few hours, gratis."

"Then why are we here?" Kelly gestured at the crowd. She'd never liked crowds and since living on her remote ranch, she was completely unaccustomed to being so closed in.

"We had to coordinate everything. We're try-ing to have everyone go in a group with their own people. Since it's in walking distance, we are all going to head over there in a few minutes."

Since he'd looked only at Kelly when he spoke, she took Mac's arm. "Ian, Mac is coming with me. Wherever I go, he goes."

A muscle worked in Ian's jaw. "That's not possible," he said. "I'm sorry, but the organizer of this thing was very specific. Tearlachs only. No one else is to be allowed inside."

Chapter 10

Mac wasn't surprised. Actually, he'd expected as much. As Kelly opened her mouth to argue, he nodded curtly at Ian and pulled her away.

"Let's go," he said, with a look warning Ian not to follow.

"Wait," Ian began.

"She'll meet you over there," Mac interrupted, steering Kelly back toward the elevator and punching the button. Miraculously, the doors immediately opened.

Stepping inside and pulling her with him, he punched their floor number. He waited until the doors closed again, and then he released her.

"Why'd you do that?" She glared at him, eyes

spitting fire. "I'm sure all Ian needed was a bit of convincing."

"He doesn't matter. Ian's not the one in charge here."

She didn't back down. "Then who is?"

He gave her a grim smile. "I was hoping you could tell me that. It's your shindig."

"I have no idea. Do you want me to call Ian?"

"Not yet. We'll figure something out."

They reached their floor. Stepping out first, Mac cleared the hallway, then motioned for her to join him.

"Stop doing that," she said tiredly.

"Doing what?" he asked, though he suspected he knew.

"Acting like my bodyguard. You're not."

He let that bit of foolishness go, aware that arguing over the small things would be a waste of both time and energy. "I need to know something. If there are all these unfamiliar Tearlachs here to attend this thing, I should be able to walk right in. After all, how is anyone going to know whether I'm one or not?"

Now Kelly lowered her face, staring at her feet. "They'll know," she told him.

"How?" Crossing his arms, he wondered why she wouldn't look at him. "Kelly? How can you tell?"

When she did raise her face to meet his gaze, her look was guarded. "We just can. I can't explain it. When we meet another of our own kind, we can tell."

He glanced around them, overly conscious that they were standing in a hotel hallway, completely exposed. So far, the area was still remarkably empty, except for the maid's cart down at one end. "Is it something in the aura?"

"Sort of." Sounding utterly miserable, she began walking down the hall toward their room, leaving him to follow her.

He caught up to her and took her arm. "Explain. Please."

"I can't, not really. It's not something that's actually visible or anything you'd be able to duplicate. We just know. It's more like a click of recognition when we look in another Tearlach's eyes."

Frustrated, he released her. "I don't understand."

She said simply, "I know."

At the door to their room, he inserted the card key. "Then explain it to me."

Opening the door, she turned to face him. "I—"

Before she could finish, a loud crash sounded and the building shook. Then the fire alarms went off and a mechanical voice came over the intercom. "Please evacuate the building immediately."

Kelly froze. "What the…?"

"I'm sure this has nothing to do with your meeting," he lied, not wanting her to panic. "Let's just go to the stairwell calmly and make our way outside."

She shook her head. "That's what whoever is behind this wants us to do, so they can capture us."

"If that's the case, we'll be ready for them." He indicated her gun, still holstered securely at her side. "Are you sure you don't have a spare one of those that I could carry?"

"No, I don't." Crossing the room to him, she took his arm. "Mac, remember how I told you that sometimes I *know* things? This is one of those times. We should not go to the stairwell."

Impatient now, he stared at her. "Then how do you propose we get out? Hotel elevators always go on lockdown when the fire alarms activate."

"We don't. We don't leave. We stay put."

Insane. But yet… Eyeing her, he considered. "The building is not on fire."

She sounded so certain he almost believed her. Even with the alarms still clanging and the mechanical voice repeating the evacuation orders every few seconds.

"Then why? What's going on?"

Moving away from him restlessly, she shook her head. "I don't know. Maybe they're waiting in the stairwells, trying to round up as many of the young female Tearlachs as they can."

He had to make her see reason. "That would be damn near impossible, given the sheer size of the numbers of you coming down the stairs at the same time. You saw how many there were upstairs."

"They may not all be evacuating. Others share a similar ability to mine. Many of us won't evacuate."

As the claxon kept on, he pushed down an instinctive panic. "And you can seriously say with one hundred percent certainty that there is no fire?"

Slowly, she nodded. "Please, Mac, let's just wait it out."

"Fine. Though I don't like this, not at all." He began to pace the perimeter of the small room.

Five long minutes later and the smoke alarms stopped blaring. Whether that was because they'd fixed the problem or the fire had disabled them, he couldn't say.

"Trust me," she said softly. "I'm never wrong when it comes to listening to my inner voice."

"That must be nice." He couldn't help but mock her. "To never have uncertainty in anything you do."

She bit her lip, looking stricken. "If you only knew…"

"If I only knew what?"

As she stared at him, not answering, a voice came over the loudspeakers and gave the all clear for guests to return to their rooms.

Her frown cleared. "See? I told you. There was no fire. It was a false alarm."

"Then what was the purpose?"

"Who knows?" She shrugged. "A distraction, most likely. But from what, I don't know. Whether the leaders of this group wanted to try and grab someone or something, I can't say. I don't even know if they've succeeded, though I guess they'll tell us in the meeting."

"Assuming I can get into the meeting."

Glancing at her watch, she gave him a confident smile. "First, we need to pick up a pair of cheap sunglasses so no one can look into your eyes."

Stunned, he nodded. "You're right. Why didn't I think of that?"

Clearly pleased, her smile widened. "With

the sunglasses, I think if we go to the convention center right about now, while everyone is still unsettled from the fire alarm, you shouldn't have a problem getting in. No one is paying attention to anything else but themselves right now."

"Is that one of your premonitions?" he asked wryly.

"No." Her smile never wavered as she took his arm. "Just a hunch."

Her hunch turned out to be right. To his relief, they breezed past the various clusters of talking people without anyone questioning them. Even those who appeared to be sort of standing sentry at the entrance doors barely glanced their way. From what he could overhear, everyone was worried about the explosion and/or fire at the hotel minutes earlier.

They made their way outside and though the morning air felt warm, he knew from past experience this heat was nothing compared to what would come. He'd once had an assignment in Wichita Falls, Texas, during August. After that, he'd sworn never to come near the state in the summertime again.

Once inside the convention center, they took their seats quietly, choosing a spot in the back, away from the main flow of foot traffic and, most important, in the shadows near the exit. He wanted to be able to make a quick getaway if something bad happened. As a further precaution, he also kept his sunglasses on, though that made it slightly difficult to see.

This entire scenario so reminded him of his time in the Protectors Academy that he felt really at home.

Kelly couldn't stop fidgeting. She twirled her hair on her finger, kept checking in her purse, pulling out her cell phone, checking the screen and replacing it, and shifted in her seat.

"What's wrong with you?" he asked, low-voiced.

"I don't have a good feeling," she said. "In fact, I have a terrible feeling. But this time, I must be wrong. Otherwise there wouldn't be such a huge crowd."

"Maybe not everyone shares your gift."

She gave him a doubtful smile and said nothing.

Side by side, they watched as the auditorium filled up with people. Glancing around him, he searched row by row. Kelly had been right. There were no children present.

Still, the size of the crowd blew his mind. Surprised, Mac watched as row after row filtered in. Group after group, sometimes in clusters of ten, others as little as two or three. The sheer number of attendees forced him to revise his estimate of the total number of Tearlachs here from the hundreds well into the thousands.

Unreal. In a way, he could understand Kelly's unease. With such numbers, one pre-emptive strike could wipe out most of the Tearlach population. Though he imagined they had to be aware of this and were prepared, he couldn't help but wish the Protectors could have been notified so they could at the very least act as guards.

These people, the Tearlachs, needed protection. After all, he was not one of them and he'd gotten in way too easily. Who knew who else might have done the same, and for what nefarious purposes?

Nefarious. He rolled the old-fashioned word around in his mind, wondering where that'd come from. Just this entire situation, with blood debts and mysterious mind reading that supposedly wasn't, was enough to creep out most men. Not to mention the way Kelly kept hinting about a binding, just because they'd spoken words of protection.

He supposed she wasn't ready to discuss that right now and, the truth of the matter was, neither was he.

Honestly, he was willing to let all that weird woo-woo stuff go if he could just locate his children and hold them in his arms. It had been far too long since he'd seen their trusting little blue eyes gazing into his, or their joy-filled smiles as they ran to him for hugs.

A stab of pain made him realize why he normally shut his mind down whenever he started thinking about them—because it hurt too damn much.

Next to him, Kelly shifted in her seat again. Glancing at her, he saw her attention was focused on a group of people who were taking seats close to the front. He spotted Ian's red head and realized they must be her family.

For the first time he realized Maggie's brother most likely would be there also. He'd have to be careful not to run into him or else he'd be outed as a non-Tearlach.

As he leaned over to whisper this to Kelly, a muscular older man with longish silver hair took the stage.

"That's my uncle Danny," Kelly told him, keeping her voice low. "He appears to be in charge of all this, doesn't he?"

Mac nodded. The overhead lights flickered on and off, signaling all those who were still standing to take their seats. In a flurry of motion, everyone rushed to do just that.

"Welcome," Danny McKenzie said into the microphone, his Scottish accent lending a burr to his words. "I'm glad to see so many of you were able to make it."

Several people cheered.

"Many of you are aware of female family members that have been taken. Most of you probably think this number is limited to two or three, all within your own clan. This is not the case. As of today's date, thirty-seven young women have been abducted."

As one, the audience gasped. Mac sat up straighter in his seat. Around him, people began to talk among themselves.

"Holy crap," Kelly muttered next to him. "This is unbelievable."

Someone from the other side of the auditorium shouted out something similar, demanding to know what was being done about this.

"I don't have any answers." Danny spread his hands. "We don't even know who is behind the abductions. We set the hotel alarms off this morning, trying to flush them out. We've hired private investigators around the world, even approached the Pack Protectors—"

At this, many gasped again. Several shouted out curse words or denials.

Looking serene, Danny waited until the group had once again grown quiet before continuing. "Despite having the best people in the world working on this, we have been unable to obtain any answers."

"That doesn't seem possible," Mac muttered in Kelly's ear. "The Pack has lots of resources. Surely they would be able to—"

Kelly shushed him, inclining her head toward the stage, where Danny was asking them for silence.

"This is the reason we've decided to all get together. Perhaps we were wrong splitting up the families. We've never faced a threat of this magnitude before. Maybe there is better safety in numbers."

"What does our council plan to do about this? These are our daughters, our sisters. We need answers!" someone from the audience shouted out.

Expression sad, Danny scanned the audience, making Mac wonder if he was trying to find out who had spoken so he could single the man out for retribution.

"No, that's not it," Kelly spoke beside him. "He's not like that."

"Not like what?" Mac whispered back, once again forced to wonder if she'd read his mind.

"He's not evil," she said, her attention still focused on the stage.

"Therefore," Danny continued, "our council has decided to put it to a vote. A ballot has been drawn up and will be distributed among you. We can ask the Pack Protectors to use their considerable resources to assist us, but as you know, their help comes with a price."

Again the crowd erupted with noise, everyone speaking at once. Several yells of *why* were heard over the racket.

"We have several theories, but we really don't know why." Danny had to shout to be heard over the crowd's noise. "Some think it's some kind of breeding program, though we all know that would be futile. Another hypothesis is some kind of black magic ritual. Many more ideas have been tossed about, though in my opinion they keep getting stranger and stranger."

"Alien abduction?" someone cried out, causing more than a few snickers in the crowd.

"That was one of them, yes. There are a few more, but to be honest with you, we don't understand why. We've had a few threats—if we try to locate the missing women, they'll be killed—but no demand for ransom or anything like that."

He looked so frustrated that Mac caught himself feeling sorry for the guy.

"We've set up a toll-free number for you to make reports. If you have a family member missing, a friend, hell, even an acquaintance, call and report everything you know. The smallest details can mean anything when they're put together."

A woman in the third row stood up. "Have you compiled statistics? What is the primary age group of the targets?"

"They are all young women, all of childbearing age, between eighteen years old and twenty-nine. They've been taken from every continent, every country. However, most of them—a staggering thirty-three percent—have come from the United States."

This time, the audience sat silently absorbing this information.

From another section, another woman stood. Danny dipped his chin at her, indicating she should speak.

"Have they all been virgins?" she asked, her strained voice conveying her nervousness.

"To the best of our knowledge," Danny answered, "yes, they have."

Stunned, Mac listened as everyone started talking again. While he heard the words *witchcraft* and *black magic* repeatedly bantered about, no one seemed to find it strange that so many virgins aged eighteen to twenty-nine existed.

"That's because we are forbidden to mate until we've found our true mate," Kelly murmured.

Startled, Mac stared at her, the implications of what she'd said clear. "Are you reading my mind?" he accused.

Shaking her head, she returned her attention to the front of the room.

On the stage, Danny tapped the microphone, repeatedly asking for silence. "The council—and myself, of course—has determined that we have few options. We can ask the Protectors for assistance to find our missing women, or we can continue to try to do this on our own."

He held up a hand, indicating he hadn't finished yet. "And finally, there is a third option. We hesitated to mention it, because it will be quite distasteful to many of you. The Vampire Council has offered to help, as well. Their Huntresses will use their considerable skills to find our missing people."

More shouting again, though this time people leapt to their feet, shaking their fists. The outrage over this suggestion was three times as strong as when Danny had mentioned the Protectors, which Mac was glad to hear.

Personally, Mac found the idea abhorrent himself. Vampires and shifters were rarely able to work together, never mind achieve results in an enterprise of this size.

This time, Danny waited a moment or two before tapping the mic and asking them to listen. When the noise level shrank, he announced that the ballots would be handed out and that they should use their code name and number as identification.

"This will, of course, be matched with our database to ensure fairness. Only one vote per person," he said. With that, Danny exited the stage and the houselights flashed back on.

Everyone began talking to each other at once.

Mac exchanged a glance with Kelly. "I need to know who they have contacted at the Protectors. We don't require payment when we help someone. Or, in this case, a group of people."

Her steady gaze never wavered. "Really? That hasn't been my experience. Every single Protector they sent to me wanted me to join the Pack."

"So?" Confused, he frowned. "But that's not asking for payment."

"Isn't it? If we were to become Pack members, that would give you access to all of our powers."

He'd had enough. "What powers?" Leaning in close, he went nearly nose to nose with her. "You keep hinting that you people are some kind of supershifters or something. I read the dossier. Yes, you can protect someone, keep them from dying, like you did with me. But what else can you do? What makes you so valuable that someone is kidnapping your young women?"

Though the answer to this question seemed vital if they wanted to find out who was doing this and why, she wouldn't answer. Instead, she would only shake her head.

The woman two seats to his left handed Mac a stack of papers with instructions to take one and pass them on. The ballots.

Though Mac knew he couldn't vote, he didn't want to draw attention to himself, so he kept one, along with one of the stubby pencils. Kelly did the same.

"Vampires," he said with disgust, reading through the ballot. "He was really serious."

"He wouldn't have mentioned it if he didn't mean it," Kelly said, sounding distracted. Since she still held her ballot and her pencil, her pre-occupation had to be on something else.

Looking up, Mac saw her attention was focused on one of the exit doors. Since it was empty, he didn't understand why.

"What's going on?" he asked.

As his gaze met hers, she stood, panic flashing across her face. Voice low and urgent, she spoke. "We've got to get out of here. Now."

Another premonition?

Pushing to his feet, he gripped her arm. "Tell me. What's wrong?"

Tossing her head back and forth, her agitation appeared to have made her unable to speak. He looked around at the rest of the crowd, and saw several others had stood and were behaving the same way.

So many did share Kelly's predilection for premonition. While he filed this information away to examine later, Kelly pulled him forward.

"Come on, let's go. Hurry," she urged him.

Moving quickly, they started up their row.

But they were too late. Before they even reached the end of their row, several men wearing black trench coats with matching black fedoras pulled low over their faces appeared in the doorway.

They were carrying MG 34's, light machine guns that were completely illegal. A quick check revealed they stood in every doorway. Blocking them in.

"Crap." Kelly's entire body sagged. "I wasn't quick enough. If anyone tries to leave, they're going to shoot us with those guns."

"Yep, and I bet they're armed with silver bullets," Mac said, pulling Kelly back down into an empty seat. "Keep low. Try not to attract their attention. I have a hunch."

Someone screamed. The crowd, most of them intent on their surveys, looked up. Mac could almost see the ripple that went through them as they all noticed the newcomers.

To their credit, no one panicked. If they did, Mac had no doubt the intruders would mow them down.

"What's your hunch?" she whispered.

"They're here to gather more captives. The ones in real danger here are their targets— young women between the ages of eighteen and twenty-nine."

She closed her eyes for a moment. When she opened them again, he saw a sort of calm resignation that scared the hell out of him.

"Like me," she said.

As if they'd been hypnotized or something,

the entire room went silent, staring at various exits. Mac looked around for their fearless leader, but Danny appeared to be conspicuously absent.

Figures. Mac just bet Danny and his immediate family had gotten clean away. But no, he spotted Ian, climbing up to the stage.

"What's he doing?" he asked.

"I don't know." She shook her head. "I just hope he's not doing something foolish."

Watching her cousin's self-assured movements, Mac had a dawning suspicion that he was part of this somehow. Then, as Danny strode out to join his son, he knew it deep in his gut.

From the stricken look on Kelly's face, she realized it, too.

Ian's next words confirmed his suspicion. "This meeting was actually a ruse." Ignoring the angry murmurs rising from the crowd, he continued, "We needed a way to get you together, all in one place."

Then, as everyone stood frozen, uncertain how to act, what to do, Ian tapped the mic. "Kelly McKenzie, please step forward."

"No way," Mac snarled, grabbing her arm. "Slide down in your seat so he can't see you."

"It won't do any good," she said, sounding miserable.

"Please," he urged, as a spotlight came up and began sweeping the audience, row by row.

"Fine." Though she did as he'd asked, her expression reflected her fear. "He'll find me anyway."

"Not if I can help it," he promised grimly, crossing his arms and pretending to be as interested in what was going on with the spotlight as everyone else.

"Kelly, I know you're here." Ian spoke too close to the microphone, causing a feedback that squealed so loudly it hurt the ears.

Someone jumped up from a section to the left of the stage. "Kelly left early," she said, speaking loudly so her voice would carry to the stage. Rose, Kelly's mom. "She's going to meet me for dinner later."

"You're lying." Ian sounded calm. "We've checked the hotel. She and her Pack friend came here." He spat the word *Pack* as though it tasted vile on his lips.

"She's gone," Rose insisted. "I watched her leave myself."

Danny stepped forward, grabbing the microphone from his son. "Rose, we've known each other a long time. It's perfectly understandable that you would try and protect your daughter, but she has broken the law of our people and must be punished."

"Punished?" Rose's voice grew stronger, more strident. "By whom?"

"By our enforcer. My son, Ian."

Rose wasn't backing down so easily. "What law did she break?"

"You know which one," Danny softly chided her. "She has become the mate of one outside our race."

Chapter 11

Listening, Mac toyed with the idea of standing up and shouting out the truth—that he *wasn't* mated with Kelly, and she'd simply saved his life. Normally, he was all for being honest and up front, but in this instance of bizarre-land, he thought it better to remain invisible and let the situation play out.

Now he had a better understanding of why they'd taken his children. Apparently, Kelly's uncle Danny and his son had elected themselves dictators over the Tearlachs. And it didn't appear to be a benevolent dictatorship, either.

Not only did they want complete control over their own kind, but they wanted to punish any-

one who broke the rigid set of rules they'd made.
He wondered what they considered punishment.
Torture? Death? Involuntary sterilization? Or
incarceration?

At the options, any of them, he winced. While
he'd been aware that mating with non-Tearlachs
was considered a bad thing among them, he
hadn't known such a deed was actually *punishable*.

And why? Just because they said so didn't cut
it with him. And from the looks of things, many
of the others were having similar issues with
that. Eyeing the two crazies up on the stage, he
realized their quest for power had most likely
been built up over time. Kelly had said twelve
years had passed since her father died. No doubt
Danny had been plotting ever since then, if not
before.

He wondered what other rules they'd set in
stone and would no doubt try to enforce. Soon
they'd be trying to tell people how to dress and
act. Did they really think they could treat people
like serfs and get away with it? So far, it looked
like they had. Up until now, it seemed clear that
no one had even been remotely aware of them
pulling the strings behind the scenes.

Though from their ranting and raving today,
their worst infraction appeared to be the one of

which they believed Kelly guilty of making—mating with a non-Tearlach.

Forbidden. Punishable. This had to be a fairly recent development. After all, Mac had been married to a Tearlach. He couldn't help but wonder why this hadn't been an issue with Maggie. While she'd been ostracized due to their marriage, no one had ever wanted to punish her. If they had, he would have known about it.

Wouldn't he? He had to believe he would.

Then he had to wonder if this offense was the reason Kelly's sister, Bonnie, and the other girls had been taken.

The spotlight kept making its slow sweep of the room, row by row.

"You know I might as well give up," Kelly whispered urgently, tugging on his jeans. "When that damn thing shines over here, he's going to know."

"Not if you stay down," he muttered from the side of his mouth, still pretending to be as interested as the others who were watching the slow, deliberate search. "That thing can't shine through seats or illuminate the floor. Stay down and he won't see you."

"Maybe not, but he'll see you," she said. "Wearing sunglasses in the dark. That's suspicious enough. And you can't take them off or your eyes will give you away."

Cursing under his breath—the thought hadn't even occurred to him—he watched the sweeping spotlight get closer and closer while he tried to figure out what to do.

As if she sensed his dilemma—and who knows, maybe she did—Kelly's mother once again stood and challenged Danny and Ian.

"You say this meeting was a ploy to make us all gather together, but you haven't explained why, other than your sick desire to 'punish' my daughter," she shouted, her chin raised in a gesture Mac recognized.

"I would think that would be obvious." Danny spoke with great dignity, acting as though he were insulted that she even had to ask. "We must keep our race pure."

"That smacks of the Aryan Nations," Rose replied. "I would think you would welcome fresh blood to mingle with ours. We are a dying people and this is the natural evolution of things."

"Natural?" Danny sneered, practically spitting the word. "Such a thing is a travesty, an aberration against our kind. How dare you believe it otherwise."

Rose continued to regard him calmly. Face

red, eyes bulging, the man looked on the verge of a coronary.

"Last time I checked, I live in a free country," Rose pointed out, adding gasoline to the fire, Mac thought.

This time, Ian replied. "Free with regard to certain things. But this is Tearlach business. This is different."

She shrugged, the overblown gesture obviously meant to show that she discounted his words. "By whose law?"

"By our law," Danny roared back, spraying spittle. Ian walked over to him, moving him back from the microphone and speaking to him, no doubt trying to calm him.

Rose was having none of that. Still she pressed on. "Since you have armed guards preventing us from leaving, it appears you have taken it upon yourself to act like some feudal king. By what right do you keep us here?"

Her belligerent tone had the effect of rousing the others. Two men and another woman also stood and shouted out, demanding answers.

Now the entire crowd appeared energized rather than just stunned. Many got to their feet, others leaned forward.

But what was even more worrisome was that the room appeared to be splitting into sides. A growing number of people coalesced around Rose, but an even greater number gathered at the opposite side of the stage, near where Ian and his family had been sitting.

"Some of these people knew this was going to happen," Mac muttered to Kelly. "Danny had to have begun organizing this a long time ago."

Danny laughed, the sound chilling Mac to the bone. He'd heard people express amusement exactly like that during assignments as a Protector. Never good, almost always a warning of worse things to come. Danny had the laugh of a madman.

But when he spoke, his voice calm and soothing, he sounded completely sane and rational. "We are the only ones who can keep us safe." He gazed directly at Rose, his expression full of compassion. "You know this, Rose. Look at what happened to my brother, your beloved husband. Before he was killed, he set in motion the plan that we follow to this day."

Appearing convinced, Rose bowed her head. Mac's heart sank. Then, just as he was about to tell Kelly that her mother had caved, Rose appeared to shake off Danny's hypnotic litany. She stepped forward again, bringing her within arm's reach of the stage.

Two armed goons moved to block her, but Danny waved them away.

"What about the missing girls? My daughter Bonnie and your own girl? And all the others. Do you know where they are?"

For a moment, Danny hesitated. While he wavered, appearing to debate carefully what he would say, Ian stepped in front of him and took the microphone.

"They are safe," he said. Whatever else he tried to say was drowned out in the roar from the crowd. It sounded like everyone spoke at once, shouting questions, crying and even screaming.

While the melee went on below them, Kelly jumped to her feet and grabbed his arm. "If we can, now we need to try to leave while they're distracted." She pointed to the armed guards. While several had abandoned their posts by the doors to move closer to the crowds, in every single exit he could see at least one man remained, assault rifle at the ready.

"I don't think that's possible," he said. But she didn't appear to be listening, pulling him along. Instead of heading for the exits, she appeared to try to make it to the stage.

Since he had no choice, he followed her.

If need be, if she tried something crazy, he'd stop her.

The two groups screamed at each other. Ian used the microphone to try and calm them down, but everyone ignored him. Mac and Kelly kept going. With everyone focused on the stage, no one paid them any mind.

When they reached the railing and steps that separated the floor seats from the elevated section, she turned right. "We'll have to climb a railing and let ourselves drop down onto concrete," she told him. "Perfectly safe. Certainly better than this insanity."

From the stage, Danny's followers had begun to get louder and ruder and more belligerent with the group of people who had doubts and questions. The yelling match raged on, and the noise level had climbed so many decibels that Mac knew Danny and Ian would have to act decisively soon if they wanted to prevent an out-and-out riot.

A quick glance at the stage revealed that for now both of the men appeared content to let the fierce debate rage below them. They stood back watching, while the spotlight continued to make its slow sweep of the crowd. Even Ian had abandoned the microphone and appeared focused on what the searching spotlight revealed.

Luckily, they were still in the dark. But not for long. Soon, the light would hit their section.

"Come on," Kelly urged. At the metal railing, she climbed, one leg over, then the other, teetering on the edge. Looking back over her shoulder at him, she flashed him a reassuring smile.

"One, two, three." She let herself drop, landing safely on both feet. Looking up at him, she motioned for him to do the same.

Moving quickly, Mac did the same, noting with relief that no guards blocked the long tunnel under the stage.

As they hurried along, he cast frequent looks over his shoulder. The roar of the still-unruly crowd had grown greatly diminished. He couldn't tell if this was because Ian and Danny had finally decided to exert some crowd control or if the tunnel muffled the sound.

"Where does this go?" he asked.

"To the dressing room area. This is the way the main act and their entourage come when some power speaker is having a seminar."

"How do you know that?"

She shot him an amused look. "I used to go to a lot of dog rescue events around the country."

"So you weren't always a recluse," he said as they slammed into double metal doors. They busted past the waiting room, and through another door, and finally found themselves in a huge underground parking garage filled with cars.

"No. I used to be quite sociable. Now we need a getaway vehicle," she told him, with a gleam in her eye that made him want to grab her and kiss her. He restrained himself, instead glancing around at all the cars in the garage.

"What do you have in mind?"

"Since we can't get to my Hummer, I want something fast. Like that." She pointed to a black, low-slung sports car.

"That's a Lamborghini. No way. First, it's too noticeable, and second, it probably belongs to Danny or Ian. And I'd definitely bet that it's alarmed."

"Too bad. I bet that thing is fun to drive," she commented, already scouting for a second choice.

Since they didn't have time to debate the pros and cons of various cars, he spotted a dark green vintage Corvette parked a few spots away.

"There." He ran to the car, tested the door and, miracle of miracles, found it unlocked. "What kind of person leaves something like this unlocked?"

"Not that car." Frowning, she pointed to a black BMW Roadster. "Take that one. While I love my 'Vette, that's my mother's ride. I don't understand why she didn't lock it, but I refuse to steal from her."

This he could well understand. However, the Beamer was locked and he had to waste valuable seconds jimmying the door. Once he had the car open, it took a few more seconds to hotwirc it, but finally the engine came to life with a satisfying roar.

"We're in business," he told her, getting out and jotting down the license plate number on a slip of paper, which he tucked in his wallet. Then he hopped back in and fastened his seat belt, trying to slow his racing heart. "A little small, but I like the dark tinted windows. Let's roll."

She clicked her own seat belt and nodded. "I'm ready."

As they pulled away, exiting the garage via a ramp and merging onto a busy side street, he grinned. "That was close."

"Too close," she said, staring at him with a dazed expression. Then she blinked and smiled back. "At least we know where we stand."

"Yeah, but it's not pretty."

"Not at all, though it eases my mind somewhat knowing my sister isn't being tortured by some strange psychopath."

He clenched his jaw, refusing to state the obvious. If Danny wasn't a psycho, he didn't know who was.

"Now I've got to figure out how to go up against my own cousin and uncle," she continued, "so I can rescue her."

"What about the other girls?"

"I'm sure Katie's fine. She's Ian's sister, Danny's daughter. Surely they wouldn't hurt her. Now, the others, I don't know."

"You don't think they're in danger?" he asked, remembering the madness he'd heard in Danny's voice.

She thought for a moment. "I don't know. I would never have believed Uncle Danny and Ian could do something like this. I just want to rescue my sister."

"Rescue her from what? I don't understand what he's doing with them. His niece? Own daughter? You mentioned some sort of breeding program. What did you mean?"

"I'm not sure." Kelly gazed out the window, fidgeting in her seat. "That was something my mother said to me last night. I'm not certain she knows anything, either. She sounded as much in the dark as we are."

"Call her," he said, adrenaline still pumping.

"She called your cell phone, so you should have her number."

Clearly torn, Kelly turned to gaze at him. "She's probably still trapped in the meeting." She sounded less than enthusiastic. "I don't want to draw attention to her."

"Then text her."

"Pushy, aren't you?" she grumbled, taking her phone out and staring at it, but not actually dialing anything.

"At least now I understand why he took my children," he said. "What I don't get is why so many of you seem to just go along with him. It's a disturbing look at the herd mentality."

She met his gaze, her own stricken. "You're right. And I don't have a good answer for you. Everything seemed perfectly reasonable. Protecting our own, and no one actually got hurt—"

"I did." Cutting her off, he let the full weight of his bitterness show in the roughness of his voice. "How can you say that? When you take children away from their own father? Of course people got hurt. And not just me, but my twins."

At his words, she bowed her head, her shoulders hunched. When she looked up again, tears streamed a silver path down her creamy cheeks.

"You're right and I'm so sorry," she told him, her voice breaking. "Though I wasn't directly involved, when you first told me about them being taken, I found nothing wrong with the idea. That was just the way things were. Tearlachs raised Tearlachs. That's how it's always been and I never questioned that. I honestly believed that children should be raised around their own kind."

"Children should be raised by someone who loves them,"

"Yes," she whispered. "And that's where Uncle Danny and my father were wrong."

Swallowing hard, staring blankly, her gaze appeared to turn inward. "When I was sixteen and forced to live with complete strangers, I would have given anything for my mother and sister. Instead, I had to learn to deal with my grief alone. I wouldn't wish that on anyone. Yet that's exactly what's happening right now with your kids."

"Does that mean you know where they are?" he asked.

"Yes. And no."

Almost afraid to breathe, he held himself absolutely still, alternating between watching the road and her face. "What do you mean?" he asked, his voice deceptively casual.

Lost in her own memories, she didn't even notice. "They're doing to your children what they did to me. It's a horrible, rootless sort of existence. While I don't know their exact location, I can tell you that they're being shunted around in a sort of Tearlach-only foster-family system. They won't be allowed to live too long in any one place, so it'll be hard to form friendships or ties. Just when they start to feel comfortable, they'll be moved."

She sounded so desolate, he used the overwhelming rush of sympathy he felt for her to push back the instinctive rage at the thought that they dared do this to his boy and his girl. His children. His babies. The only beings he loved in the entire world.

"Why?" he managed, aware his attempt to come off as unaffected failed. "That's no kind of life for anyone, especially toddlers. They lost their mother and then got yanked away from their daddy. Most of all, they need security, a feeling of permanence. Instead, they're being shuttled around like unwanted pets. What's the logic in that?"

She grimaced, reminding him that he'd just described her exact situation twelve years earlier.

"Doing that makes it a lot more difficult to find them. That's the intention. And I guess it works, because no one ever found me as a child." Her voice was so full of loss and regret it made his chest ache.

"Where do you think the kids are being kept, then, if all the Tearlachs in the world are here?" Holding his breath, he waited for her response.

When she raised her head, the hope shining in her eyes took his breath away. "You're right," she whispered. "For a meeting of this size and scope, they must have all the children in one location."

"With non-Tearlachs guarding them, since they wanted all Tearlachs at the meeting."

"Exactly."

"Then all we need to do is figure out where they're keeping them." Almost afraid to hope, he kept his voice steady.

She covered his hand with hers. "We'll find them. Somehow."

Exiting the freeway, he took a side road.

At the first red light they came to, the second the car had come to a complete stop, he leaned over and kissed her. Hard, lingering and hopefully full of promise.

When they broke apart again, she was breathless. "What'd you do that for?"

Wondering about that himself, he focused again on driving. The light had changed to green. As they pulled forward, he told her the truth. "I don't know. I've been wanting to do that ever since we escaped the convention center."

With a half smile, she dipped her head, clearly pleased. "We'll get your children back."

"Oh, I have no doubt about that. And when we do, Danny—or whoever is responsible—will pay," he vowed.

She nodded. "I'm feeling kind of bloodthirsty myself."

On the outskirts of Fort Worth, on I-35W, they found a motel in a place called Burleson.

"Kelly Clarkson's from here," she said.

At his quizzical look, she elaborated, "You know, the first American Idol?"

He didn't know, nor did he care. "Let's check in to that motel and use this as our home base. We've got to figure out some kind of plan that doesn't involve us turning you over to them. First, we need to find out where they're keeping your sister."

"The only way to do that is to spy on them," she mused.

"Exactly."

As he was about to elaborate, her cell phone rang.

Glancing at the caller ID, she nearly dropped

the phone. "It's Ian," she said, sounding horrified.

"Perfect timing. Answer it and see what he wants."

Swallowing hard, she opened the phone, pushing the button so the sound was on speaker. "Hello?"

"Kelly, it's Ian. Where are you?"

"Not at your meeting," she replied.

"That's obvious. We kept everyone here until we could screen them, one by one. When we finished—no you." He sounded peeved.

"Sorry." She couldn't resist taunting him.

"Our security cameras showed how you got away," he continued, as if she hadn't spoken. "By the way, we have reported the black BMW stolen, so the police are on the lookout, as well. Sooner or later, we're going to find you," he said.

"Maybe not."

"Oh, we will," he said. "Because if you don't turn yourself in, your mother and sister will die."

And he hung up with a sharp click.

Kelly sat frozen, staring at her phone. Finally, she closed it and looked at Mac. He could see the sheer terror in her expression, along with a hopelessness that broke his heart.

"Deep breaths," he advised, keeping a firm grip on the steering wheel to stop himself from touching her. "Keep taking nice deep breaths."

She nodded, doing as he asked. When she'd taken three or four, she lifted her head and looked at him. The haunted look in her eyes was enough to make him pull the BMW over to the shoulder of the road and take her in his arms.

"What am I going to do?" she asked, face pressed up against his chest. "If he touches one hair on their heads, I'll…"

Smoothing her hair back from her face, he kissed the top of her head. "We'll save them, somehow."

Lifting her head, she nodded. "We need to ditch this car."

Relieved that she hadn't lost her focus, he kissed her cheek. "Agreed. But not here. Not yet. Someplace where we haven't been, where we have no connection. Someplace where we can't be traced."

Moving out of his arms, she pulled down the visor and busied herself fixing her mussed hair. "I'm okay," she said. He wasn't sure if that was for his benefit or hers.

Again he ached to touch her, to offer comfort. Instead, he forced himself to sound upbeat and optimistic. "I know you are. We'll be fine."

"But will they?" She turned a tortured gaze to him. "My mother, my sister, my cousin? Your children?"

"He's not going to kill anyone. I have to believe that and so do you."

Still, she looked unconvinced, so he pressed on. "Ian's making empty threats. Remember, they want to keep the Tearlach race pure. Therefore, they need all the females they can get."

Expression finally relieved, she managed a slight smile. "You're probably right. At least, I hope you are."

His stomach growled loudly, making her smile widen, for which he was grateful. "You know, I could eat. Maybe we should stop and get lunch or dinner or whatever. We've got to keep up our strength."

"Okay." She glanced around them at the plethora of fast-food places and casual restaurants. "I feel sick to my stomach. Maybe food will help." She sighed. "What are you in the mood for?"

Unbidden, he almost said the first thing he thought of, which was *you. I'm in the mood for you.* But, since he wasn't in the habit of making corny remarks that sounded like a bad pickup line, he forced himself to focus on their choices. "Let's just grab something at the first fast-food place we pass."

She opened her mouth to agree and her cell phone rang, making her jump.

Glancing at the caller ID, she grimaced. "Ian again."

He felt a surge of anger so swift, so violent, that for a moment he saw red.

"Answer it," he managed, wishing Ian was in front of him so he could put his hands around the other man's throat and demand answers.

Kelly nodded, punching the button for speaker. "Hello."

"Let me talk to your friend, Mac," Ian demanded.

"You're on speakerphone," Kelly told him. "You're talking to him now."

"No. What I have to say to him is private."

"Anything you have to say to me can be said in front of Kelly," Mac put in, making his voice hard. "So speak your piece."

"Take me off speaker."

In response, Mac said nothing. Instead, he waited. The silence grew, taking on a life of its own.

Unable to take it, Kelly began fidgeting.

Finally, Ian swore. "I have your brats here. Do you want to talk to them? If you do, take me off speaker and we'll converse privately."

Heart leaping into his throat, Mac didn't immediately respond, because he didn't want to give Ian the reaction he wanted. Instead, he counted to three.

When he spoke, he had a clear, unemotional tone. "Of course I want to talk to my children, you sorry sack of…" He reined himself in, just in case the twins actually were there and possibly listening. Though he really doubted that was the case, a little niggle of hope wouldn't go away.

False hope was worse than no hope at all. He despised Ian McKenzie for pulling his strings that way.

Mac glanced at Kelly. She nodded, her eyes wide.

Grabbing the cell, he punched the speaker button again, turning it off. Holding the phone up to his ear, he swallowed hard.

"You're off speaker. Now what do you want?"

Ian's voice was silky smooth. "I want to cut a deal, Mac Lamonda. I want to make a trade. Your kids for Kelly."

Chapter 12

Words failed him. Mac wanted to curse, to scream, to call Ian McKenzie every name in the book and then some.

He did none of those things. Instead, he simply punched the off button, ending the call.

Kelly's gaze searched his face. "Your children weren't there?"

"I don't know," he told her grimly. "He's playing games. I refuse to do that when lives are at stake."

The phone rang again.

"Don't answer it," he barked. Then he instantly reconsidered.

Some of his indecision must have shown in

his face because she shook her head and pressed the speaker option.

"Daddy?"

Isobel. His sweet, tiny baby girl.

"Honey?" he managed, aware he could barely sound coherent and unable to do anything about it. "Izzy? Are you and Caleb all right?"

"Daddy?" she repeated, her high-pitched toddler voice wavering. "The bad man says you won't come get us. Why, Daddy? Why?"

She started crying, then outright wailing, in the dramatic way toddlers have. Right before Ian disconnected the call, his little girl screamed for him. "Daaaaddyyyy."

Then she was gone.

Mac doubled over in the driver's seat, feeling as though he'd taken a blow to the abdomen. Consumed by pain, he wanted to lash out, punch something, scream and curse and plead—anything, to bring his daughter and son back to him.

Kelly touched his face, her fingers gentle. "You're crying," she said. "I'm so sorry."

Though on a conscious level he hadn't even realized he was weeping, he wasn't surprised. He turned his face toward hers, letting her see his agony. "What kind of sick man could use a child that way? She's only a baby."

"I would never have guessed my cousin could

do such a thing," she mused. "But then I guess I never knew Ian very well."

"I just don't understand the logic." He'd begun to get himself back under control, shoving the grief and the terror back into a steel-encased box in a back part of his mind. "What's the reasoning?"

"I don't know. Uncle Danny never told us. It all comes back to that breeding program that my mother mentioned, I guess. If we could figure that out, we might have a few more answers."

"Maybe I should just ask Ian," he said. "He seems pretty fanatical and those sort of people love talking about their cause. If it is a breeding program, I don't understand what it has to do with my twins. They're only toddlers."

"At least you know your daughter is all right." She stroked his arm. Though no doubt she'd meant only to offer comfort, her comment raised another question.

"True, but then that makes me wonder what they've done to my son."

"I'm sure he's fine." She leaned over, wrapping her arms around him and giving him a tight hug. "Mac, I'm so sorry. I had no idea."

Taking what comfort she was able to give, he thought again of Ian's offer, the one he hadn't wanted Kelly to hear.

Trade Kelly for his children. Even considering such a thing disgusted him. Even if Ian could be trusted to deliver Caleb and Isobel, did he really think Mac was that unscrupulous, that he was actually capable of trading one life for another so coldly and callously?

Then he heard Isobel calling for him and the words his little girl had spoken replayed in his mind. Suddenly he realized that when it concerned his children, he might be capable of just about anything.

Oblivious to his thoughts, Kelly pointed to a fast-food restaurant located at one end of a strip shopping center. "Let's eat there. I don't know about you, but I'm starving."

"First, let's get rid of this car," he said. They drove the BMW to a discount store parking lot, where they abandoned it on the outer edge of one of the rows, well out of the range of any security cameras.

This done, they walked the half mile or so back to the fast-food place they'd seen earlier.

They shared a quick meal at a hamburger joint. The food was surprisingly tasty and though Mac would have bet he couldn't choke down anything, once he started eating, he found he was ravenous.

A shabby motel was within walking distance.

Once there, they checked in, only this time when Kelly went to dig out her credit card, Mac wouldn't let her. They paid with cash, which the desk clerk appeared loath to take until Mac slipped him an extra twenty to convince him.

They were assigned a room on the second floor across from the emergency exit stairwell. Seeing this, Mac was glad. He wanted to have an escape route near in case they needed to leave quickly.

A faint sense of guilt nagged at him. He still hadn't mentioned Ian's offer to Kelly. Worse, he wasn't sure he was going to. He tried not to think about what that might mean.

Stretching out on the bed while Kelly took a shower, he attempted to clear his mind and focus on his objective the way he'd been taught in Protector school. But instead his baby girl's voice kept playing over and over inside his head, breaking his heart anew each and every time.

Yet Kelly had not only saved his life, but sometimes he thought she might have saved his sanity. They'd been lovers, something closer than partners, and he couldn't imagine letting her down.

A flash of fury seared him. How exactly was he supposed to decide? It wasn't like he really even had a choice.

The second Kelly emerged from the bathroom, he pushed himself up off the bed and headed for the bathroom, meeting her halfway.

Grabbing her, he pulled her in for a quick hug and then, before he thought better of it, crushed her mouth in a deep, soul-searing kiss, hoping to release some of his pent-up anger.

When they broke apart, they both were breathing fast.

"What was that for?" she asked, smiling shakily, her voice uncertain.

"Just because." Feeling a twinge of guilt over his glib answer, he moved past her and closed the bathroom door behind him.

Only then, when he was alone, he was able to release a breath he had barely been conscious of holding.

Staring at himself in the mirror, he berated himself silently, trying to reconcile the action he'd been briefly considering with the man he considered himself to be.

There was no way he could betray Kelly. But he would save his children. There had to be a way other than the one Ian proposed. He just had to find it.

Ever since the terrible phone call, Mac had been different. Kelly couldn't exactly blame him, but with that insight that never failed her, she sensed an undercurrent of anger directed at her.

Why? Because Ian was a member of her family? Or was it more complicated than that, something to do with the Tearlachs and their archaic rules?

If only he'd be honest with her, tell her what was on his mind. She sighed, aware she hadn't exactly been forthright with him, either.

In the bathroom, she heard the shower start up. For the space of a heartbeat, she allowed herself to fantasize about joining him in the shower and finishing what he'd started with that kiss.

But no, even though the flash of heat, of desire, still lingered, it was time to come clean in another way. When Mac rejoined her, she'd tell him everything. What the words they'd spoken meant, and what would happen to each of them if they were separated, forcibly or not.

Only when he knew the truth would he be able to make his choice. Then he could make his own decision about whether or not he wanted to be her mate in all the ways that mattered.

Of course, if he wanted to live…he had no choice. Neither did she. They were now bound for life. Wincing, she remembered stories she'd heard of involuntary bindings where one party grew to despise the other. She didn't want that to happen with her and Mac.

Slightly nervous, yet exhausted from the dramatic events of the day, she stretched out on the bed in the exact same pose Mac had adopted earlier. She marveled at the softness of the bed—pretty amazing for such a low-budget motel.

While she only meant to rest, her eyelids felt heavy and she closed them—only for a moment.

When Mac emerged from the bathroom, she was deeply asleep.

In the morning, she awoke alone in the bed. The digital clock said 6:00 a.m. Blinking back sleep, she sat up and looked for Mac, finding him asleep on the couch. With his body too long for the sofa, his legs hung off one end and he looked extremely uncomfortable. She didn't understand how anyone could sleep like that.

While she studied him, he opened his eyes and smiled sleepily at her before swinging his legs to the floor and sitting up. Brushing the hair from his eyes with his hand, he looked past her to peer at the bedside clock.

"It's early," he said, sounding surprised.

"I thought we might get an early start. We can get coffee and breakfast and then we've got to work up a plan."

He nodded, his expression distant.

As she got up to head into the bathroom, she felt his gaze following her. She paused, glancing over her shoulder at him. "Before we leave here, I've got something I want to tell you," she said.

With a grimace, he nodded. "Me, too," he said, to her surprise. "And I know you're not going to like it."

"Neither are you," she said under her breath as she closed the bathroom door. "So that makes two of us."

Later, while she waited for him to emerge from the bathroom, she rehearsed what exactly she was going to say. Though how she told him wouldn't really matter, since it all came down to the same thing in the end, she wanted to put as positive of a light on it as possible.

The bathroom door opened and she tensed, watching as he crossed the room to the door.

"Where are you going?" she asked, trying not to panic.

"I need coffee." He flashed a smile that chased away some of her fear, sending warmth into her frozen heart. "Caffeine before revelations, okay?"

"That works for me." Relieved and ashamed of being so, she jumped to her feet and followed him to the door.

"Let's walk to the coffee shop next door, have a couple of cups and something to eat, then we can come back here and spill our guts," he said.

She could barely muster a smile in response. "Coffee sounds good," was all she could manage.

Casting her a curious glance, he took her arm. "Are you all right?"

"Just a little nervous," she confessed. "And hungry."

This earned a laugh, which made the tightness in her chest ease somewhat.

Outside, the humidity felt stifling. Though the sun had not yet come out full force, the early-morning heat made it plain that the day was going to be a scorcher.

Thinking of this, she longed to be a wolf, running through quiet, cool woods in search of game.

As she pictured this, his grip tightened on her arm.

"You know, it's been a while since we've shifted," he said, his tone conversational. "I don't know about you, but I get antsy if I go too long without my wolf time. We'll need to look for a safe place while we're out today."

Heart in throat, she nodded. "I was just wondering about that."

With a chuckle, he kissed her cheek. "Why am I not surprised?"

She had difficulty preventing herself from jerking away. This had to be due to nerves, since any other time she would have turned her face so they could share a genuine kiss. Maybe her reaction was due to the edges of the anger she still sensed simmering within him.

Her heart squeezed. The way he was acting—like they were an actual couple—made things worse. Until she told him, she knew she would continue to be a mess. She truthfully didn't know how she was going to make it through coffee and breakfast with the words locked inside her.

She took a deep breath, coming to a decision. It made better sense to tell him now, before she completely lost her nerve.

As they crossed from the motel parking lot to that of the coffee shop, she grabbed his arm. "Hold on a minute."

Stopping, he looked down at her. "What's wrong?"

"There's something I need to tell you," she began, rushing the words. "And I really can't wait until after breakfast."

"Impatient, aren't you?" he teased.

She nodded again, unsmiling.

"Fine." He shrugged. "Out with it, then."

Now that she'd been given the go-ahead, she found herself unexpectedly tongue-tied. A jumble of words chased themselves around inside her head. How do you tell someone something that will completely and unalterably change the course of his life? Where to begin?

Taking a deep breath, she knew. At the beginning.

Willing her racing pulse to slow, she glanced at him. "You know how everyone thinks we're mates?"

Eyes narrowing, he nodded.

"Well, actually we are." Heart pounding so hard that she wondered if he could see it, she forced herself to continue. "When we spoke the words of binding, it was to save your life, true."

"And I'm thankful for that," he put in, apparently trying to help her out.

"Yes, well, among my kind, we only speak the words of binding once in our lifetime. That's because when we do, we're truly mated for life."

"Until the divorce," he said dryly. "Or one spouse dies."

At his unknowing trivialization, she felt a flash of temper. He didn't know, he really didn't know. "Will you let me finish, please? This is serious."

"Sorry. Go ahead."

"Among our kind, the words of binding actually *are* binding. Saving your life came with a price." Swallowing hard, she lifted her chin and held his gaze. "We cannot be separated for very long, or we die."

On the highway, traffic continued to rush past. In the hotel parking lot behind them, someone started a car. Mac, who'd gone absolutely, utterly still, continued to stare at her.

"What happens if one of us dies first?" he finally said.

"Then the other one will also die."

For a frozen moment, he simply stared at her. Then, he took an audibly deep, shuddering breath. "More than simply being mated, like Maggie and I were. She died and I'm alive. Why?"

"Because you never took the vows of binding."

He searched her face. "She said she didn't believe in them," he muttered hoarsely. "But now I understand. What you've just told me—that's why my wife would never speak those words with me. She knew this. She always made a little joke of the fact that we hadn't said them and I didn't even realize how important they were."

Looking away, his gaze fixed unseeingly on the horizon. "She had to know, didn't she?"

Kelly hadn't meant to cause him pain. "I'm sorry," she said.

Raising his head, his eyes flashed. "If that's the case, what about your mother? She remained alive after your father was killed. Are you telling me they never were bound?"

Slowly, she nodded. "Many of our people refuse to say the binding words unless absolutely necessary to save a mate's life. They don't consider themselves any less mated. I'm sure that's why your wife never spoke them with you." It stunned her how thinking of another woman being Mac's mate brought her so much pain.

"I know she and I were mated. Our children together prove it."

"It's a good thing the words were never spoken," she told him gently. "Because if Maggie and you had exchanged the vows that bind, you would have died when she perished in that fire."

He nodded, his expression shuttered. "And our children would have become orphans."

"Yes."

"What kind of system is that?" he raged. "Pointless oaths and deadly magic."

"Not a good one, I admit." The rawness in his voice made her ache.

"Then why?" he asked, his gaze bleak.

"I don't know. We—the Tearlachs—didn't make it like this. We are bound by the laws of nature, just like everyone else. We can complain all we want, but in the end we have no choice in the matter."

Opening his mouth, he started to speak, then apparently thought better of it. "Go on."

She sighed, forcing herself to continue. "The binding is irrevocable. If the vows are broken, death is the result. That's simply how it is. And this fact has caused many a sleepless night among my people, let me tell you."

"Why did Maggie never tell me? And why is this not known by the Pack? I read nothing about this in the literature I was given."

"It's a closely guarded secret among our people. It's forbidden to tell anyone, unless you are bound to them."

"How can you live with that?" he asked.

"We do. Like I said, we have no choice. It's just one of the myriad ways we are different than the other shifters, than your Pack. Like Healers, Tearlachs are bound by their own rules, created by nature. We have been since our kind came into being."

Studying her, he didn't move. Gradually, the bleakness disappeared from his eyes, replaced with…nothing. In turn, she studied him back, searching his face, hoping for something— anger, relief, confusion—any emotion rather than this blankness. To her, it felt as though he was shutting her out.

"I'm not," he said, startling her. "Instead, I'm trying to calmly consider our situation. Give me a moment."

So she did, though each breath felt like torture. She thought she knew now how the accused might feel in court, waiting for the verdict to be read. Even though she knew she was not guilty of anything, what the jury—in this case, Mac—decided would determine everything.

Because in the end, the binding went both ways.

Finally, he spoke. "So you're saying that we're bound together for real, you and I? That we'll actually die if we're separated?"

"Yes." Holding her breath, she waited for his response. Would he curse and rage, yell and storm off? Or would he retreat from her with icy indifference, trying to pretend this had never happened?

In the end, he did none of those things.

Instead, he gave her a wry smile. Then, while she was still puzzling over that, he hugged her, holding her tightly and giving her a quick kiss before he released her.

"If that's the case, then you're absolutely going to love what I have to reveal," he said.

"What do you mean?"

"I'll tell you. But first, unlike you, I need about a gallon of coffee and some protein in the form of bacon and eggs before I can even think about it. Are you ready to get something to eat now?"

Stunned, she managed a nod. She let him take her arm and they continued to the coffee shop, sliding into the booth that the hostess gave them.

Immediately, Mac requested coffee. The waitress brought a carafe and two mugs, telling them she'd come back once they had time to decide what they wanted.

While Kelly pretended to peruse the menu, she instead studied Mac, cataloging the features that she increasingly found so compelling, so masculine and beautiful. She'd dreaded telling him the truth for what seemed like an eternity and couldn't get over his nonreaction to her news. She wasn't sure if she should press him or leave well enough alone.

Partly, she had to admit his response worried her.

She truly didn't understand why he hadn't

had much of a reaction at all. The only reason she could come up with was that he really didn't believe her.

Not believing her could have deadly repercussions if he were to decide to put it to the test.

Closing his menu, he gave her a lopsided smile that tugged at her heart. "Have you decided? I need nourishment. Now."

She nodded. "Double bacon and a three-egg ham-and-cheese omelet with hash browns."

"That's exactly what I'm ordering." With a grin, he leaned across the table. "I don't know if I can ever get used to this mind-reading stuff."

She couldn't help but smile back. "Not entirely. All true mates do that. And we can't exactly read each other's minds. It's more like an impression."

"So you have no idea what secret I've got to reveal after we eat?"

"No. And I have to admit I'm more than a tiny bit curious to hear whatever you have to tell me." Whatever it was, he hadn't yet dropped a single hint, though she suspected it had to do with whatever Ian had said to him.

As if thinking his name brought his attention to them, her cell phone rang.

"Ian again," she told him. Then, before Mac could speak, she pressed the button to refuse the call. "No more of his crap until we get this sorted out."

Mac rubbed his temple like his head ached. "I agree." He signaled for the waitress, who hurried over. Once he'd placed their order, he poured them both fresh cups of coffee.

"Are you going to tell me now?" she asked softly.

"Impatient again?" he teased, making her think whatever it was, it mustn't be too serious. But then, his smile faded and his expression hardened. "You won't have much appetite if I tell you right now. Enjoy your breakfast, then we'll do a little shopping and find us a new vehicle. Okay?"

Since she didn't have a choice, she nodded, waiting impatiently for the meal to arrive. When it did, she dug in, devouring her bacon with an intensity that woke the wolf inside her.

As the beast paced and tested the boundaries, she pushed it back down. She'd need to change soon and she knew if she felt the need this strongly, Mac most likely did, too.

Once the plates had been cleared and the check arrived, she waited for him to speak. Instead, he put the cash on the table and got up, holding out his hand to her.

Slipping her fingers into his, she realized

how perfectly their hands fit together. Once they straightened this mess out, they'd be doing this for the rest of their lives.

This thought pleased her. Until she remembered the alternative. If they failed, they would die, and not necessarily at the same time.

Once outside, she saw that the heat had ratcheted up considerably higher. "I'll bet it's close to ninety out here," she said, trying to make conversation.

Instead of answering, he led her back to the motel. They rode the elevator in silence up to their room.

Once there, she busied herself making sure everything was packed away. "I assume we're going to get a vehicle next," she said, avoiding using the word *steal*. In her heart, she considered they were only borrowing, even if it was without the rightful owner's permission. Again, it was another of those things where they didn't have a choice.

"Kelly?" Something in Mac's voice alerted her, making her heart begin to pound. He meant to reveal his secret now.

Slowly she turned. He beckoned her over and she went, conscious of each and every footstep. He patted the bed to indicate she should sit and she shook her head, preferring to stand.

Mac's eyes were dark when he looked at her, so dark she couldn't read them. "When Ian asked to speak to me off the speaker, he offered to make a trade."

"A trade?" One moment, she didn't understand, and the next, she understood far too well.

"You for my children," Mac continued. "I'm ashamed to say I actually considered it."

Though she should have suspected this was coming, hearing him say the words felt like a blow to the stomach. Had he actually considered it? Why had he waited so long to tell her?

Somehow, by dint of sheer willpower, she remained upright, unmoving and expressionless. "And now?"

Expression grim and unsmiling, he met and held her gaze. "Now, I'm actually positive that we should consider doing exactly that."

Chapter 13

"What?" Open-mouthed, she gaped at him. If he'd meant to simply diffuse her angry disappointment, he'd certainly succeeded. Though she still felt faintly nauseated, shock trumped everything else. "Are you serious?"

"Deadly serious." His eyes glinted as he continued to hold her gaze. "Ian has no reason to believe that you've ever told me the truth about the binding. He'll know we can't be separated and will think I'm not aware of that. We'll set a trap and use Ian's own offer to grab my kids. Once we have them, we'll be free of them forever."

"Uh, no." She discovered that resentment still

simmered away inside her. "You're forgetting about my sister and my cousin. And anyone else those two have taken, like my mother. Getting in and grabbing your children is a great idea, but there are more lives at stake than just theirs or ours."

He lifted his chin. "I understand that. No worries. We'll just have to free them all."

Easy to say. Not so easy to actually do.

"How? The only way to do that is to shut down Uncle Danny and Ian's group."

"Again, to bring them to justice, we need to involve the Protectors."

"No."

He cocked his head. "Okay. Then what do you suggest—involve people, let the humans bring them to justice?"

"Now you're being ridiculous," she told him. "Since all shifters are forbidden to tell humans anything, you know that's not even a possibility. We need to infiltrate the group. Find out who we need to bring in to shut it down."

She could tell from his set face that he didn't like her response. "Infiltrate? To me that suggests going undercover. Not only is there not enough time for that, but we don't have any operatives."

She conceded his point. "Maybe that was a

bad choice of words. Of course we can't go undercover. But we do need to get more information about the group."

He frowned. "I agree. Right now, we know nothing about them, other than your uncle Danny appears to be in charge, with Ian as his second in command. We don't have any idea how many people are part of this, and what type of elaborate operation he might have going."

Crossing her arms, she met his gaze. "Exactly. We need to find out everything before we go rushing in blindly."

"Again, we need the Protectors. We're only two people."

"Two very determined people," she said. "What we need right now is to talk to someone on the inside."

He straightened. "Do you know of anyone?"

"Not this second, but all it will take is a couple of phone calls. Like everyone else, I have all the phone numbers programmed in my phone. Let me start making some calls. I haven't enabled the GPS function, so no one can track me."

Finally, he cracked the bare beginnings of a smile. "Are you sure you didn't study to be a Protector?" He sounded so irritated, she couldn't keep from crossing the space between them and kissing him.

"No, I did not," she murmured up against his mouth.

When the kiss ended, he held on to her, holding her tight. When he released her, he gave her a rueful smile.

"I should have thought of that," he said. "I'm the one trained in this sort of thing, not you."

"Cut yourself some slack. The reason you're not thinking clearly is because you're letting your emotions get involved. I think on some level, you know this, too."

"You might be right." He sighed. Holding her gaze, he reached out and tucked a stray hair behind her ear. "You know, the Protectors are very good at gathering intel. I really wish you would consider involving them."

"No."

He held up a hand. "Now who's being emotionally involved? Will you really risk everything on the basis of an unsubstantiated murder? Think, Kelly. Really think. What would give us the best chance of success?"

"I..." Finally, she sighed. "I'll consider it, but only as a last resort. First, we'll see what we can find out on our own. And you'll need to let Ian know you're considering using me as bait."

"And then what?" He sounded so disgruntled that she couldn't hide her smile.

"Then we'll make our plan. I'm sure in the end, we'll end up going with your original idea. I'll willingly be bait."

"Yes, but without the Protectors helping us, I'm not sure about the safety of that. Like you said, I'm too close to the situation. I thought it was perfect," he said, stressing past tense. "I thought it might work. In fact, I even went so far as to believe it couldn't possibly fail."

"And now?" she prompted, knowing he wanted her to.

"Now I have my doubts. Tell me everything you know."

This time, she hid her smile. "First off, Ian is smarter than you give him credit for. Whether I've told you about the binding or not, he knows we can't be separated too long or we'll both die. All he has to do is keep me for six months and we're goners."

Mac winced.

"Or," she continued darkly, "even better, not to mention quicker, he kills me and you die. Not a good situation, any way you look at it."

He moved restlessly. "Kelly, the more I think about this, the more I believe that we've got to involve the Protectors. They can help us. In fact, they're our only hope."

"Not yet," she said flatly, letting him see her annoyance. "Please stop trying to bludgeon me into agreeing. I told you, no Protectors unless it's as a last resort. I'll never trust them. They killed my father."

Grabbing her, he pulled her up against him, kissing her hard. "Have you ever stopped to consider that good old Uncle Danny might have actually done the deed? After all, he knew your father was talking to the Protectors."

"He wasn't talking to them. He was avoiding them, just like the rest of our family." She gave a halfhearted struggle, not really wanting to leave the warmth of his embrace, but knowing she should.

"But he was," Mac insisted. "I've seen the transcribed documents. He was trying to get help for his family. He was worried about someone, though he never said who. I'd hazard a guess it was Danny."

"His own brother?" Though she didn't push him away, she didn't really want to hear it. Voicing such a thing almost sounded like sacrilege. And yet…it kind of made sense, knowing what she now knew about her uncle. "Do you have proof of that?" she asked.

"Not with me. But back at headquarters, there are tons of tapes. And yes, before you ask, your father knew his conversations were being recorded."

Unable to think coherently with him so close, she finally backed out of his arms. "I'll consider it. This isn't a decision I can make lightly. You'll have to give me some time."

"Fine, but please don't take too long." His gaze searched her face. "I'm not sure how much time your cousin is going to give me before he reneges on the deal."

They checked out of the motel. Then, carrying their bags, they walked over to the discount store to purchase some basic supplies, such as deodorant and toothpaste. Even though it was midday on a weekday, the place was packed.

Inside the crowded store, she watched the myriad humans hurrying about, some intent on keeping their children from destroying something, others on completing their shopping trip as quickly and painlessly as possible, rushing from aisle to aisle with single-minded intent, and was glad she was different. For the first time she could remember since childhood, she actually rejoiced in what she was, in her true shape-shifter, Tearlach nature.

Inside, her wolf, who'd waited patiently since

they'd eaten, made another attempt to break free. Though Kelly was successful in pushing her lupine nature back into submission, she knew she couldn't wait too much longer before allowing the wolf to escape.

An overwhelming urge to leave shook her, so hard she had to stop and refocus on her purpose. But now all she could think about was becoming wolf, of running free on four paws, guided by her instinct, her nature, wild and free. As animal, all her petty concerns fell away, and she was one with her body and the earth, using her astounding sense of smell to see more than her eyes.

While she struggled with herself, Mac came up behind her and put his hand on her shoulder as though he sensed her distress. "Kelly? Is everything all right?"

Swiveling her head wordlessly, she let him see the wildness in her gaze. She watched as slowly his eyes shifted, turning almost yellow to match hers.

His wolf wanted out, as well. Inside, her beast thrilled to this.

"You need to change," he said. "And so do I. Let's hurry up and buy what we need and get out of here."

Unable yet to speak, she simply nodded.

Moving quickly, they finished shopping and chose the self-checkout lane so they wouldn't have to wait in line. Paying with cash, Mac carried their few bags out, then swore.

"I forgot we no longer have a method of transportation," he said. "What do you want to drive now?"

"My Hummer," she responded, only half joking. "Even though that's not possible. So let's take whatever we can find."

They settled on a late-model Ford F-150 pickup that was parked between the store and the motel, hopefully out of range of the parking lot surveillance cameras. The Ford was white and nondescript, exactly like five thousand other pickups on the road in the area. Again, Mac jotted down the license plate and tucked it in his wallet. She decided not to comment.

They stowed the shopping bags in the truck and took off, all without calling attention to themselves.

"We didn't buy anything that will spoil, so let's find a nice wooded area where we can change. Though," he said wryly, glancing around them at the freeways and the traffic, "that might be easier said than done since we're in such a congested area."

"Yes." Testing her voice, she was pleased

to see it had returned. "I remember reading in a magazine an article about the best places to shape-shift in urban areas. If I remember right, there are nature trails somewhere near here, in a suburb called Irving. If we can find those, that might be the best place."

He pointed to the GPS on the dash. "See if you can put it in that thing."

Once she got it running, she typed in a search for nature trails and, to her surprise, got back several hits, including the one she'd read about in Irving.

"It's near the monastery," she said, surprised that there even was such a thing in the heavily trafficked area. She selected that and the GPS's metallic voice began to give them directions.

It took less than ten minutes to locate the nature trails. On such a hot weekday, there were only a few other cars in the parking lot. A sign boasted acres of wooded trails.

Both smiling savagely, they got out of the car. It felt like the temperature might be a hundred degrees, but anticipating the cooler woods, she didn't mind.

Holding hands, they started up the trail, looking for a perfect place to change.

As soon as they entered the forest, she felt a significant drop in temperature. "Amazing what some shade and damp earth will do to help you get through summer."

He shot her a sideways look. "It might be cooler, but it feels twice as humid. We won't notice it so much as wolves, though."

As wolves. She felt almost giddy with the knowledge that in a few minutes she could let her lupine nature free. Though they'd shifted together before, this time, walking as humans hand in hand down the wooded path, there was an amazing sense of intimacy in the knowledge that they would share something so vital.

They were going to change together again, but this time with the full knowledge that they were a mated pair. As a child, she'd watched other couples lope side by side among the pack, hunt as a team and soak up the sun in dappled clearings. Though she'd been young, she'd yearned for the day when she'd have her own mate.

The day had finally arrived. Mac was her mate. She'd told him the truth and, while he hadn't rejoiced at the news, he hadn't rejected it outright, either.

Of course, what choice did he have? What choice did either of them have in the end?

Still, with her hand clasped firmly inside his

large one and her wolf pacing inside, eager to break free, she felt a moment's contentment.

Then she thought of his children and her family, and that feeling vanished. Suddenly, she realized what she must do. Once again, as seemed to happen so often in this life of hers, she really had no choice.

"Mac?" Squeezing his hand, she stopped and faced him, taking his other hand in hers. "I've been thinking and you're right. After this, let's tell Ian that you'll trade me for your kids. As long as we have a good plan, I see no reason why we all won't get out."

He searched her face. "Are you sure?"

She wasn't, but both for his sake and because destiny kept pushing them forward, testing their resolve, she managed a smile and nodded. "Very sure," she lied.

The look of sheer joy that transformed his handsome face made it all worth it.

"We'll work on a plan," he promised, pulling her close and giving her a long, deep kiss that had her head spinning.

She nodded. "It'd better be a hell of a good one. Otherwise, we're both as good as dead."

His grim look let her know that he understood. "And my kids will be orphans."

Though the presence of other cars in the

parking lot told of humans, they didn't run into anyone as they went deeper into the forest. Veering from the trail, Mac led her to a glade lit with dappled sunlight.

"Here," he said simply.

Side by side, they began removing their clothes, folding them and stacking them neatly on a large rock.

When they were both completely naked, they faced each other. Kelly took note of the flare of desire in his eyes, felt her own need swell up, warring with that of her wolf.

Instead of giving in, she channeled that energy into the change. Across from her, Mac did the same.

Her own transformation was swift this time, fueled by her inner beast's raging need to break free. Even so, when she opened her eyes as wolf, Wolf-Mac stood across from her, his fur burnished copper in the sun, his dark eyes gleaming.

And they were off running, side by side, tongues lolling. Only as wolf did Kelly feel so completely alive, free of human constraints like time and manners. Living fully through her senses, alive with a single-minded focus that mankind could never experience.

Wolves and their mates. Never before had

she realized what it would be like, to run wild, free and unfettered, yet irrevocably tethered to another.

She felt liberated somehow, knowing he was with her, that he'd have her back. Her companion. Her mate.

Glancing at him, again she marveled at his sheer size, his strength. As wolf, her thought processes were completely different—no abstract thought or complicated equations. That was one of the things she loved about existing as her other self—she lived in the immediate here and now. Completely in the present, living moment by moment, no worries about past or future. Just now. With the virile male wolf running at her side.

Reveling in the sheer joy of being wolf, they ran. Each time they scented humans, they veered to another direction. Rabbits fled from them in a panic, and doves and mockingbirds took flight.

Side by side, they ran until spent, until they could run no more. Then, panting, they lay on their bellies in the damp wet earth and enjoyed simply existing in the here and now.

This day, they didn't hunt, as having fed recently while human meant their wolf selves were not hungry. Instead, after a brief rest, they looked at each other and turned as one to return to the place where they'd left their clothing.

Then, flanks touching, they gazed deep into each other's eyes and began the change back to human.

Bare seconds passed before she found herself on the ground, completely naked and fully aroused. One glance at Mac showed he was the same.

They came together, passion exploding. There in the forest where they felt most at home, with leaves and trees and wildlife all around them, they cemented their partnership, mating with more than just their bodies. They mated with their hearts and their minds, as well.

Afterward, fully spent, she lay in his arms and allowed herself to relish the moment. All too aware that in an instant they would have to go back to reality, and trying to deal with the awful situation.

Thinking of that, she rolled over, away from him, and retrieved her cell phone.

"One missed call," she read out loud. Of course. "Ian."

Mac jumped to his feet and began getting dressed. After a moment, she did the same. The knowledge that Ian had called, though not completely unexpected, put a damper on her mood.

Actually, that was putting it mildly. It felt like the sun had gone out of the sky, the joy sucked from the air.

"We have to deal with him sooner or later," Mac said, fully dressed. He held out his hand for her to take. "Let's find a bench somewhere and start making phone calls. Maybe you can find someone willing to talk."

She nodded, slipping her fingers into his. "Maybe," she said. But now she didn't really believe it.

They located a bench in a sunny spot near the trailhead. Taking a seat, she pulled out her phone and scrolled through her contacts.

"I'm just going to go alphabetically," she told him. "The first one willing to talk to me will be the one."

The first three numbers rang, then went to a generic, computer-generated voice mail, per protocol. The fourth went to a recording that stated the number was not a working number, which sent a chill up her spine.

Finally, on the fifth attempt, her second cousin Siobhan answered, her voice hushed.

"Who is this?" she whispered. "If you think you can find me, you've got another thought coming."

Then, before Kelly could speak and identify herself, Siobhan disconnected the call.

"She hung up on me!" Kelly told Mac, immediately pushing redial. This time, the phone rang three times before going to voice mail. Shaking her head, she closed the phone. "She thinks someone is after her." She repeated what Siobhan had said.

She'd barely finished when her phone rang.

"Ian again?"

Glancing at caller ID, her heart leapt. "No. It's Siobhan, calling me back."

"Hello?" Barely had Kelly gotten the single word out when Siobhan began to speak, rapid-fire.

"Kelly, if this is you, you'd better hide. Danny and Ian have gone crazy and they're trying to make their own harem or something. From what I hear, they've got some sort of compound out in west Texas. So far they've impregnated ten or more women, including both our sisters."

Kelly gasped, shocked. "I didn't know they'd gone that far." She swallowed. "Where are you, Siobhan? Wait, don't answer that. Just tell me, are you safe?"

"As safe as I can be for the moment." Siobhan sounded weary and far older than her twenty-three years. "This constantly being on the run is exhausting. I don't understand why the men won't get together and stand up against Danny and Ian."

"I think it's because of the way he's presenting this. Everyone believed outsiders were taking the girls. We thought my sister, Bonnie, had been kidnapped. Until yesterday, no one even realized what Danny and Ian were doing."

"I did," Siobhan said darkly. "Ever since Ian tried to force himself on me. What do you mean? What happened yesterday?"

Kelly filled her in on the big gathering. Siobhan groaned. "So right now they have everyone held at gunpoint. That makes no sense."

Suddenly realizing what Siobhan meant, Kelly's heart dropped into her stomach. "You don't think they'll…?" She couldn't complete the sentence.

"I hope not. But Kelly, how did you escape?"

Again, Kelly gave her the details. Hanging up, Siobhan promised to pass on any new information she learned.

Once Kelly told Mac everything, he sat silently, lost in thought. "Everything is beginning to make sense. Even the attack with the silver bullets when I first met you."

She crossed her arms. "Yes, but if they were

coming to capture me, which I'm assuming they were, why the silver bullets?"

"Because that's the only thing that can make you weak. Especially since it won't kill you, but it's usually enough to bring your kind down for an hour or two. Long enough for them to subdue you and get you transported."

"And the fact that they shot you?"

"Incidental. I was in the wrong place at the wrong time. I got in their way, so they killed me."

"And now I'm of no use to them." Now the time had come to tell him the rest of what their binding meant. "Since you and I are mated, my body will accept no other seed. I cannot get pregnant, except by you."

He stared at her, his gaze narrow. "In other words…"

"I'm completely useless to Danny and Ian. The only reason they could want me is to make an example of me, to punish me for what I've done—mated with an outsider."

"You mean they'll—"

"Kill me. I think so. Yes."

"I won't let that happen." As he looked away, she could see from his stunned expression that another thought had occurred to him. "What about Maggie?" he said, his voice low with pain.

"She and I never spoke the words of binding. Does that mean Isobel and Caleb aren't really mine?"

He deserved an honest answer, but she couldn't bring herself to destroy what little he had left. "Until we take the vow, we can get pregnant by any man of our choice, human or shifter or Tearlach. It's only after we do so that our bodies will accept only one man."

For the space of a heartbeat he continued to stare at her and she thought he might challenge her. Then, jaw tight, he nodded and she almost let herself sag with relief.

"There are DNA tests, you know," he said, almost to himself. "I could find out the truth about their paternity and settle things once and for all."

"Would that really matter to you?" she asked gently, touching his arm, relieved when he didn't jerk away.

"No." His rough voice was laced with pain. "I don't think Maggie would have done that to me. And even if she did, this is not about her. I love them. They're all I have left of their mother and they're a very real part of me. Regardless of biology, Isobel and Caleb are mine."

Tears pricked her eyes at his words and she

nodded. She suddenly realized exactly how much she loved this man.

He leaned over and kissed her. "Come on. We already know more than we did yesterday."

She allowed him to pull her to her feet. Side by side they walked the path back to the parking lot and their truck. "Now what?" she asked.

"Now we've just got to find out where in west Texas they are. That's a vast area, so we need to narrow it down some."

"How do you propose to do that?"

Opening the driver's-side door, he got in, waiting while she did the same. Once she'd buckled in, he turned the key in the ignition and started the truck. "I think it's time for me to call Ian and up the stakes a little."

Chapter 14

Her eyes widened, but she nodded. Pleased that she agreed, Mac held out his hand, waiting patiently while Kelly dug out her phone.

When she handed it to him, her fingers trembled. He wanted to hold her and tell her everything would be all right, but he couldn't lie. And, he reflected wryly, even if he could have, she'd know. Right now he had his own doubts. About everything, including the very foundation he'd built his entire existence on. He couldn't help but wonder if his whole life had been based on a completely false premise. If everything he'd believed in and fought for was nothing but an illusion.

He thought back to something Ian had said the first time they met, back in Fort Worth. He'd asked why Mac was still alive. A horrible thought occurred to him. Though he tried to shake it off, it just wouldn't go.

"Kelly?" He touched her shoulder, needing the contact for support. "Do you think it's possible that Danny and Ian had something to do with Maggie's death?" he asked. "That they could have killed her as punishment for mating with me?"

Once the ugly words were out in the open, he almost wanted to take them back. But he couldn't. The possibility was just too real. He had to know, even if it ripped his heart from his chest.

Expression miserable, Kelly met his gaze. "Maybe. I don't know. But it's entirely possible, knowing what Ian and Danny are up to. They would have had no way of knowing you and she hadn't spoken the words of binding. By killing her, they would have believed they were killing you, too."

"And leaving my children alone, ripe for the plucking." He swore, a string of virulent curses that he'd learned in the first year of Protector Academy. Maybe that was why Maggie had refused to speak the damned words with him.

She hadn't wanted to leave their children alone, as unprotected orphans. The back of his throat ached with emotion, though he'd be damned if he'd cry. He'd only cried a few times in his life—on the day his wife was killed, and then when he'd returned home to find his babysitter unconscious and his children missing. Most recently, the sound of his daughter's voice had brought him to tears.

No, he wouldn't cry now. He'd vent his rage instead. Looking about him wildly, needing to punch something, hit something, destroy something, he found nothing but the interior of their stolen pickup and Kelly. Sweet, patient Kelly, watching him with sympathy in her lovely green eyes.

So he swore some more, though mere words were an inadequate substitute for a punching bag.

When he finally wound down, she reached for him and wrapped her arms around him, holding on tight. Her scent, light and feminine, smelling faintly like roses, calmed him.

They sat together like that for a moment, unmoving. He felt a faint flicker of desire, which he ruthlessly quashed. Despite that, as she held him, he welcomed the warmth that flooded him, making him feel alive and giving him hope.

Maybe, despite his pessimistic estimate of their chances of success, things would work out. He'd rescue the twins and together with Kelly, they'd become a happy family.

He decided he'd cling to that hope and use it to propel him through what was to come.

"Thank you," he murmured against the fragrant skin of her neck.

When she raised her head, her gaze was troubled. "You and Maggie had something special, didn't you?"

Realizing her fear, he kissed her cheek. "We did. But I have room in my life for you, I promise. We're mates, for better or for worse."

If she noticed he made no mention of love, she didn't comment.

Pulling away from her, he connected his own seat belt. He hesitated before he put the shifter in Drive, though he kept his foot on the brake.

She watched silently while he studied her phone. Though he sensed the questions in her eyes, he didn't raise his head. Instead, he punched the button to redial the last missed call.

Ian answered on the second ring. "Talk to me."

Finding this ironic and amusing, Mac had to bite his tongue to keep from popping off with a remark about Ian having watched too many detective shows. Instead, he made his tone cautiously civil.

"I want to meet," he said. "As soon as possible."

"Have you considered my proposal?" Ian asked, his voice an odd combination of jovial and guarded.

"Yes." Mac glanced at Kelly, sitting ramrod straight in the seat next to him, her eyes troubled and still full of questions. "I'm thinking it's a go."

Ian made a rude sound. "I don't believe you. Does she know?" His voice rose, became sharper. "Have you told Kelly about my offer?"

"Of course not." Mac didn't have to fake his disdain. "Stupid question. Now, do you want to meet or not?"

After a thoughtful pause, Ian chuckled. "Point taken. I'd say the sooner we can make this exchange, the better. Are you available this afternoon?"

Something in the smoothness of his tone told Mac that Ian was lying. He had no intention of trading anyone for anything. The bastard probably didn't even know where the twins were being held.

Wishing he could take hunches as truth, Mac grimaced. On the off chance that he was wrong, they would have to go through with this cha-rade. "Where and when?"

"I'm no longer in Fort Worth." Ian sounded pleased. "I have a vacation home on the shores of Richland Chambers Reservoir. It's isolated *and* heavily guarded, just in case you're plan-ning on pulling anything. Meet me there at four o'clock. Come alone, you and Kelly and no one else."

"Understood."

"And, Lamonda? Remember I not only have your children—and such adorable little tykes they are—but Kelly's sister and mother. I won't hesitate to kill them one by one if you don't do as I ask."

"Point taken." Repeating the other man's ear-lier words, Mac almost disconnected the call. But one thing he'd learned over and over in the Protector Academy came back to haunt him.

Know your enemy.

"Ian," Mac asked impulsively, trying to catch him before he hung up.

"What?" Ian snapped. "Don't tell me you've already had a change of heart."

"No, not really." Swallowing hard, he forced himself to continue. "I just want to know why."

"Why? Why what?" Ian's impatience showed in the staccato way he spoke. Mac could picture the man checking his watch to see how much of his precious time this conversation was wasting.

"Why are you doing this?" Mac asked softly. "I don't understand why. Capturing these women, kidnapping my children, trying to impose a sort of dictatorship on the other Tearlachs. Help me to understand."

"That's none of your business," Ian said, his tone lofty. But one thing Mac had learned about psychopaths was that they couldn't resist any opportunity to talk about themselves, whether to explain their convoluted rationales or methodology, or to expound on their heartfelt (and often irrational) convictions.

"Look, I know I'm not as evolved as you," Mac said, struggling to sound sincere. "But I really would like to understand the logic behind all this. It all seems so nonsensical to me."

On the other end of the phone, Ian sucked in his breath in shock. Mac felt a flash of triumph. Evidently he'd found exactly the right phrase to get Ian to spill.

"Think about this, Protector." Since this was the first time Ian had acknowledged Mac's status, Mac found this significant. He believed that might mean that Ian would tell the truth.

"There are millions of regular shifters in the world, but only a few thousand Tearlachs. While you Pack shifters don't seem to mind your blood being weakened and diluted by marrying and breeding children with humans and creating Halflings, we have seen how these mutts weaken your abilities." Ian sounded disdainful.

Mac held his tongue, waiting for Ian to continue his diatribe.

After a moment, he did. "As a result of this mixed breeding, you are weak. As we would be, were we to allow such a travesty to occur. This is why we must be vigilant."

Ian's words had the tenor of an often used and familiar speech. Mac surmised that perhaps Ian spoke these words as part of an indoctrination of his recruits or whatever he called the others he wanted to convert to his way of thinking.

"Years ago," Ian continued, warming to his subject, "my father decided the time had come to make new laws for our people. Most specifically, he wanted to purify our race. By selective breeding, he believes we can develop and refine the perfect Tearlach."

In silence, Mac listened, struggling to contain his mounting horror. He wondered if Ian realized how much he sounded like a certain human someone who'd lived in Germany in the late 1930s and early 1940s.

At least Danny and Ian weren't attempting

to round up others and exterminate them. He supposed he should be thankful for this.

Or were they? Did they kill those who disobeyed their laws? Like Kelly. And Maggie before her.

"Did you kill my wife?" Mac interrupted, his tone low and cold and hard.

This stopped Ian in his tracks. "What?"

"Did you kill Maggie? Simply because she'd married me?"

"I believe she perished in a car accident," Ian said.

"That's not a denial. It's not a difficult question. Answer me. Did you or your people kill my wife?"

Ian's bark of laughter was answer enough. "You need to understand that we are serious. We will not be deterred from our goal."

"Understand this," Mac snarled. "If I ever get a chance, I will make you pay for what you've done to me and my family."

"Really?" Ian sounded unconcerned. "And will Kelly also try to gain retribution for the death of her father? How pointlessly stupid." He laughed again.

"You son of a—"

"Leave my mother out of this, boyo." Steel once again hardened Ian's Scottish burr. "Just remember who holds all the cards." With that, he disconnected the call.

Mac sat in stunned silence, anger simmering away inside him. He took a deep breath before closing the cell and handing it back to Kelly.

"What'd he say?" she asked, eyeing him with something like concern in her expression.

He gave her a recap, including the part about using their family members as a guarantee, but omitting the mention of her father. Ian hadn't confessed to killing him and until he did, Mac wanted to spare her the pain.

"He wants us to go to Richland Chambers?" Consulting a map, she frowned. "That's not in west Texas. It's a man-made lake southeast of Dallas."

"So your cousin got her information mixed up. Right now, it's all we have to go on."

"Either that, or he's not letting us get close to the compound." She regarded him curiously. "What are you planning to do? Surely we're not going to drive there and just give ourselves over? He'll kill us or, worse, torture us to exact retribution for my imagined crime."

"I agree." Praying she would see his point this time, he put the truck back in Park, though he left the engine running so the air conditioner still worked. "Do you have any ideas?"

Slowly she shook her head. "No."

"Well, then, I hate to beat a dead horse, but if we are to have any chance of coming out winners in this, I see no alternative. We've got to involve the Protectors. One phone call is all it will take."

For a moment she simply stared at him, her eyes narrowed. After what seemed like an eternity, she finally nodded. "All right. You win. But only because I can't see any other way. Call them. I'm trusting you on this."

Shock, followed by crushing relief, had him reaching for her. "Thank you," he said, pulling her into his arms and kissing her once, then again. "Now we actually have a real chance of succeeding."

Holding his gaze, she gave him a worried smile and nodded. "Just make sure you trust whoever it is you contact over there at the Protectors. I'm pretty sure Ian and Danny have a mole or two working for them."

While this should have surprised him, it didn't. He was also unsurprised to realize he no longer completely trusted his own employer, when once he would have given his life in their service if necessary.

"I'd trust him with my life and yours," he said simply. "As well as the lives of my children."

The worry vanished from her face. "Then that's good enough for me."

He dialed Simon Caldwell's private number. Simon had gone through hell and back a few years ago, when he'd had to fight against the evil that had corrupted the very organization to which he, like every other Protector, had dedicated his life.

Simon had won, the Protectors had purged themselves and Simon found his own happy ending. He'd fallen in love and married a formerly Feral shifter named Raven and together they'd settled in Colorado. Though he was no longer officially a Protector, he did consulting work for them and would know exactly who to trust. If anyone could help in this situation, Simon could.

When Simon answered, Mac exchanged a few pleasantries, then told him why he was calling. "I need your help. You remember the stories we used to hear about Tearlachs?"

"Yeah." Simon laughed. "We put about as much credence to those as we did to Healers. And, since a bona fide Healer turned up a few years ago, I expect you're going to tell me Tearlachs are real, too."

"Exactly. They're more than real, and I'm mated with one."

Simon laughed. "Congratulations. Now, while I'm happy for you, I know you must have had another reason for calling. What's going on?"

Filling him in on the entire situation took several minutes. When Mac finished, he waited in silence while Simon processed the information.

"Why haven't you contacted me until now? This is not good."

"I know," Mac said. "I didn't want to involve you until I had to."

"You need my help," Simon interrupted. "I know you. You thought you could handle this alone. Let me see if I can get a hold of Beck, as well." Beck was another Protector who'd bucked the system and won. Mac had heard he'd married a vampire Huntress and lived in New Mexico with their daughter.

"I'd—we'd—really appreciate it," Mac told him, wondering if the other man sensed his desperation. Beside him, Kelly nodded as though she definitely did.

"Let me assemble a team and meet you." Simon sounded energized. "How long do you have before you're supposed to meet this Ian guy?"

Checking his watch, Mac saw it was nearly noon. "Four hours," he said. "Even if you left right now, we'd never make it. It's an hour-and-a-half to a two-hour drive from the airport. Plus flight time."

"See if you can postpone the meeting," Simon urged. "That'll give me time to gather more information. Can you do that?"

Imagining Ian's reaction, Mac grimaced. "I'll do what I can."

"Great. Keep me posted. I'll call you with an ETA for me and my team."

Closing the phone, Mac looked at Kelly. "We've got to get Ian to reschedule the meeting for tomorrow."

She grinned. "That's an easy one. I'll pick a fight with you and make you call him."

"That won't work. You're not supposed to know."

"Oh, yeah?" Raising a brow, she cocked her head. "Then how were you going to get me to agree to drive out to this lake place?"

"I meant you're not supposed to know about the deal I made with Ian to trade you for the twins. He left it up to me to figure out how to get you to go willingly. If I were doing this for real, I'd probably tell you Ian dropped a hint and I think that might be where he's holding your sister. We'd head out there with the intentions of rescuing her."

"But you forget, we're mated," she argued.

"I can sense something is wrong. Therefore, I don't believe you."

"Stalemate." He grimaced. "In this imaginary scenario of yours, where do we go from here?"

"That's easy. We can do like they do on television and demand to speak to her. Ian has to produce her or it's a no-go. I'll tell him I don't believe she's really alive."

Straightening, he felt a pang of longing as a thought occurred to him. "I wonder if I could ask to talk to my children."

"You could." She sounded doubtful. "But in this context, it would seem out of place."

"Still...wouldn't you try, if you were their mother?"

He could tell by her expression that he'd hurt her. "I didn't mean—"

"I know." She waved him away. "If you want to talk to them, we can put in the request at the same time I ask to talk to my sister. Who cares what he thinks? We have no reason to trust him."

Hope glimmered so brightly it was painful. "All right, then. That's what we'll do. I think this might work."

"Of course it will." This time she smiled, reaching for her cell. "I'll call him now."

"Let's wait until closer to the meeting time," he said.

"Why wait?"

"Because what if he puts your sister on the phone right away? Then we're out of excuses."

She nodded. "Good point. So we'll wait."

"That'll give Simon time to assemble a team."

"How long do you think that will take?" Her mischievous smile made him smile back.

"Why?"

Leaning in, she gave him a long, lingering kiss. "I don't know. We could go back to those natural trails and change?"

He suspected she didn't mean only shape-shifting. When he came up for air, he touched the tip of his nose to hers. "Do you mean…?"

With a throaty laugh, she nodded. "That is, if you're up for it."

To his surprise, he realized he'd never been more up for anything in his entire life.

She had to trust Mac. Though, as far as she was concerned, he was her one true mate, she knew in his eyes she'd never live up to the mate he'd chosen of his own free will and lost. Maggie. The love of his life.

Briefly, she closed her eyes, wondering if the hurt at knowing she loved him more would ever lessen. She could only hope it would with the passage of time. Now, though, they actually had a few hours to waste.

"Do you think they're still looking for us?" she asked, wondering if he was as tired of being hunted as she was.

"I doubt it. We've agreed to a meeting. I think they'll concentrate their resources on whatever trap they're setting for us."

"So we have…"

"Time to ourselves?" Smiling, he finished her sentence, which really shouldn't have surprised her. The more they spent together, the more like true mates they'd become.

"Exactly."

"You sound so wistful." Cupping her chin, he studied her. "Where is my fierce she-wolf?"

Amused and enchanted, she held his gaze. "Oh, she's still here, I promise you. I just need some time to reenergize."

Releasing her chin, he nodded. "I see no reason why we can't have a couple of hours to ourselves. Especially if doing so will help us face what is yet to come."

Walking the nature trails together, they revisited their secret glade as humans and made love again. This time, slowly and unhurriedly. She explored his body with her fingers and her mouth, eager to experience every inch of him. This experience only made her realize how much she'd come to care for this man. She was secretly glad that the binding between them could not be undone.

Even if it meant their deaths? She refused to even consider such a possibility. They'd enlisted the help of the Protectors. Now they couldn't lose.

After making love, they drove to a local restaurant and had a late lunch. Both of them opted for the specialty of the house, called the Ole Cheeseburger. When their meal arrived, huge juicy burgers seasoned with cilantro and chili powder, topped with thick slices of ripe tomato, lettuce and onion, she knew she'd made the right choice.

Though she could have sworn she'd never be able to eat anything that large, she devoured the entire burger, bun and all, and polished off most of her French fries. Plate clean, Mac finished off the rest of them.

Despite being unbelievably full, she smiled when Mac ordered a blueberry pie for them to share, along with two coffees. As soon as the waitress moved away to get it, he leaned across the table.

"Any place with burgers this good has to have amazing pie," he told her.

A few seconds later, the waitress carried over their huge slice, the golden crust bursting with blueberries. One bite and she had to agree. "Heavenly," she said, rolling her eyes.

Once the pie was gone, they lingered over their coffee, both too full to move just yet. Suddenly nervous again, Kelly chattered away about small, inconsequential things. Mac responded in kind, though she saw evidence of his tension in the way he jiggled his left leg under the table. She supposed neither of them wanted to voice their apprehension over the events to come.

When her cell rang, she jumped. Heart racing, she looked. Caller ID showed a private caller from area code 303. Colorado. Mac's Protector friend. Their too brief time had come to an end.

Wordlessly, she handed him the phone. She listened while he confirmed the time of his friend's arrival, jotting notes on a napkin.

When he finished the call, he flashed her a huge smile. "They'll be here in a couple of hours."

"Do we need to meet them at the airport?"

"Nope. They're renting a car. We're going to meet up in Corsicana, at the big home improvement store right off I-287."

Relieved, she nodded again. Feeling at loose ends, she consulted her watch for the tenth or twentieth time and sighed. "Then all that's left is for us to call Ian and stall him, right?"

"Right. We've got to be convincing."

Easier said than done. But she didn't speak her doubts out loud. Instead, she glanced around at the nearly deserted restaurant. "Not here. We need someplace private."

Signaling for the check, he agreed. "Especially if we're going to stage a big, fake fight."

Even full of the delicious meal, her stomach clenched.

"I can do it," she said, meaning her words. "For my sister and my mother and your children. This will be the most believable fake fight you've ever been in."

He laughed out loud. "It's nearly two. We need to go."

After the waitress brought the check, he paid with cash, leaving a generous tip. Arm in arm, they walked to the truck. Kelly wondered if he could feel how fast her heart was racing.

Climbing inside, she froze when a police car cruised slowly past. "He's checking us out."

Mac cursed. "Stay calm. I doubt this truck has even been reported stolen yet." Starting the ignition, he put the truck in Reverse, backing from the slot.

As he pulled out onto the feeder road, the police car did the same.

Chapter 15

Feeling trapped and helpless, which he hated, Mac drove exactly the speed limit, staying in the right-hand lane and hoping the cop would eventually pull past them. Instead, the squad car settled in right behind them, not exactly tailgating but riding their back bumper pretty darn closely.

"Damn." Mac began to perspire. "Don't turn around, but I'll bet he's running a check on our license plate."

"Where he'll see this vehicle has been reported stolen."

"Exactly."

"This isn't good," Kelly muttered. "Not good at all."

Behind them, the patrol car turned on his lights and hit the siren once, *whoop,* making Kelly jump.

"What are you going to do?" she asked.

"Pull over," he told her. "Then, once the officer gets out of his car, I'm going to take off. It's our only chance. If this truck's been reported stolen, he's going to arrest us."

Up ahead of them, a motorcycle careened out of a side street, doing at least seventy-five, maybe more. Weaving in and out of traffic, the bike picked up speed.

"That guy's an idiot," Mac said, momentarily diverted from their own problem. "He's an accident waiting to happen."

As soon as the words left his mouth, a panel van turned onto the access road, just as the motorcycle swerved out to pass another car.

With a loud boom, the two collided. The biker went airborne, the bike, too.

Kelly gave a little scream.

Traffic, which had been moving along well, came to a complete standstill. The police car, lights still flashing, whipped around Mac and Kelly and, driving on the shoulder, headed toward the accident.

Unable to believe what had just happened, Mac looked at Kelly. She gave a nervous laugh and shrugged. "What now?"

"We've got to get out of here," Mac said.

"I agree." She looked wildly around them. "But how? We're hemmed in by cars."

Sirens sounded in the distance, indicating the police officer had called the accident in.

"More cops and emergency vehicles are on the way." Mac flipped on his blinker and began inching toward the shoulder.

People had begun getting out of their cars and walking over to see what was going on.

Eyeing the accident and the increasing crowd of onlookers, Kelly sighed. "I just hope that cop forgets about us by then."

"He won't," Mac put in grimly. "Not if he ran a check on this vehicle. We've got to get out of here. I need to try and make it onto that side street."

"The one the van pulled out from?"

He nodded. "I know it's blocked, but if I cut through the gas station…"

Behind them, flashing lights signaled the approach of police backup. A fire truck and an ambulance, sirens wailing, blazed past on the shoulder, with two more police cruisers directly on their tail.

By the time they all pulled up to the accident site, the side road had been thoroughly blocked.

"Next they're going to set up someone to direct traffic. They'll have to use that side road," Mac predicted, trying to sound calm and feeling trapped.

"I feel like a sitting duck." Kelly rubbed her arms as though she was cold. With the air-conditioning blasting, maybe she was.

"Come on. Let's get out and walk. We can pretend we're like them." He pointed to the cluster of people on the side of the road near the police cruisers. "We're leaving the truck here."

She stared at him. Then, biting her lip, she unbuckled her seat belt and reached for the door handle. "You're right. It's our best chance. We'll disappear into the crowd of people over by that shopping center."

"Yeah. We can find a new vehicle later."

Caught up in either the spectacle unfolding at the accident scene, or their own irritation at being stuck in traffic, no one honked or yelled, as Mac had half suspected they would.

Holding hands, he and Kelly headed toward the accident scene, and then they cut across the shoulder, down a grassy embankment and into a half-full parking lot. They slipped among the parked cars and mixed with a group of people heading to shop at a large grocery store.

"We need to get out of this immediate area," Mac told her, keeping his voice low. "Once they get that accident scene cleaned up, and everyone back in their cars, they're going to realize that pickup was abandoned in a lane of traffic. If they didn't realize it was stolen before, they will now."

"Okay, then pick one." She glanced around them, gesturing widely. "There are a lot of cars here to choose from."

Wincing, he grimaced. "I really didn't want to steal another vehicle, but we've got to meet Simon and his crew in Corsicana."

"And we've still got to call Ian," she reminded him.

He couldn't believe he'd managed to forget about that. Checking his watch, he saw it was a little after two-thirty. "We'll call him around three," he said, "an hour before the meeting, and try to delay it. Right now, let me get us some transportation."

This time he chose a black four-door sedan, a Chrysler 300. Common enough not to attract notice, spacious and roomy and completely different from the pickup and BMW they'd used before. Again, he jotted down the license plate number and put it with the other two before climbing in and starting the car.

"Why do you do that?" she asked, clicking her seat belt into place. "I noticed you writing down the tags on the other two, as well."

Slightly embarrassed, he gave her a rueful smile. "I'm guessing I'll have a lot of karma to pay back when this is all over. Stealing three different vehicles isn't a good thing. I can look the owners up with the license plate number. That way, I can at least try and make some kind of retribution."

Her eyes widened. "You plan on contacting total strangers and telling them you're the guy who stole their car?"

He laughed. "No. Actually, I plan on doing everything anonymously. If I told them who I was, most people would just call the cops and have me arrested. But I'll try to make it up to them somehow, if I can. Without them knowing who or why."

She stared at him. He couldn't tell if she approved or not. He told himself he didn't really care, but the truth was, he did.

"Have you always done this?" she finally asked.

"Nope. But then I've never stolen anything before."

"I like that." Leaning over, she brushed a kiss on his neck. "Since I stole with you, I want to help you make amends."

If he could have, he would have pulled the car over and given her a real kiss. He settled for grinning at her instead.

Ducking her head, she blushed. Then, while he was still grinning like a lovesick fool, she lifted her chin and met his gaze. "Where are we going now?"

Back to business. She was right. He needed to stay focused. "We're taking 287 down to Corsicana. When we get to the Home Depot, we'll wait for Simon."

"Meanwhile, we need to call Ian." Pulling her cell out, she looked at it. "I am so dreading this."

"We'll be fine." He hastened to reassure her. "Do you want to practice or anything?"

"No. We'll be fine." She turned her head to look out the window.

Driving, he felt glad of the silence. Normally, before being sent on a mission, he was pumped up, ready to go, uber-confident that things would go well. This time, it was too personal, there was too much at stake. If he even allowed himself to think about what could go wrong and what was at risk, he would make mistakes.

He stared straight ahead at the road, not really seeing it. He needed to shut down, get in the zone and focus. Maybe once Simon and his team arrived, he would find it easier to do just that.

"Mac?" Kelly's voice startled him out of his thoughts. "It's five after three. Are you ready to call Ian?"

He nodded, keeping his face expressionless, as though his heart hadn't leapt into his throat.

"All right, then." Locating the stored number, she pressed it, putting the phone on speaker before handing it to him.

"I assume you're calling me because you're early," Ian answered, going directly to the point.

"There's a problem," Mac said. "Kelly doesn't believe her mother is even there. She wants you to put her on the phone and let her talk to her, as proof."

"I'll do no such thing," Ian replied, anger sharpening his tone.

"Then we won't be coming." Shooting Kelly a quick glance, Mac terminated the call.

"Whoa." Kelly exhaled loudly. "I wonder how long it'll take him to call back."

"That depends. If he has your mother handy, it will be only a few minutes. If, on the other hand, he's bluffing, then the phone should ring just about now."

Silence.

Forcing a chuckle, Mac tried again. "Just about now."

To his relief, the cell rang as if on cue.

"How did you know that?"

He shrugged. "Just know his type. Go ahead and answer it."

Again on speaker, Kelly answered. "Hello."

"You impertinent little bitch." Ian's voice dripped venom. "You have no right to try and test me."

"I have every right," Kelly rejoined, an edge in her voice. "This is my mother and my sister you're claiming to have captive. How do I know you're not lying?"

Ian cursed, using another lyrical language that made the swear words sound like poetry. They waited until he wound down, then Mac spoke. "Get her mother and her sister and put them on the phone, or the deal's off. And," he added, pretending it was only an afterthought, "I'd like to speak to my children again, as well. Both of them this time."

"Impossible."

Flashing Mac a grin, Kelly gave the thumbs-up sign. Then she let loose. Screeching like a shrew, she called her cousin every name in the book, and then some. Amazed, Mac sat back and watched while she worked herself up into a lather.

Ian made several attempts to interrupt. Each time, Kelly drowned him out, her voice shrill and furious.

"Mac, get your woman under control," Ian finally shouted.

Obligingly, Mac said her name, the first time in a normal voice, the second in a sharp tone of command.

Immediately she fell silent, unable to keep from smiling at him. She thought their acting was pretty darn convincing.

"Go ahead, Ian," Mac said.

"I don't have time for this nonsense," Ian snarled. "This is your last warning and your last chance. If you don't show up here in less than an hour, the deal's off and you can forget about ever seeing your loved ones again. Understand?"

Kelly shook her head and opened her mouth. Lifting his hand to forestall her, Mac replied to Ian, "We're not going anywhere or doing anything until we know our family members are alive," he said stubbornly. "And if you can't provide that assurance, the deal is off."

With that, even though Ian had started to speak, he closed the phone and ended the call.

"Let's see what happens now," he said. Glancing at Kelly, he saw she was staring straight ahead, tears running down her cheeks.

Damn. Swearing softly under his breath, he immediately signaled and turned into a fast-food-restaurant parking lot. Once they'd parked, he reached for her and pulled her into his arms. "What's wrong?"

She raised her face to his, her gaze tortured. "He's not going to let us talk to them. I'm beginning to think he's already killed them. My mom and my sister. Dead."

He wanted to say something reassuring, but the same thought had also occurred to him.

Gently he brushed the tears off her face. "Why do you think that?"

"Why else would he refuse to put them on the phone?"

Kissing her cheek, he shook his head. "I can think of several reasons. Chief among them being that he's not at the same location as they are. Remember, you heard there was some sort of compound out in west Texas. Obviously, this is pretty far from there."

She peered up at him, then slowly nodded. "You've got a point."

"So stop worrying," he said, aware he was also speaking to himself. "Everything will work out fine."

They continued heading south on 287. Outside, the cloudless sky and bright sunshine made the temperature steadily rise. By the time they reached the exit for I-45, the car's outside thermometer showed ninety-three.

About to comment on the heat, Mac realized that Kelly had fallen asleep. Leaning on the door with her hand under her head, she looked so peaceful dozing that he didn't want to wake her.

Finally, they took the Richland Chambers exit. Turning left and going under the freeway, they made a right turn and pulled into the Home Depot parking lot. Checking his watch, he saw that they were way too early to meet Simon.

Since Kelly slept, he kept the car running and listened to the radio.

An hour or so later, Kelly's cell phone rang, waking her. Blinking groggily, she fumbled in her purse and, without looking at it, handed it to him.

It was Simon.

"We've landed in Dallas and are en route," Simon said. "We should be there in ninety minutes or so. Meanwhile, I've had my assistant working on finding out about this Danny McKenzie and his son, Ian."

Sitting up a bit straighter, Mac dragged his hand through his hair. "And?"

"The west Texas rumors were exactly that, only rumors. But they do have some sort of compound or encampment near Corsicana. Five hundred acres of mostly pasture. They've built a huge house, thirty thousand square feet, and most of them are living there, sort of like that Branch Davidian thing years ago in Waco. I've got aerial photos that were actually taken by the FBI."

"The humans are watching them? That's not good."

"Nope. Foolish. Your agency has been keeping an eye on them, too, but the Protectors don't seem to be aware that they're Tearlachs."

"Faulty intel. What about this lake house where Ian wants us to meet?"

"The upper echelon spends quite a bit of time there. Danny McKenzie and his son and an odd assortment of women. They're rumored to have quite a harem, but nothing illegal, so other than keeping an eye on them, the various agencies aren't doing anything. Their hands are tied."

Mac relayed the earlier conversation he'd had with Ian. "We need to strike soon. He won't be expecting us."

Simon was silent for a moment. "Where?" he finally said.

"The compound. I want to rescue my kids, Kelly's family and anyone else who wants to leave. We can take them into protective custody."

Beside him, Kelly shook her head. "No," she mouthed. "No custody. A rescue, free and clear."

"I'll have to alert the Pack authorities," Simon said, unaware of what Kelly had said. "It'll be a full-scale raid on the place, minus the human media. Are you sure you're up for that?"

Once again Mac glanced at Kelly. He saw the determination in her eyes, the desire to make this go her way. While part of him—fine, *all* of him—completely understood, his children had to be his first priority. And the only sure way to get them out was to go in there with a small army. As for Kelly, in the end she'd get what she wanted, too. Her mom and her sister would be free. They'd negotiate the conditions later.

"I am," he told Simon. "Get the ball rolling."

"All right. See you in a few. Oh, and better tell Kelly you'll be wearing riot gear. You know as well as I do that this thing can go either way."

"It won't." Mac was positive of that. "Standard operation. Women and children first. Talk to you later."

As he closed the phone, Kelly shifted restlessly. "What'd he say?"

"He'll meet us in a few. And he's ordering up reinforcements."

Now that it was a done deal, he shouldn't have hesitated to tell her the entirety of it. But he told himself he didn't want to worry her, and he kept his mouth shut.

After all, she'd find out everything soon enough.

Kelly couldn't shake the dread coiling in the pit of her stomach. Mac was hiding something from her, she was certain of it.

Women and children first. Like they were evacuating a sinking ship or something.

What had he meant by that? What the hell had Mac asked this Simon person to do?

Since they had time to kill, they went inside the Home Depot and wandered the aisles. After an hour had gone by, they returned to the car and waited.

Thirty minutes later, a black Jeep Cherokee pulled up.

"That's them," Mac said. "Wait here." He got out of the car, obviously not expecting her to follow.

"Wait here?" Muttering under her breath, she opened her own door and followed him over to the other vehicle, where the other men were slapping each other's backs and shaking hands.

"There's a lot of male bonding going on here," she said.

Mac turned around, frowning. She ignored him, focusing on their leader, Simon.

"I'm going, too," she informed them, using her best no-nonsense voice, the one she used when working with a stubborn dog.

Of course all the men began to protest. All of them, that is, except Simon. He stood watching silently.

"Enough." She waved her hand, cutting them off midprotest. "If our theory is correct and they've got all of the kids in one place, and you're going in with guns and riot gear, there are going to be a lot of terrified children. They're going to need someone to help them through this. That someone will be me."

Mac opened his mouth, then closed it when she glared at him. She looked at each man, one by one, daring them to contradict her.

Studying Mac's—friends? Coworkers?—she was struck by one trait they all shared. Each and every one of them radiated a raw masculinity, from the breadth of their broad shoulders to their narrow, fit waists.

They ranged in height, a smorgasbord of testosterone, yet, standing near them, she felt petite and feminine. Protected.

Paradoxically, this infuriated her. Until Mac had shown up on her doorstep, she'd managed just fine, thank you very much.

Now, even if their lives weren't eternally tied together, she didn't know how she'd endure a life without him. Thanks to the Tearlach binding, she wouldn't have to.

Eyeing Mac's friends, she hoped their expertise would be enough to ensure that they'd succeed.

Talking together in low voices, they began outlining their plan. Since she couldn't hear, Kelly moved closer, pushing herself in between Mac and another man.

The man—whose name she didn't remember—gave her an indulgent look that set her teeth on edge. "You don't need to trouble your pretty little head about any of this, ma'am. We've got it under control."

Both Mac and Simon groaned in unison.

"Now you've done it, Spider," Simon said wryly.

Mac put his arm around Kelly's shoulders and squeezed, making her close her mouth before she let loose with a scathing remark.

"She's coming with us," he said, his voice sharp.

Spider glanced at him, then at Simon. Finally, he shrugged.

"Whatever."

"Not whatever." Simon rounded on him. "She's Tearlach, going up against her own kind. Her family is being held captive there. Of any of us, with the exception of Mac, she has the most to lose. She's to be protected and assisted, at any cost. Do you understand?"

Suitably chastened, Spider nodded. "Yes, sir." Turning to her, he inclined his head. "Sorry, ma'am."

She smiled to let him know she was no longer angry. "It's important we all work together as a team," she said.

After a second of startled silence, Mac laughed. "You're preaching to the choir, sweetheart. This is a team, and a pretty airtight one, from what Simon tells me. They've worked together many times."

"We can be depended on," Simon put in. "We trust each other with our lives. Now let's go over this plan one more time."

Kelly listened, though to her it sounded like their so-called plan was basically to break in, disable any guards and round up anyone who didn't want to be there. Not much of a plan, as plans went, but damned if she could think of another.

Simon passed out wireless communicators, and they spent a moment testing them. They fit inside the ear, with a tiny mic that clipped to the shirt.

"As far as you know, this place is the only

location where they're holding captives?" she asked Simon.

"Yes," he told her, without hesitation. "And we have people monitoring Danny and Ian. They're still at the lake house. We'll know the moment they decide to head out here."

She stepped close to Mac and gave his arm a quick squeeze, drawing strength from the scent and feel of him.

"Then I'm as ready as I'm going to be," she said. "Let's do this."

Chapter 16

Mac kept glancing at Kelly, trying to put himself into full Protector mode so he wouldn't worry about her. He didn't like the fact that he couldn't seem to detach himself. This was why the Society wouldn't let an individual work a case if he'd become personally attached.

Nevertheless, this was one case he had to work himself, because of that very same attachment. He'd do it not only for himself and his children, but for his mate.

Finally they'd hammered out a plan, reviewed the satellite photos on Simon's laptop, went over the remarkably unsophisticated alarm system and piled into the Jeep.

"Ready to roll?" Simon asked loudly.

"Ready to roll," his entire crew answered in unison, letting Mac know that this dialogue was a sort of ritual when they began a mission.

And they were on their way.

Once outside the small city of Corsicana, they took to the back roads. Kelly wished the sun would set, but it was still too early.

"We tried to stall Ian, but he's never called us back. My guess is he's having to make a run out to the compound," Mac said. "That is, if he intends to let us speak to the captives." Sitting too long in silence only gave him too much time to think and too much time to worry.

"Let's just focus on getting ourselves there," Simon said.

Kelly seemed absorbed in her own thoughts. She simply huddled as close to the door as she could sit, apparently as an attempt to distance herself from the rest of them.

Mac felt a stab of hurt. He could sort of understand her need to separate herself from the Protectors, but even from him?

"Hey." He touched her shoulder, sliding his hand around to the back of her head, where he massaged her neck. "How are you holding up?" he asked, keeping his voice low so the others wouldn't stare at them.

"Fine," she said shortly, without even looking at him. In fact, her distant expression and the way she focused her gaze on the passing landscape out the window told him she wanted to be somewhere else. Anywhere else.

Given her inherent distrust of Protectors, this was probably understandable. The way she lumped him in with them was not.

The fact that he actually was a Protector didn't help. He might be, but he was her mate first and foremost.

This realization stunned him. Even when he and Maggie had been married, he'd always considered himself a Protector first, then a husband and father. Sure, he'd given them equal billing, at least in his own mind, but Maggie had always complained that he kept that part of his life closed off from her and their children. She'd been right.

Pushing away those thoughts—after all, he couldn't change the past—he focused on their route.

Sensing him watching, Simon turned and flashed him a grin. "We're about to leave the blacktop. Get ready for a bumpy ride."

True to his word, a moment later they turned left, immediately hitting a rut hard enough to send them all bouncing.

"How much farther?" Kelly asked.

Spider consulted a printout. "Three point seven miles, ma'am."

She fell silent again, retreating back to her inner world. Mac didn't know whether to try and reach her or let her come to terms with whatever was troubling her alone.

The Jeep slowed. "We're nearly there." Simon clicked off the radio. "Everyone check your gear. As soon as we pull up to the main house, take your positions."

Mac touched Kelly's arm. "Are you ready?" he asked.

Barely even glancing at him, she nodded. "As ready as I'm ever going to be."

Though most of the group had been given solo assignments, Mac had wanted to keep Kelly close to him. To his surprise, rather than starting an argument, she'd agreed.

"If your little ones are asleep, you'll need someone to help you carry them out," she'd said firmly.

He'd loved her for that. Instead of worrying about her mother and her sister, her first concern had been for his twins—kids that she'd never even met.

Ahead, the house loomed into view, the massive log structure easily as large as a Super

Target. Several upstairs windows were open, though most of the downstairs appeared closed.

Wait—two windows on one side were open, the screens black.

The Jeep coasted to a stop. All four of its doors opened at once, and they all climbed out.

"One, two, three," Simon counted quietly. And they were off, slipping into the trees. For this mission, they'd decided to remain in their human form, saving shape-shifting into wolves for if and when it became absolutely necessary.

Mac hoped it would not. Because if it did, that would mean things had become unfathomably bad.

Kelly close to Mac's side, they crept along the back of the house toward the first of the open windows, which should have been closed against the August heat. Through the screen and open curtains, they were able to see inside.

A group of children was gathering around a middle-aged woman who appeared to be brushing one of the girls' long hair. Several others seemed to be waiting in line for their turn. Though he searched in vain for Isobel's bright red shock of hair, he saw only blondes and brunettes.

"Do you see your daughter?" Kelly whispered.

"No," he whispered back. "These kids are older, maybe four or five."

"Let's check the next window."

But that one, though also open, had the blinds completely closed, making it impossible to see within.

"Guess we're going in blind," Mac said. He thumbed his mic and adjusted his earpiece. "What do you see?" he asked.

Two others had been assigned perimeter detail, with Simon and Spider scoping out the other side of the house.

"All the closed windows are empty rooms," Simon said back. "And every one on the first floor that I've tried so far is locked."

"I'm at the back door," Spider said. "And a man just exited. I'm gonna take him down, so we'll have entry."

He clicked off.

Exchanging a glance with Kelly, Mac took off at a run, with her right beside him. They reached the back portion of the house at the same time as Simon and the other two men, just in time to watch as Spider dragged the unconscious man into the bushes.

"He'll be out for a while," Spider said, standing up and dusting his hands on the front of his black jeans. "But I tied him up and gagged him, just in case."

Simon tried the back door. "Unlocked," he said. "Perfect. Now we don't even have to worry about disabling the alarm."

Single file, they slipped inside. The building, rather than being laid out like a residence, on the inside much more resembled a school or a dorm building. Long hallways stretched out in both directions, with multiple doors lining both sides.

"What now?" Kelly asked, sotto voce. "We can't just stroll along, trying out every door."

As she spoke, a door ahead of them opened. Kelly's mother walked out into the hall and stood staring at them.

"Mom!" Kelly hurried over, stopping short at the distraught look on the older woman's face.

"Oh, Kelly," Rose said, her voice a weird mixture of dismayed and triumphant. "What on earth are you doing here?"

Glancing over her shoulder, Kelly met Mac's gaze before turning back to her mother. "We've come to rescue you, Mom. You and Bonnie and Katie and anyone else that Danny and Ian are holding prisoner here against their will."

Rose crossed her arms. "Rescue us? What if we're perfectly happy exactly where we are?"

Simon's crew all looked at Simon, who looked at Mac, who lifted one shoulder in a shrug. This was a new development, though not completely unexpected. Captives often began to identify with their captors. Though not usually this quickly.

Unless…

Kelly gasped, apparently having reached the same conclusion on her own. "How long, Mother? How long have you been working with Danny?"

Lowering her gaze, Rose studied her hands, twisting a large diamond ring. "You have to understand. After your father died and I had to send both my daughters away, I was so alone. More lonely than I'd ever been in my life. Danny has been a good friend to me over the years."

"What about Aunt Teresa?"

Lifting her head to meet Kelly's eyes, a glint of anger flashed in Rose's gaze. "They divorced four years ago."

"I didn't know," Kelly said softly. "No one told me. So Danny was a friend, and now he's more?" Waiting for the answer, she crossed her arms.

"And now he's more," Rose agreed simply. "Much, much more."

Mac saw the hurt in Kelly's expression an instant before she shut it down.

"I should have known," Kelly mused. "What did I expect from a woman who would send her kids away?"

Rose slapped her, so hard that Kelly's head snapped back. Lifting her hand to her rapidly reddening cheek, she stared at her mother.

Mac stepped between them to prevent further violence. To his relief, Kelly made no move to stop him. "What about at the big meeting?" Mac said, unable to believe what he was hearing. "You confronted Danny and Ian, I heard you. And you stood up for Kelly. What was that all about?"

A brief expression of sorrow crossed her patrician features, before being replaced by a look so confused that it made Mac want to shake her. "I was punished for that. Danny only wants what's best for you, Kelly. For everyone."

Clenching his fists, Mac put his arm around Kelly, who, he belatedly realized, was shaking. "You betrayed your own daughter for that man?"

"Daughters," Kelly put in, her voice rough. "Where is Bonnie?"

"Oh, she's safe." Rose waved her hand vaguely. Mac couldn't help but again notice the huge diamond prominently displayed on her left ring finger. An engagement ring? Or worse, a wedding band?

"Your sister is happy here," Rose continued. "She's pregnant with Ian's child."

Kelly reeled back as if she'd been struck. "He's her first cousin," she cried out in disgust. "That's sick."

"We had such plans for you," Rose continued as if she hadn't spoken. "Pity you had to go ruin things by mating with this shifter." She cut her gaze to Mac, dismissing him with her dazed eyes like he was vermin. "Bonnie was extremely fertile, conceiving immediately. We all had such high hopes for you."

"And now?" Kelly asked harshly, clinging to Mac as if he was her lifeline.

"Now, you'll have to take your punishment just like the others who are stupid enough to refuse."

As though her words were a signal, all at once about ten of the other doors, both in front of them and behind, opened. Men carrying assault rifles poured out.

Men being a relative term. To his disgust, Mac realized most of them were vampires. Most likely the same ones that had shot him and Kelly in Wyoming.

Urgently, he moved his thumb over his mic, speaking loudly and deliberately so they all could hear. "Those vamps are armed with silver bullets. Only Tearlachs are immune."

"Exactly." Rose's smile chilled him to the bone. "So nobody better move. Danny's men will escort you to a holding cell, where you'll wait for him and for Ian to arrive."

Despite the riot gear, which meant they had body armor, but nothing to protect their heads, in a terse voice Simon ordered his men to comply.

Mac's heart sank. Someone had tipped them off. That had to be it, otherwise how could they have known what Mac and Simon were planning to do?

A glance at Simon's face revealed nothing. The man once known as The Terminator had always been, in times of crisis, able to shut down everything in order to function with the precision of a machine. It was one of the traits that made him so effective.

"Danny is already on his way and will be joining us shortly," Rose McKenzie said, managing to combine both satisfaction and longing in one sentence. She sounded, Mac realized, drugged or hypnotized.

At her words, Simon turned to Mac and

flashed him a grim, pleased smile. Nothing else, but it was enough to make Mac realize that Simon had planned for every possibility, even this.

Silently, they allowed themselves to be herded like cattle into a large, windowless room. No one made any move to relieve them of their communication equipment or even check for weapons. Mac supposed they were that confident of the power of the silver bullets. He kept Kelly close, whispering to her not to say anything out loud.

She nodded to show she understood.

As the door closed, they heard the sound of the lock.

"We're trapped," Spider said, fury and panic mingling in his voice. "What are we—?"

"Be quiet," Simon ordered, turning to face Mac. Moving close enough to whisper, he told Mac to be careful what he said, that the room was most likely bugged.

"Thanks for the tip," Mac whispered back. "Listen. Both Kelly and I are immune to the silver bullets. We'll have to be the ones to get out of here."

"Good." Simon even managed to sound like he'd planned this, too. "I have silver bullets as well, though I imagine most of the folks here are immune if they're Tearlachs."

"True." Mac squeezed Kelly closer. Though she'd seemed stunned and out of it since learning of her mother's betrayal, she bent her head in so she could be included in the conversation.

"We have men on the outside ready to grab Danny and Ian," Simon murmured. "I'm hopeful they'll stop them before they make it here. The plan is to run them off the road and take them down before they know what hit them."

Relief flooding him, Mac nodded. "Then we can use them to negotiate for our loved ones' return."

"Exactly," Simon said. "Assuming any of them actually want to leave. We can't force anyone who's an adult."

"I've got to find my children," Mac said. "They aren't old enough to have any choice in this."

Just then, the lights went out.

"That's the signal." Simon's voice rang in the darkness. "As one, we'll charge the door."

If they were worried about the vampires with silver bullets, they didn't say it.

Moving as one, the team rammed the door. Hard. It splintered on the first try, though not enough to allow them to leave.

"Again."

This time, the wood gave way.

"Follow me." Simon led the way. His men followed him without question. Struck by the confidence in his voice, Mac realized what made the former Protector such a valued leader. Simon was definitely a good shifter to have on his side.

They moved double file into the dimly lit hallway, Mac keeping a firm grip on Kelly. Luckily, shifters had better vision than humans, though not nearly as good as vampires.

Silently, they jogged down the hall toward the same door they'd used to enter.

Now Simon thumbed his microphone on. "Team Tres, report."

"We're behind them, sir." Because all mics were open, Mac and everyone else who had one could hear the exchange. Kelly squeezed his arm hard, in what might have been excitement or relief.

"In a minute, we'll be making our move."

"Good," Simon said. "Notify me when your mission is accomplished."

Mac liked the way Simon had utmost faith in the success of his men.

Simon flashed Mac a thumbs-up sign before moving past.

Nearing the door, Mac's heart raced. Closer,

closer. Freedom almost upon them, they burst through the door and outside.

Illuminated by candlelight, four armed vampires waited for them.

Mac didn't hesitate. Neither did Kelly. Holding hands, they moved to the front of their small group, using their bodies to provide cover for the others.

One of the vampires laughed, displaying his shiny white fangs.

"One, two, three." In unison, Mac and Kelly drew their weapons and fired, mowing down two vampires almost simultaneously. At the same time, Simon and his men fired, having moved out from behind them to do so. The other two vamps fell without any of them getting off a single shot.

"Hurry," Simon urged. "They won't be down long and the gunfire will draw the others. We need to get to the Jeep if we want this to work."

Mac had already started moving in that direction, towing Kelly, who for some reason didn't want to go.

"Come on," he urged. "We've got to hurry. Don't endanger the plan."

"We can't leave without your children," she protested as he ushered her into the Jeep. "And

I've got to talk to my sister. I want to hear it from her own lips that she wants to stay here."

Everyone piled in and Simon started the engine. As they raced off back the way they came, a voice came over their headsets.

"Mission accomplished. Both Danny and Ian McKenzie are now in custody."

"Now we can get everyone else," Mac told her, pulling her in for a hug, then thinking he needed more, maybe they both needed more, he claimed her mouth in a kiss.

At first, she held herself rigid, passively resisting, then finally she sagged her entire body into him, giving herself up to his kiss.

"Hey, get a room," Simon said, laughing. Lifting his head, Mac met his old friend's gaze in the rearview mirror.

"Sorry," he told the others. "But I can't guarantee it won't happen again."

They all laughed, even Kelly.

Later, once what seemed like an entire army of Pack Protectors had arrived, the people of the compound were sorted out. The adults were separated by sex, men in one room, women in another. There were many more women, outnumbering the males three to one.

To no one's surprise, almost all of them wanted to stay.

Including Bonnie, Kelly's sister. They located her by accident, while searching room by room for his children.

"I want to raise my baby with his or her father," she said, resting her hand on her rounded belly.

"But..." Kelly sputtered. "He's your cousin."

"No," Bonnie said. "That's where you're wrong. You were too young to remember, but I was adopted. My parents were Rose's friends. They died in a house fire when I was an infant. The last thing my mom did was save me. She got me out before she burned to death. We're not really sisters."

Kelly lifted her chin. "Maybe not by blood, but we are in my heart."

"Then you'll understand. I love Ian. I want to stay with him."

"Even if you have to share him?" Incredulous, Kelly appeared to be struggling not to cry.

"Even so. It's for the good of our race."

Mac felt he had to interject here, just so Bonnie was clear. "You do realize that Ian's probably going to go to jail for a long time."

Bonnie's gray eyes flashed. "On what charges?"

"Kidnapping, for one. I was at that meeting when he held everyone hostage. Plus, the treaty between the vampires and shifters has been broken by him employing them to do bodily harm. They shot me, as well as my wife."

Beside him, Kelly inhaled sharply at his choice of word, though she made no comment.

"I still want to stay," Bonnie said. "I'm sorry, Kelly. You could have known the same contentment, if you weren't so stubborn."

"I love her," Mac stated, hoping in his heart that Kelly felt the same. "Believe me, I'll give her much happiness, once this is all over."

Bonnie's bright gaze never wavered from her sister's face. "What about you? Is this what you want?"

Kelly nodded. "It is. He is. I love him, too. We'll make our own life. I'm going to be happy with our future the way it is."

Rose came to stand beside her adopted daughter, putting her slender arm around Bonnie's shoulders in a show of solidarity. "You love him," she said.

Glancing up at Mac, Kelly's expression softened. "I do."

"Ah, but there's the catch of it," Rose said slyly. "Does he love you, or is he with you only because you bound him to you?"

Kelly immediately stiffened. Leaning down, Mac nuzzled her, kissing her lips lightly before straightening to face her family. "I love Kelly more than life itself."

With a cry, Kelly turned to him, burying her face into his shirt. He held her for a moment, watching as her sister and her mother turned away, withdrawing what little support from them that she'd had. He'd hoped for more, but should have known better.

"Come on, my love," Mac said softly. "Let's go find the rest of your new family."

They left that room and went in search of another. They found all of the children had been herded in one place, and then separated out by age. Thirteen and older were taken to another room, and the youngest, of which there were twenty-six, huddled together, wide-eyed and frightened. The larger children held as many of the younger ones as they could hold, but terror showed in all of their young faces.

That they honestly thought their rescuers were the enemy made his chest hurt. Children so young shouldn't be made to feel such fear.

"Those whose parents choose to stay will be remaining," Simon told them. "Word of caution. Don't get too attached to any that aren't yours."

"I won't," Mac said, but seeing them like this made it difficult. He wanted to take them all home and ease their fears. A quick glance at the suffering on Kelly's expressive face told him she felt the same.

"It's okay," he said, repeating himself over and over, his voice soothing. "We're your friends. It's okay. We aren't going to hurt you."

None of them moved. Several cried softly, hiding their faces behind their fingers.

Still holding Kelly's hand, Mac spotted his twins in the back, in the middle of a cluster of kids of varied ages. He caught his breath. His babies. No, that was wrong. They weren't babies any longer. At nearly three years old, they were capable of stringing words together to form a complete sentence, capable of strong emotions and definitely capable of expressing them.

Moving closer, he worried. Despite Isobel's forced phone call when she'd called him Daddy, he couldn't help but wonder if they'd recognize him. He'd been missing over half their short little lives.

As he moved closer, several hunkered down even more, as if they expected him to lash out and strike them. Beside him, Kelly was openly crying, tears streaming down her cheeks.

Slowing as he reached Caleb and Isobel, he stopped and held out his arms. They shrank from him, crying. Avoiding his gaze, Isobel began sucking her thumb, as though the action brought her some comfort.

"Isobel, honey. It's me. Your daddy. Caleb, you're such a big boy. Don't you remember me?"

Shooting him distrustful looks, they shook their heads vigorously.

He took another step closer.

"Go away," Caleb shouted out. "Bad man. Go away."

"No," Isobel whimpered. "Scary man go."

Dimly aware that Kelly had pulled her hand from his, he tried once more, entreating them.

"Remember our house, with your swing set out back? And your rooms. Isobel, you had mermaids, and Caleb, yours is done in *Toy Story*. I've kept everything just the way Mommy had it, the way you remember…"

He let his words trail off into silence, finding no sign of recognition on their baby faces.

Now Kelly moved forward, singing a song in a lilting voice directly to his two children. Mac couldn't understand the lyrics since she apparently sang in another language, but all of the children shifted, watching her closely.

He could have sworn the tension vanished from them, in a single, magical instant.

She continued singing, and gradually, one by one, they joined in. When she reached first for

Isobel, then Caleb, they took her hands willingly, mouthing along to the music, singing the words they knew and making up others when they didn't.

Now all of the children had joined in. Tentatively at first, then finally singing with wholehearted abandon.

Amazingly, unafraid, Isobel and Caleb allowed her to lead them out of the group, over to where Mac stood. When she finally finished singing they stood in front of him, gazing into his face, completely at ease for the first time since he'd entered the room.

"Tearlach's original language," Kelly whispered haltingly. "We all instinctively trust it."

Overcome, he could only nod, eyeing his children, afraid to make a move.

"He's your daddy," Kelly prompted. "Go to him now, and say hello."

"Daddy?" his baby girl asked, pulling her thumb from her mouth to study him. "Is that really you?"

So choked up he couldn't speak, he nodded. This time when he held out his arms, both of his children rushed into them, allowing him to kiss them and touch their beloved hair and hug their sturdy little bodies close.

"We're going to go home," he told them

fiercely. "Me and you and Kelly." Holding out his hand, he drew her into their little circle. Content, they all held on to each other as if they never wanted to let go.

"Is Miss Kelly our new mom?" Caleb asked solemnly, his owlish expression serious.

Even Kelly seemed to be holding her breath waiting for his answer.

"Yes, pumpkin." Mac kissed the tip of his son's nose, then his daughter's. "She is. Now and forever."

Epilogue

Instead of sunshine, storm clouds gathered on the horizon. Rain. Mac shuddered, more from habit than anything else, then realized such things couldn't hurt him anymore.

Mo Anam Cara. We are one. After the simple ceremony today, once they exchanged their self-written vows, they'd be joined in marriage by the laws of Wyoming, as well.

With one final glance out the window, he straightened his tie and realized that of course the weather was perfect. If he'd asked for a sign from above, the cosmos had certainly given him one. At least he didn't have to drive anywhere. A little rain certainly wouldn't hurt anyone.

The crowd gathering at the ranch didn't seem to mind, either. Watching them arrive out his window, he saw most had come armed with umbrellas. And all of them had brought their dogs.

According to Kelly, it wouldn't be much of a party without dogs. Grinning, Mac had to agree with her.

Finished dressing, a glance at his watch told him it was time. Leaving the kennel office where she'd nursed him to health what seemed like an eternity ago, he walked past the newly built house that had gone up with surprising speed. A new house for a new life, everyone had said. They'd come from miles around, likening the event to an old-fashioned barn raising. The home had been completed in less than a month. Just in time for Kelly to become Mac's wife.

The sounds of chaos beckoned as he drew near the backyard. Dogs—too many to count— chased each other around in circles, barking happily. People talked, children played. His children, spotting him approach, ran to him and attached themselves to his legs, one on each side.

Gently he pried them off, taking them by the hand and leading them to Kelly's friend Ben, who was supposed to ensure that the flower girl and ring-bearer did their jobs. They exchanged smiles as Mac made his way up the makeshift aisle in between the rows of folded chairs to the front, where the minister awaited.

Simon, the best man, grinned as Mac joined him. "Are you all right?" he asked quietly. "You look a little green."

Before Mac could answer, thunder rumbled in the distance. Because of the gently rolling landscape, they all could see the storm as it moved toward them across the prairie.

Just then, all the noise died down. Mac looked up to see a vision in white floating up the aisle toward him. Kelly. His other half, his love, his mate.

Throat closing, Mac blinked hard. Radiant as she drew closer, she flashed him a smile so full of love that he could do nothing but smile back.

When she reached him and took her place at his side, he knew his life was complete.

Mercifully, the rain held off as they spoke their vows, words of love they'd written for each other, knowing only three words truly mattered.

Mo Anam Cara. We are one. Mac repeated them after the minister, feeling the power of them electrifying the air.

Mo Anam Cara. Now Kelly spoke, and the instant she finished, the sky opened up, drenching them.

Hurriedly, the minister shouted his part, eager

to finish the ceremony. "I now pronounce you man and wife. You may kiss the bride."

Mac needed no prompting. Claiming Kelly's mouth, he crushed her to him, aware that all around them the guests watched from under their umbrellas. The dogs, glad of the cooling rain, still ran and played.

When finally the newly married couple broke apart, the rain abruptly ended. A colorful rainbow shimmered across the sky, garnishing *oohs* and *aahs* from the guests and promising magic for the rest of their days.

* * * * *

Special Offers

Every month we put together collections and longer reads written by your favourite authors.

Here are some of next month's highlights— and don't miss our fabulous discount online!

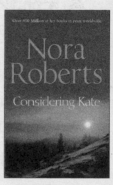

On sale 16th March　　**On sale 16th March**　　**On sale 6th April**

Save 20% on all Special Releases

Have Your Say

*You've just finished your book.
So what did you think?*

We'd love to hear your thoughts on our
'Have your say' online panel
www.millsandboon.co.uk/haveyoursay

- 🌹 Easy to use
- 🌹 Short questionnaire
- 🌹 Chance to win Mills & Boon® goodies

*Visit us
Online*

Tell us what you thought of this book now at
www.millsandboon.co.uk/haveyoursay

YOUR_SAY